For Goodne Sake

By

John Britten

In memory of my father

Lawrence Francis Britten

1917-2006

2

Index	Chapter Title	Pages

The Author

John Britten was ordained in the Congregational Church and inducted into a church in rural Leicestershire. He became a teacher, and ran his own education/ business company with his wife Katharine. They then joined the Church of England and was a churchwarden and worship leader. They now live in south west France. 'Goodness Gracious draws on all those experiences to create a church and village in rural Cambridgeshire. The humour is often subtle and gentle but vividly explores issues encountered by 'real people' in real churches.

In 2015 he was shortlisted for the PG Wodehouse New Comedy Writers Award with a short story taken from the book.

A synopsis

This series of short stories begin as Graham West arrives with his young family as the new Vicar of St Wulfstan Church. With enthusiasm and naivety he throws himself into the everyday life of a 21st century parish with all its quirkiness, foibles, feuds and festivals. Things do not always go his way, but with goodwill and the help of the new Archdeacon, issues are eventually resolved. The story unfolds in the rural setting of Random, a small Fenland town in East Anglia, where the people like to pride themselves on their modern attitudes, honesty and straightforwardness. Although they don't always succeed, Graham West is there to pick up the pieces and smooth ruffled feathers.

Graham West is a 40 something Vicar from the parish church in Random, a small Fenland town in North East Cambridgeshire. He is married to Judy, a management consultant, and they have two children, Stuart and Sally.

Chapter One introduces us to the village and the family and some of the issues into which the new vicar is asked to take sides.

Chapter Two reveals that rural calm is not all it seems when the Church Choir who are not all in favour of change, want make sure the Vicar understands that most have been there a lot longer than he has.

Chapter Three brings the Vicar up against two issues. He does not feel comfortable with either. An attractive single woman moves to the village and creates confusion with her piano playing and her Information Technology skills.

Chapter Four creates a moral dilemma when a member of the church wins the lottery. The windfall could benefit the church but will the Vicar put aside his doubts.

Chapter Five illustrates a feature of many country towns when the music society tries to maintain enthusiasm for the AGM with a quiz.

Chapter Six will 'ring' true for many churches when the bell ringers strike out for new members and leave the vicar in a quandary.

Chapter Seven demonstrates Graham West's expertise as a batsman. Games on Saturdays tend to clash with services and especially weddings.

Chapter Eight involves the hierarchy of the Church of England and in particular the Archdeacon, in effect the Vicar's boss.

Chapter Nine describes a now somewhat old fashioned Harvest festival, in which the flow of new wine has unintended consequences.

Chapter Ten illuminates the role of other churches in the area and how the search for ways of working together can prove somewhat difficult.

Chapter Eleven picks up the music society on its annual trip to a live performance. and the Vicar turns out to be something of a hero.

Chapter Twelve Christmas in the village of Random brings lots of help to set things up, some of it unexpected.

Chapter Thirteen reminds us that churches need money to survive and much time is spent in devising new ways of fund raising. The Vicar realises where their priorities should be.

Chapter Fourteen The church newsletter is under threat from new technology. The editor moves from opposition to developer with the support of a Sikh student.

Preface

My father Lawrence Francis Britten was born in 1917. He went to Enfield Grammar school but lack of funds curtailed his education. He was a Conscientious Objector during the Second World War and became a member of the Non-Combatant Corps. When he was demobbed in 1946 there were few jobs and in desperation he took an emergency six week training course in bricklaying.

 His first love was books and he passed his passion on to me. His favourite characters reveal his sense of humour and Jennings, Jeeves, Don Camillo and Rumpole could always be quoted at length and were part of my upbringing

When he retired in 1981, tired from long years of physical work as a bricklayer, he often mentioned the idea of writing a book. Dad often had ideas that were seldom put into practice, so the family would smile knowingly.

 But he started the book. It was called 'Random Reflections' and he managed a page and a half describing a man posting a letter. It was typical father, observant well written and funny. He read it to me and we agreed it was a good start.

As time went on I would occasionally ask about its progress but he got no further. Dementia set in his later years and that was the end of it.

When he died in 2006, I vowed to finish the book for him. It has taken me a long time.

It is my tribute to a lovely man who gave me an appreciation of the best things in life. I feel that I have done for him the two things that he would have loved to do but circumstances prevented him.   I graduated from the University of Manchester and I have written his book. I was very proud to have been his son.

Thanks are due to many people who have given me ideas, read through the pages, commented on plots etc. Katherine Rose, Rev. Wendy Thomson, Chatteris Parish Church; Geoff and Heather Squires; Jane Carlisle; Camelot Lottery; Melton Mowbray Congregational Church; Students of Northern College, Manchester 1964-1969.

Any mistakes in the text are entirely my own for which I apologise in advance.

All characters are fictional; any resemblance to existing people and places are coincidental.   John Britten May 2018

For Goodness Sake

]Chapter One

Random Reflections

There is a hill in the middle of the Cambridgeshire Fen and on it sits the village of Random. At one time it must have been an island which became attached to the mainland by causeway when the Fens were drained in the seventeenth century. Monks from Peterborough had seen it as a seaside retreat, but since those times the monks and the sea have receded. The causeways are still the main thoroughfares between the higher ground, and the modern day traveller, now above the low lying fields, observes that as far as the eye can see there is flat land, criss-crossed by rivers, canals and ditches punctuated by the browns and greens of the flat fields. In autumn and winter the dark black earth fills the gap between the pale blues and greys of the water and sky and the Fen blow sweeps down from the Russian steppes, through a house, a barn or a copse, placed like draughts on a board. In spring and summer the colours change to red and yellow and purple flowers. Summer growth produces the country's vegetables, carrot, potato, leek, which fill the fields to feed the city masses. The high expanse of sky spreads to the low horizon where the field meets the road;

In any other part of the world the hill would not have been thought of as a hill; more a gradual slope. In the fens, hills are merely land above sea level and even at its highest point Random could manage no more than forty feet.

The main road from Cambridge strolls up to the church at its highest point and then down and out into the widening landscape and on towards Ely. It is not in a hurry.

 At the top of the hill the village follows the contours. The church stands at the centre surrounded by the village green. In the immediate area around it there are a number of fine Georgian mansions in a crescent, clustered around the green. Once residences of the landowners, bankers, doctors and lawyers of the area, they are now the offices of the aforesaid bankers, doctors and lawyers who have all moved out into large modern homes on the outskirts.

The area was not built for the motor car. It is pleasantly pedestrian with a wide pavement available, originally required for the horses and carriages of the occupiers and their friends. It has become a mall for those who wish to visit the doctors' surgery, the bank, or the solicitor who doubles as an insurance broker on the second floor. There is no parking in the mall. It is prevented by a set of black iron posts at the junction with the main road. Parking for ten cars is to be found in a lay-by opposite the hairdresser, and these bays are on weekdays taken by those who work in the mall. It has been a source of controversy for many years because on most mornings those who stop to visit, leave their cars wherever they feel it is most convenient for them.

'I'm only going to be a minute,' they cry to no one in particular and dash across the road to the post box or across the green to the bank for the cash machine. For the mothers taking their infants to school down the hill it is a danger as they are forced off the pavement and on to the road.

It was in the autumn sunshine that the Reverend Graham West drove across this landscape to begin his ministry in Random. Beside him in the somewhat battered Ford Escort was his wife Judy. In the back, the children, Stuart and Sally, were beginning to get restless.

His curacy in Norfolk had been a delight but he was ready, if a little daunted at the prospect of his own parish. As he drove across the fen towards Random he became acutely aware of the history of the area and his place in it.

As he drove up the hill into the town Graham could see the spire, and around the bend, the roof of the nave, and then finally the parish church came into full view; his church. His sense of responsibility brought butterflies to his stomach. He parked in a bay on the edge of the green and the family tumbled out blinking in the late autumn sunshine.

Graham stood for a moment looking at the church. It was his church.

'Which one is our house?' said Stuart looking around the crescent.

'Oh, that one' and he pointed to a house at the far end of the crescent. 'Let's go see it! I've got the key. Stuart, run and open the gates and I'll bring the car.'

'We need some milk, I for one need a cup of tea, I won't be a minute' said Judy

So saying she made her way across the road towards a small 'SPAR shop. Graham leaned on the side of the car; arms folded, and took in the view. The children ran around on the grass until they found some conkers and were busy stuffing them into their pockets

.Graham's reverie was soon disturbed.

'You're parked in the place reserved for the disabled!' said a voice behind him.

Graham turned towards the voice, unable to see the man clearly in the shade of the trees.

'Am I? I'm so sorry, I didn't see a sign.'

'There isn't one,' said the voice, 'Used to be, it got knocked down.

'Aah' In a second he resisted the temptation to enquire how was he supposed to know it was a reserved bay for the disabled if there was no sign. Instead he resorted to 'I won't be a minute; my wife is in the shop.'

'That's what they all say!' Doesn't help those us who are disabled, does it?'

'No, I suppose not. Were you wanting to park? Here's my wife now, we'll be gone in a moment.'

'Bit late now.'

Graham walked towards the voice with his hand held out.

'So sorry, I'm Graham West by the way, I'm the new Vicar, just arrived.'

The man turned away, ignoring the hand.

'Then you ought to know better than that,' he said, and crossed the road.

They had arrived in Random.

The vicarage was on the corner at the far end of the crescent as it met the main road. It was the building with a curved gravel drive and space for a garage. It had been the practice of the previous vicar, the Reverend Hawksmore, to leave his drive gates open and his parishioners, not being discouraged, began to see parking in it as a kind of perk for being a member of his congregation.

'Good morning Vicar, mind if I leave my car in your drive while I nip to the bank?'

In the first one hundred and fifty years of its life there were few cars and mobility for the incumbent. It was more a case of putting on the cycle clips than starting the car. Life for the vicar of today is different. He has a group of parishes to look after; the crematorium is five miles away; diocesan meetings are often held in Ely.

'I mean, I can't get in or out of the drive some mornings. One wants to be of service, but this is too much. What can I do, dear? I don't want to upset people in our first month,' said Graham West to his wife Judy.

'Wait until the second month then, darling.'

'Oh Judy you know what I mean.'

'I can't see what the problem is. Close the gates to the drive, dear,' said his wife, without looking up from toast and marmalade. 'Are the children dressed, dear? Do hurry them up, or I'll be late and you will have to take them to school.'

'Stuart, Sally, hurry up please.'

The Wests, Graham and Judy and their two children, have settled into the Vicarage, the village and the area. Judy is now a commuter to her new job at Shire Hall in Cambridge, an hour away by car. As she folded the 'Guardian' newspaper and finished her coffee, the children arrived for their juice and crispies and the morning tension familiar to all those with school age children had begun.

'Ok kids, if you want a lift to school you've got two minutes or daddy will have to walk you down. I'm late.'

An hour later, Graham West returned to his study. On Monday morning he liked to start thinking about what he might preach on the following Sunday. One sermon per week was not too burdensome but he liked to give it time to develop. He turned to his lectionary and looked up the readings for morning worship in the lectionary. As he turned the pages in his bible he thought about his first two months in Random and wondered whether he was meeting the expectations of his flock and recalled moments which encouraged him to think so. Then he also knew there had been times when things could have gone better. He recalled with embarrassment his second Sunday. He really must ensure that the pulpit had been properly repaired and the wooden balls secured. He certainly wouldn't close the pulpit door again.

Events had gone against him that Sunday morning. He was rushed, struggled to get to the 8 o'clock communion on time and it put everything else out. He liked to be ordered, leaving plenty of time between things. That morning, his preparation had been rushed. In a fluster he had left his sermon in the vestry and had climbed the pulpit to preach unaware of the fact. He had closed the small pulpit door behind him. Only then did he realise he didn't have his papers and turned to go back down the five steps to retrieve them. He was thwarted by the door which for reasons known only to itself, had stuck. He had no time to think about what to do; he simply gave it a fierce bang with his knee. It opened with an almighty bang, crashing back against chancel wall. The congregation waiting patiently gave out an 'oooh', like a football crowd responding to a bad tackle. He limped down the steps to the vestry and back up again with his script. On his return he paused at the door and decided not to tempt fate again and left the door open.

He began the sermon red faced, stumbling through the introduction to his theme. He took a deep breath and after a while he got back into his stride and became more confident. At the critical point of emphasis he had raised his arm to make a point and brought his hand down sharply on to one of the wooden balls which lined the front perimeter of the pulpit. It came away in his hand. Only those who have some experience of public speaking will know that kind of 'out-of-body' sensation in which one continues speaking, but one's mind is elsewhere. In this case, as he continued his theme, the mind asked, 'what should I do with the wooden ball?' Unfortunately he tried to fit the ball back on its plinth without looking and he failed. He gave up as it became clear that the congregation were more interested in the ball than what he was saying, wondering whether he would succeed in the task. Eventually he leaned down and placed the ball at his feet and continued his sermon. This would in most circumstances have been a sensible and mature reaction if the floor had been level. It wasn't. Slowly the ball moved towards the now open door of the pulpit. The first that he became aware that the ball had taken on a life of its own was the series of six staccato thuds. That would have been bad enough, but sadly the nave had a slight incline down towards the west door. This was enough to propel the ball the ninety degrees required for it to continue unimpeded down the central aisle, gathering speed as it went. It is difficult to know whether it would have been better to have ignored it and let it eventually find its own level, but the church warden didn't; he got up from his chair at the end of a row and with knees bent, hands forward in a wicket-keeper like stance, he fielded the ball, held it up, and as in a moment of triumph cried. 'How's that Vicar!'

Graham's reverie was interrupted by the telephone and for a moment he thought he must have dreamt the embarrassment, then reality kicked in and he reached for the handset.

'Vicarage, Wicketkeeper speaking, no...uh ..sorry.....Graham West speaking.'

'Is that the Vicar?' said a voice.

'It is yes...sorry....my mind was elsewhere.'

'We haven't met before but my name is Adams, James Adams.'

'Good morning, Mr. Adams, what can I do for you?'

'Well I wondered if you could spare me half an hour of your time. I'm clerk to the Parish Council and I have been asked to sound you out on a particular matter concerning the village. Have you time in the next few days?'

'I'm sure I could find you half an hour.'

'Would tomorrow morning be convenient?'

About 11.00 would be fine with me.'

'Excellent, I'll see you then, goodbye.'

George Wilson had been the village postman for over twenty-five years and he wondered whether the job would last just long enough for his retirement. He was 64 years old; it was 11.30 am and he had just finished his letter round. He was drinking his tea in the sorting room contemplating the stint at the customer window that would be the next object of his attention.

Across the green, in the morning shade of the chestnut trees stood the National Westminster Bank. Inside Mrs. George Wilson, known to everyone as 'Em', was sipping her tea in the small staffroom, relieved by her colleague from duty at the customer window. She was 59 and wondered whether the job would last long enough for her retirement.

They were both suffering from a severe attack of ambivalence, a nasty disease caught only by the indecisive. Although nice to be valued by the community in which they lived and glad of the support of the village for their individual establishments, they had realised that the closure of their branches would lead to their redundancy and with less than a year to go before retirement, it is an opportunity to gain a nice injection of capital for the Wilson nest egg.

'I really wasn't sure what to say,' 'Em confided in George, as they sat down to supper,

'Mrs Baker was so enthusiastic when she came in to cash her cheque this afternoon.'

'Don't worry, my dear, we're all behind you,' she said. She's been with the bank since 1964 when it was the Westminster Bank, because it sounded so safe, she said. Apparently she told them that if they close the branch they will lose her account. She's written to head office, she said.'

 George nodded his head.

'I know! She was just the same in the Post Office. Apparently she has suffragettes in her ancestry and for two pins she would lock herself to some railings.'

'In the end it's not really about us, is it dear? It's about the village, especially those who don't have their own transport. The young and the old, they're always the ones that suffer.'

The two financial establishments had much in common; but they were also in competition; for the current accounts of most in the village; for loans and insurance. However they also have their own niches for stamps, pensions, benefit payments and driving licences, and for mortgages and investments. But the national mood seemed to favour cutting costs, maximising profits, getting rid of waste. The rural economy is always the victim in such circumstances. There were large long plastic signs outside their premises on opposite sides of the green. One read, 'Save our Post Office,' the other, 'Save our Bank.' Across each poster was a further one angled as an afterthought which announced a village meeting at the end of the month.

Across the road on the left hand side was the SPAR grocery shop. It had a small car park at the back. It was popular because it was convenient for people who wanted to use the bank and the post office. Mr.Gulam Singh had put up a large notice saying, 'For the use of customers to the shop only.' The word 'only' was underlined. Mr. Singh's world was split into two kinds of people, those who take any notice and those who do not. Those who take notice sometimes turn themselves into customers for the sake of convenience, polo mints being his best seller.

Mr. Singh turned to Mrs Singh, 'I am a convenience store not a convenient car park. But what can I do? If I complain they park on the pavement.

'You can order more polo mints, my husband,' she replied. 'It is the least of our worries. You should be worrying if the bank and the post office close. That would solve the parking problem permanently. Fifty percent of our sales are from people visiting the bank and the post office.'

'What shall we do about the petition, my husband?'

'What petition?'

'It is on the counter over there. You must have been at the cash and carry when the very, very nice young mothers came in. They want a road crossing out here because many of the children live on this side of the road and the school is on the other. They all have to cross it in the mornings and afternoons. They wish people to sign a paper.'

'Is it wise for us to take sides, my wife? Those for and against are all our customers.'

'We have children too, my husband. It will be good for us especially if the crossing is outside the shop. But first we will have to convince the council it is required.'

'Mmmm… it is 'we' is it now? Be careful, my wife, remember what the Guru said, 'It is deer, falcon and government officials who are trained to be clever.'

The following morning at exactly eleven o'clock, James Adams, neat and suited, his briefcase tucked under his arm, smiled as he stood at the vicarage door. The doorbell was playing 'Abide with me.' It was one of the things that the West's had planned to change but had not yet found the time.

'Come in Mister Adams, sorry to have kept you waiting. Go on through to the study, straight ahead on your left. How would you like your coffee? White no sugar?'

Eventually they were seated in the broad leather armchairs of the kind where one is uncertain as to where to put ones elbows. James Adams opened his briefcase and began his pitch.

'First of all Vicar, can I ask you where you stand on Banks and Post Offices?'

'I'm sorry, I'm not sure I understand the question?'

'Ok let me try another tack. If you went to the SPAR shop where would you park?'

'I wouldn't, it's only just across the road.

'Ah how would you cross the road?'

'I'd walk. Mister Adams, I don't understand what you are getting at. Why don't you get to the point?'

'Ok sorry Vicar. I have been asked if you would consider chairing the meeting that the Parish council has called to get feedback from the village on a number of issues. Normally the chair of the Parish Council would preside, but as an employee of Nat West he feels that he must declare an interest; not only that of course, it does place him in an invidious position. He wants be there at the meeting as an observer. The Council came up with a few suggestions but eventually thought you would be neutral, and because you haven't been here very long, you haven't had time to upset anyone yet.'

'Well thanks for that anyway. Is this the one at the end of next month?

'Yes.'

'Where are you holding it?'

'In the Black Bull; Jacob has offered us his back room.'

'Is that the normal venue for meetings? What's the matter with the village hall?'

'The drama group have it booked solid for their summer production, and they won't change it.'

'Well I am a little surprised. Meetings which have an element of protest are likely to be more difficult if alcohol is available.'

'Jacob has agreed not to open the lounge bar until after the meeting. You don't need to worry about the agenda by the way, we'll deal with that. Each item will be introduced by a councillor and then opened to the floor. You just have to control or rather guide proceedings. You know the sort of thing; one person speaking at once; some semblance of order and calm authority. Do you think you could do that?'

'Oh I think I might manage, compared with my PCC meetings it sounds like a piece of cake.'

'Excellent, thank you Vicar; I better report back. If I could have your e-mail address, I'll send you the running order in due course. In the meantime I'd be grateful if you could keep it to yourself.'

'But the meeting's been advertised.'

'Not the meeting, but that you are chairing it.'

'Why the secrecy?'

'Well we don't want you being badgered by some who may have,' he paused for effect', '...let's say a vested interest.'

'Don't we? No I suppose we don't.

The following day Graham walked into the playground of Kingsmere Primary School with Sally and Stuart in tow.

He had just finished his 'Have a nice day darlings, try hard,' watching his little ones skip to their classrooms, when he was surrounded.

To be surrounded by two people takes some doing, but with empty pushchairs and the assistance of the playground wall, he was penned in. He tried to turn with a 'do excuse me' but nothing moved. The larger of the two young women wasted no time.

'Are you the new Vicar then?'

'Y-e-s, though I have been here a while. What can I do for you?'

'What do you think about the main road up at the green? Dangerous innit?

'Well yes, the traffic can be quite busy, especially at this time of day.'

'You seen the petition?'

'No I can't say that I have.'

'It's 'ere look.' She fished in the bag attached to the pushchair, withdrew a group of papers and passed them across to Graham. 'You can sign it at the bottom on the second page.'

The moment of hesitation evident in the two of them was broken by the smaller women. 'We're asking the Council for a crossing.'

'Oh really,' said Graham, slightly puzzled, and for a moment he felt they might be talking about a railway crossing, but since Random had no station he dismissed that thought. He waited and the second women continued.

'Yis really, most of us live on the wrong side of the road.'

'Oh do we, I mean do you?'

'Yis. So we went to the council and they suggested this 'ere petition, so that they'd know 'ow many thought the same and then they can go to the other council who can put it in. Do you see?'

'Oh yes very sensible.'

''Ave you got a pen?'

'Yes I believe I 'ave....' er have ,' said Graham. He reached the inside pocket of his jacket and retrieved a biro, 'Yep.'

He flourished it as if to confirm it was actually a biro and reached for the papers. 'Second page you said.'.

'Better read it, make sure I know what I'm signing. Might be signing my house away Ha Ha There you are Thank you very much. Ok?'

The larger woman replaced the papers in her bag and grasped the pushchair handles as if to go.

'May I know your names ladies?'

The smaller one responded, 'I'm Tracey and this is my friend Margie, we started this you see, all the mums are behind us.'

Graham couldn't help looking over her shoulder.

'We don't want to wait before anyone's killed, do we?

'No of course we don't.'

'We'll be at your meeting of course.'

'Which meeting is that?'

'The council meeting at the Black Bull of course; 'aven't you seen the posters?'

'Oh yes. But it's not exactly my meeting.'

'We 'erd you're runnin' it.'

'I'm not sure that it's been finally decided?'

'Oh yes, it 'as, you'll see, Bye.'

'So much for confidentiality,' thought Graham, as he made his way back to the Vicarage.

Reverend Graham West was in jeans and tee-shirt, which he thought were the most appropriate garb for lunch in the pub. He walked down the hill to the Black Bull ready to kill two birds with one stone. Lunch first and then if possible a sneak preview of the room that would be used for the village meeting. It was better to be prepared. The Black Bull public house, prop Jacob Babcock, according to the faint white hand painted script over the entrance. On the sign outside, beneath the head of the black bull with red horns and a red ring through its nose, are two words in capitals; 'FREE HOUSE.'

It was a great joke to the group of motor cyclists who have stopped for lunch on their fenland outing.

'Thought it said this was a free house,' says their spokesman, who had been presented with the lunch bill, to the raucous accompaniment of his mates.

'Gosh, I've never heard that one before, responded Jacob, the landlord, but the sarcasm was lost on the bikers.

The pub has changed little in a hundred years. It is compact. It is a pub of signs. All entrances and exits proclaim the interior as a no smoking zone. A small group huddle beside an aluminium table close to the front door has on it a large ashtray which is barely able to contain the overflow of countless cigarette butts. A door at the rear of the pub leads out into the garden and has the sign: 'Play Area'. The small print underneath takes up more room than the initial announcement and warns the unsuspecting of the dangers of leaving children unsupervised; and if they do they do so, it is at their own risk; and in any case the management of the establishment accept no responsibility for any accident or damage which may result from such a decision.. It has an undertone of irritation as much as warning and seems to contradict the sign on the lounge window which announces 'Children Welcome!' There are two bars, saloon and lounge, a toilet, a kitchen and a cellar, with a two-bedroom flat above. The lounge bar has been filled gradually with small dining tables seating twos and fours, increasing in number as the profit has moved from beer to food. The signs indicate where food is served, where it can be ordered and what can be ordered. Beneath the menu is a sign indicating the direction of the toilet, though one hopes the two things are not connected in any way. The toilet is in the corridor between the two bars and is separated into men and women. There are signs on the wall between the two to warn you that the hot water is hot, that one is not expected to leave the taps running, nor put things down the toilet. Children are to be supervised at all times and we are all expected to leave as we found it. Since there is only one exit, there is no other option. The multitude of signs is not helpful for those visiting for the first time and who may be in a hurry. One might expect a sign warning those who pause to read them that the management takes no responsibility for any accident that might result from the delay.

The saloon bar is smaller than the lounge but bigger than the toilet, with a large open fireplace that suggests it was once intended to warm a bigger room. This is the place for the regulars, the locals, who gather on the four stools which run along the bar, making it difficult for those not part of the anointed few to order their drinks.

Graham decided to eat in the loungebar. His eye was again drawn to a sign which indicated there was 'no waiting service' and that food should be ordered from the bar. As it was just after midday, there was no one else in the bar other than a short stocky bearded man behind the counter whom Graham took to be the landlord Jacob Babcock.

'What can I get you to drink, Vicar?'

'A pint of bitter please; Jacob is it?'

'It is sir. And I guess you must be the Reverend West, am I right?

'You are. I thought I'd explore the village a bit more today and lunch here seemed a good idea.'

Welcome to you then; how long is it since you moved in?

'Oh about two months, seems longer though.'

Oh I know what you mean, it's only a village but it's amazing how much goes on, and you'll have been invited to everything at the start, with everyone wanting to meet you, I expect.'

An hour went quickly, beef sandwiches had come and gone, a second pint consumed, and conversation with Jacob in his light Norfolk drawl, as he came in and out of the bar, made for a pleasant and relaxing lunchtime.

'By the way Jacob, you know the village meeting at the end of the month. I understand it's being held here. Only I'm chairing it and I wondered if I could look at the room; though at the moment I can't see where it would be?

18

'It's the extension through there, he said pointing to the wall opposite the entrance. We pull back those doors and it doubles in size. I think it should be big enough unless we get absolutely everyone from the village here.'

'And I hear you're going to close the bar.'

'This one, yes; I have to keep the saloon bar open for the regulars. I'll open this one after the meeting. There might be one or two who might like a drink and a bit of supper.'

'Well I hope we get a good number then. '

The next time Graham West walked into the lounge bar, the folding doors had been pulled back and chairs had been set out in rows with a centre aisle to aid access. It was a warm evening and the glass doors to the garden had been left open. A lounge table had been placed at the end of the extension with three chairs. The clerk to the council was already seated in one of them with his laptop open on the table. Next to him was someone Graham didn't recognise.

'Good evening Mr. Adams.'

'Good evening Vicar, all ready for the fray?'

'Yes, yes and I see you are prepared. I don't think we've met,' said Graham addressing the stranger.

'Oh I'm sorry,' intervened James,' this is Gordon Smith, the district planning officer. He's here to observe.'

'Oh! Pleased to meet you. I wasn't expecting anyone from the district. James, thank you for the agenda; I understand the arrangements; but if it's alright with you, I'd like to say a few words by way of introduction, to set the tone; to explain what's going to happen and what I expect by way of behaviour; if that's Ok?'

'Be my guest, Vicar, if you're sure?'

'Thank you.'

As the clock above the bar approached seven o'clock, numbers in the room had grown, and in the relatively small area of the bar the temperature had become rather warm. One or two men drifted in and stood at the back with pints of beer in their hands.

Graham turned to the clerk and more by way of an observation than anything else said, 'I don't suppose we can stop people bringing beer in, can we? It is a pub.'

'Do you want me to have a word with the landlord?'

'No we don't want to provoke anyone at this stage. Let's see how it goes. Are you ready to start?'

'Ladies and gentlemen, it is now seven o'clock and with your permission we'll begin the meeting.' Graham began.

'On behalf of the parish council can I welcome you all and thank Jacob for allowing us to use the Black Bull. Sitting next to me at the table we have James Adams, the clerk to the Council who will make a note of the meeting. Next to him is Gordon Smith who is the district planning officer. Gordon is here as an observer. Ok we have three issues on the agenda; the threat of closure for the post office and the bank; car parking around the green and the need for a zebra crossing. We are going to take these in order. A member of the parish council will outline the issues on each topic and then we will throw them open to the floor.'

Everyone agreed that the closing of the bank and the post office would affect their quality of life and they gave the parish council a mandate to do everything in their power to prevent closure. There was even talk of a community run post office.

It was agreed that the zebra crossing was a good idea in principle but difficult to site because of other issues like the width of pavements. Even the announcement that the chair of the meeting had signed the petition in favour had no effect on the friendly atmosphere, merely the colour of Graham's face

The issue of car parking prompted a bright spark to suggest turning the green into a car park, and the parish council was asked to look at every alternative.

Graham looked at the clock and at half past eight thought that the meeting would soon reach a conclusion..

Mr.Singh commented how lovely it was to serve such a friendly community and he was happy to be the chief supplier of polo mints.

'I'll invite Gordon Smith to have the last word. I'm sure he's been impressed by the way we do business here.'

'Thank you chair. What you may not understand at the parish level is the bigger picture. The pressure we have on housing, on roads and on the budget in general. The rural economy is under severe pressure and in that sense small is not beautiful.'

The last comment did not go down well. The audience had been basking in self satisfaction and did not want to be reminded of how difficult things were. Graham sensed the change in atmosphere and intervened.

'Thank you Mr. Smith' Graham intervened in an attempt to move the meeting to a climax, 'we are all mature enough to see that things are not always easy, but I hope you will listen to local people.'

'It does, of course, depend on what you see as local,' Gordon Smith continued, jutting out his chin and waving his paper in the air. 'District is local; county is local; country is local. it depends on your perspective. As far as the local economy is concerned, roads are the key. I'm incredibly surprised that a discussion on car parking, zebra crossings within the village has not mentioned the obvious planning solution- a by-pass. I know the budget has not been finally approved, but it will be.'

The silence was deafening. A by-pass? In an instant everyone was speaking at once; talking became shouting and sitting became standing. Graham tried to restore order

'Quiet please, can I have some order?'

In the lull that followed he turned to the district planner.

'What by-pass is this?'

'I am surprised you appear to be unaware of it- it is confidential of course-but these things usually get out.'

Graham continued, determined to support the residents.

'I think, Mr. Smith we deserve an explanation. We have spent almost two hours on what we all thought was a real exercise in local democracy which you have undermined with a bombshell.'

'Hear hear! Hear hear!'

One or two smiled and nodded and Graham felt he had tapped into their thinking and the mind of the meeting. He turned to the parish clerk. James Adams was looking at his feet.

"The idea was mooted to the parish council three weeks ago,' boomed Mr. Smith. 'I'm sure the parish clerk must have been aware of it.'

All eyes swung thirty degrees and landed on the unfortunate clerk who was still looking at his feet.

'Well, I was aware of the proposition of course but we haven't had a meeting to discuss it yet. It's supposed to be confidential.'

That did it. The audience began booing and insults flew; arms were waving and fingers pointing; people were on their feet.

The Black Bull had begun to serve food in the saloon bar, and some of it flew through the air towards the top table.

Graham turned to his table companions, 'I suggest you two leave through those doors, quickly!'

They did.

Without the chief culprits, the crowd calmed down, leaving Graham alone at the front.

'Ladies and gentlemen, ladies and gentlemen, please ….will you please sit down.' Eventually he gained attention.

'Might I suggest that we leave this issue at this stage to the members of the Parish Council, who are no doubt as surprised as we are at this evening's revelation. I trust they will take note of our reaction this evening, and ensure that consultation is extensive and thorough. I now declare the meeting closed.'

As people began to drift out, Gulam Singh turned to his wife, 'It seems that in this part of the county it is only deer and falcon that can be trained to be clever. The guru was obviously wrong about government officials.'

'I told you not to worry about polo mints, my husband.'

It was a week later when Graham West was opening his post that he recalled the events at the Black Bull. The letter that brought it all back read as follows.

'Dear Rev West,

Thank you very much for sticking up for us all at the meeting. Many of us were very angry at the way we had been treated, and we have written to the chairman of the Parish Council to complain about it, and we are going to attend their next meeting to make sure we know what is happening.

We know you haven't been here very long, but we want to ask you if you will be the chairman of our new protest group and help us fight the planners. We have many of the businesses on our side.

We are deciding on a name for the group and hope you will have some ideas.

To date we have suggestions for 'Don't by-pass Random', 'Against the by-pass;' and 'Bugger the bypass.'

Please reply soon as we are anxious to get started.

Yours sincerely

Tracey (for the committee.)

Graham West smiled and turned to his wife Judy, 'I think we've arrived.'

For Goodness Sake

Chapter Two

The Church Choir

The word 'dapper' is seldom used now, but exactly described the appearance of the Archdeacon of Huntingdon. He was a short man in his early fifties, gold rimmed glasses, balding but always neat and tidy. His well lit front garden exactly reflected the man, thought Graham West, the Vicar of Random, as he made his way past the trimmed edged lawn and neat herbaceous borders, to the front door

He did not get the chance to ring or knock. The door flew open to reveal the archdeacon, arms spread in welcome, like a conjuror producing a rabbit from a hat. 'Hallo, Hallo! Do come in dear boy, how nice to see you,' said the Archdeacon, as the Vicar of Random, Reverend Graham West stood in his doorway on a rather dark evening in November.

'Let me take your coat.'

'Thank you Archdeacon.'

'Oh, Bruce, please. When I hear the word Archdeacon, I find myself looking round to see who you are talking to. Still pretty new to the job myself, you know. Come on through to the study, can I get you a drink?'

'Coffee would be nice,'

'Nothing stronger?'

'Sorry I'm driving.'

'Of course, dear boy, make yourself comfortable. I'll just be a minute.'

Graham placed his briefcase against the coffee table, examined a couple of nice watercolours on either side of the large fireplace, and then sank into a large armchair.

The Archdeacon returned with two steaming mugs of coffee and placed them on the small table in the middle of the room.

'Help yourself,' said the Archdeacon, walking towards his desk at the far end of the room.

Since Graham had sunk into the large arm chair, he pushed himself forward with some difficulty and then upright to step towards the coffee table and take one of the cups. The cup was full, so after a moment's hesitation, he decided that launching himself back into the chair was a non starter and rather than try he perched sideways on the end of it.

The Archdeacon had picked up from his desk a red wallet file. Graham noticed it had 'Random' in black felt tip written on the flap. He pulled his desk chair across the room to sit opposite the armchair where Graham sat, opened the file and crossing his legs, revealed a pair of red socks

'Now Graham let's get down to business. You've been in Random for almost six months now and the bishop likes his clergy to have some sort of plan for the future of their churches. 'Pastoral Action Planning' he calls it, unfortunately PAP, and you and I have to put together an outline of what you think you might need to do over the next couple of years say. It's not fixed in stone and we can change it whenever we want, but it gives him an idea of progress over time and he likes that.

So, before we leap into specifics, let's start with your general impressions of the place so far.'

There was a pause. In that moment Graham assessed the distance to his briefcase and his notes; calculated the degree of disruption he would cause; the chances of spilling the coffee over him, the chair or the carpet; and then how he would extricate the notes with his one free hand, avoiding disaster. He gave in.

'I wonder if I might get my notes. I'm rather afraid I might spill this on your lovely furniture.'

'Oh dear boy. I'm so sorry. This is not supposed to be a test of your juggling skills. Allow me.'

Graham lifted his cup at the same time that the Archdeacon reached for it. The timing was off and in the collision, the cup overflowed onto Graham trousers.

'Oh goodness,' exclaimed the Archdeacon, not quite knowing what to do.

What followed was a kind of dance drama. The coffee was hot, the actors were anxious, cloths, handkerchiefs were retrieved, dabbed, and each took the blame, leaving Graham with the slight embarrassment of a wet crotch.

Eventually peace returned; the ice was broken; Graham retrieved his notes; and the Archdeacon repeated, 'General impressions then?'

'The problem as I see it is um..how ....'

'Woah Woah. Just let me stop you there. Don't you think it's better to start with the some positives? Oh and just a word of advice. The bishop would say that we don't have problems only challenges and opportunities. You and I may think that is semantics but negativity can be a bigger problem.'

'You mean challenge?'

'Touché.'

'Let's start again then. Give me a few positives about the place which might help us further down the track.

Ok, there is commitment and passion and energy, decent numbers in the pews, and a relatively healthy bank balance.

'That's helpful- so what is holding it back?

'We have an aging congregation and we should be more representative of the community as a whole.'

The Archdeacon looked across at him, smiled and nodded his head as if to encourage Graham to continue. Somewhere a clock was chiming the quarter hour.

'Our current offerings don't attract young families. The pattern of Sunday worship has not changed for years. Eight o'clock communion is attended by an average of sixteen souls, mostly regulars who have been brought up on the 1662 service and couldn't really understand the need to change anything. They meet in the Lady Chapel. Symbolic really, it's a kind of sideshow and I think many of them feel that they had been pushed out to the extremity of the early morning; they are on the far right of the building which in the circumstances seemed an appropriate place for them to be. They have to stay in place as it helps us to ensure we fulfil the requirement of a weekly Eucharist.'

'Good, I see.' The archdeacon took off his glasses and began to polish them with his coffee stained red handkerchief.

'The main church service with communion is on the first and third Sundays, morning worship on the others. It's at ten thirty and sometimes well attended. The forty or so 'persistents,' as I call them, are mostly elderly with a sprinkling of those of working age. Special services at Christmas and Easter are full to overflowing. Then we have Evensong, which is once a month, and is only attended by one of the churchwardens. They take it in turns.'

Graham found the words more easily than when he had practised in his study. He seemed to have the Archdeacons full attention

'The priority for the next two years has to be work with families, children and young people. For that I need to change the service arrangement. There will be resistance I fear.'

The Archdeacon stretched his hands behind his head and his legs under the coffee table. 'So what are you proposing?'

'Because we know the church is full at Christmas and Easter, there must be potential; the aim would be to attract those people to other services You know the sort of thing, a family service, an alpha course and a service for young people.

'Ok. Excellent. So what's stopping you? Are there significant barriers to change do you think?'

It was some time since Graham had the opportunity to talk about his concerns to someone who would listen, so encouraged, he continued.

'Yes there are some. The choir would be one. We have most of the big hitters in the choir, the opinion leaders, and they want to preserve at least the four part harmonies. Most of the new music simply doesn't cater for them. Do you know what I mean?'

'Indeed I do dear boy, indeed I do.'

The Archdeacon hesitated, as if unsure whether he should continue, then did.

'I remember having the same problem in my first parish. Like you, I wanted to change everything but in the end I had to decide what the priority was and get there gradually. Give a little, get a little! The French have a saying I believe, *Petit a petit le oiseau fait le nid.* Little by little the bird builds its nest. But I didn't start out that way. I told them I was going to change every service, bring in guitars, move the pews, introduce a coffee shop in the nave and open a tramps shelter in the chancel.'

Graham laughed.

'A tramps shelter in the chancel. I bet they liked that. So what did you do?'

'I had a family service once a month.'

'Is that all?'

'Yes. They were all so relieved they accepted it. We have to try not to demonise groups. Sometimes it seems as if everyone's against us, but it is rarely so in my experience. Try and get some on them on board, ask them what they think and try and see if you can incorporate some of their ideas in with your own. You don't have to give way on the central issues, but around the edges you might find some compromise. Do all hymns have to be new music?'

'I'm going to talk to them on Friday evening after their practice time.'

'What all of them? Then I can only say blessings be upon you, dear boy, and good luck.'

The first opportunity to outline his vision came the following day. Graham had been invited to speak at the women's group that met the in the late afternoon. The 'Ladies for Chat and Char' meeting was not well attended but he did his best to speak with some passion about the future of the church.

Elisabeth Walters, who chaired the group was clearly in charge. She sat straight backed and spoke with a slightly clipped southern accent. She thanked Graham and suggested it was time for tea, purposefully emphasising the alliteration with the tip of her tongue.'

Jane Winters interrupted. 'Are we not having questions this week?'

The look on Elisabeth's face suggested the intervention was not an unusual occurrence, but she didn't get the chance to respond.

Graham took over. 'Oh yes please, I'd be delighted to hear what your vision is and how this group could contribute to the future of the church.'

Elisabeth was not about to relinquish her control so easily.

. 'If you could all be patient for a moment we can have a discussion with a cup of tea in our hands.'

The rattle of cups and saucers became the predominant sound and when everyone had been served, Elisabeth invited the group to ask questions.

Jane seized the opportunity.

'Thank you Elisabeth,' said Jane without looking at her. 'Now Vicar, you want more people to come to church. I know you're trying to be nice to us but we haven't had one new member of this group in the last five years. How on earth can we contribute to your plans? To begin with we meet during the day when most women are at work. But that suits us fine; it's how we like it.'

This provoked a reaction from the others.

'Oh no Jane I'm sure you are wrong. What about that Deidre woman? Didn't she come with you Joan? Such a nice lady very refined I thought.'

. 'Yes but she only came the once,' said Joan.' The place where she worked changed her hours. Nice lady though; except she didn't drink tea I recall. Don't you remember Elisabeth, it was the meeting when Jane wanted to change the name of the group to *Ladies who drink.'*

'I did not,' said Jane. 'The point I'm trying to make is that the only way we can bring more people in is to change things. Existing activity leads to existing results. Isn't that so? The Vicar wants us to meet in the evening so that women who work can join us.'

All heads turned towards Graham.

'With respect I think that is a rather narrow interpretation of what I said. I was trying to be broader than that and talking about outreach, serving the community, and the role of women. There is no single right answer.'

There was a silence and Graham felt a roomful of eyes staring at him.

'Well Vicar thank you again for speaking to us,' said Elisabeth. She turned to her members. 'Ladies I'm sure when the Vicar has been with us a little longer he will get used to our ways and see how our little band already supports the church. More tea Vicar?'

Graham got up from his chair. 'If you'll forgive me ladies I must go and pick the children up from school. Thank you for the tea.'

With that he beat a swift retreat.

'Jane did you have to be so argumentative. I think you frightened him.' Elisabeth said, returning to her seat having made sure the door was closed behind Graham.

'I just wanted some clarification. I'm on his side. It's about time we changed a few things or we are going to be the last generation of church goers. There's a whole new world out there just waiting for us,' Jane replied.

'My goodness. Christian suffragettes unite. It depends what he wants to change. I remember the black bins, Elisabeth said, looking round the room for support.

Jane was not going to concede the point.

'Oh Elisabeth There is more to faith than the colour of rubbish bins; though I do remain to be convinced that a tramps shelter in the chancel is the way forward.'

'It's always the same with someone new. They want to make their mark and change things. We just have to be firm and break him in gently. I declare the meeting closed.' Elisabeth banged the table with a flourish.

It was Friday evening.... Supper was finished; dishes were washed and put away. The children were tucked up in bed. Graham had wound the clock, put a log on the fire and started the crossword. Then for the fourth time that evening he got up from his chair and carefully folded the 'Daily Telegraph', placing it, with a degree of reverence worthy of the source of all cricket scores, on the seat from where he got up, walked to the mirror and adjusted his dog collar. His humming, something akin to 'Amazing Grace', was off key, absent and indecisive. He turned, paused, picked up the paper and sat down again.

'For goodness sake, Graham, do make your mind up. If you are going to choir practice , go. If not, stop pacing around and let's settle down for a pleasant evening'. His wife Judy, head in a Sebastian Faulk's novel, did not need to look up. She knew what he was thinking. He'd been talking about it for the past three weeks. She just wished he'd get on with it.

Graham and Judy West fitted most people's idea of what a vicar and his family should be like. He was tall, with his dark brown hair beginning to show the first signs of greyness at the temple, a pair of modern round rimmed glasses, and a broad forehead that Judy said made him look intelligent. She was blond with blue eyes that looked straight at you as you talked, making you feel important. She made the most of her post-baby figure wearing dresses that showed off her ample curves. Her shoulder length hair made her look younger than the forty two years. From the start of their marriage they had agreed to support each other's careers. Nowadays it was more by listening than action. She was a teacher and had become a primary school advisor and was based at Shire Hall in Cambridge. So far everything had fallen into place. Random was their first parish, that's if you didn't count the curacy in Norfolk, and Graham had been in post for just six months. It was long enough to settle into the vicarage, but not quite long enough to feel comfortably in charge. They talked about the people in the church with strong opinions about how things should be done, and whose initial instinct was to resist change. They both knew that this concept, sooner or later, would have to be challenged. Things could not stay as they were.

As Graham sat in his armchair that Friday night, he mentally rehearsed what he might say. He had decided that the choir represented things as they had been, and had within its membership some of the key opinion leaders in the church. If things were to change he would need their support. His problem was a simple one. If they were to attract more young families to the church, they needed to change the morning service. His 'big' idea, agreed with the bishop himself, was to introduce family worship in place of the traditional morning service on the second and fourth Sundays.

He suddenly grasped both arms of the chair, heaved himself up, kissed his wife on the top of the head, checked his dog collar in the mirror, and set off for the church approximately one hundred yards away.

In the church, the choir were bathed in the chancel lights, in full swing, rehearsing the hymns for the following Sunday service. As Graham entered through the west door, the large handle and iron latch clanked and rattled. All choral heads turned as one to the left and having identified the intruder turned back as one without missing a note.

Graham raised a hand in acknowledgement and tiptoed extravagantly down the aisle to sit in the front row of chairs.

The events of the next five minutes might best be described as a Mexican stand-off. Graham felt he needed to wait for an appropriate moment to interrupt. Some of the choir continued to sing, whilst others felt they should stop. The organist and choirmaster Fred, a self taught musician, had been schooled in the church by successive vicars who had encouraged him to develop his skills. During his working life he had been a bricklayer's labourer and had found it impossible to leave the language of the building site behind him. He was very proud of his achievements and highly sensitive to criticism. At this point he was blissfully unaware of Graham's presence and carried on regardless.

Eventually to 'the Church's one foundation' last verse- 'on high may dwell with thee' the choir slowed down, came to a stop, and waited.

Graham stood up, walked up the two steps and sat down in the stalls directly opposite the choir.

'Good evening Fred. Good evening everyone, sorry to interrupt.'

'Let's do that last verse again,' said Fred still wrapped in his own world..

'Fred. Fred, Fred, it's Graham,' chimed the choir, not in unison.

'What the bloody hell is going on,' said Fred appearing from behind the organ screen. 'Oh It's you, vicar. Sorry …about the bloody… and the hell.'

'Sorry Fred, I didn't want to interrupt things, but it's the only time I can see you altogether, except Sundays of course, but we're all so busy then.'

'No problem. Have you put your Christmas calendar together yet? You won't forget that we do need rehearsal time will you. We were much too late last year. We've also got a suggestion for a Lent anthem. Now I know it's only a month away, but we can fit it in can't we?'

As the conversation between Fred and Graham proceeded, the choir lost interest and began to chat about how many anthems they used to sing at Christmas and how church festivals weren't the same anymore either. How they used to bring tins of baked beans to put on the altar at harvest; how the goods were given to the poor.. Graham ended the conversation. 'Ok I'll come back to you on all those things, but that's not why I'm here.'

He got their attention. The choir sat up and listened.

'I want to share some ideas with you and ask for your views about the best way of going about them.'

He paused as the choir put down their hymnbooks.

'I want to introduce a family service.'

The choir of St Wulfstan Parish Church in the deanery of Huntingdon in the diocese of Ely was small in number and consisted on most Sundays of three sopranos, two altos, a base and a tenor. On special occasions it could be supplemented by itinerant singers from the area and boosted to twice that number.

Elisabeth Walters, Jane Winters and Doris Panther were the sopranos, John Panther the base and Jim Walters the tenor. The altos were twin sisters, Julie and Joan Watson, whose elder brother Fred was both choirmaster and organist.

They had all been in the choir for some years. Indeed in the choir vestry there was a picture of the choir some thirty years before. Not only were they on it but their parents and their children were also featured. The parents had died, the children moved away, leaving the present core to carry the burden.

'Reverend Hawksmore tried that and it didn't work,' the deep voice of John Panther echoed around the chancel.

'That was thirty years ago John', said Doris.

'Still didn't work, we got no children and half the congregation left,' continued John undeterred.

'Not that many surely?' chimed the sisters.

The conversation in the choir turned operatic, in that several people speaking at once in high and low tones were trying to outdo each other by producing the list of people who might or might not have left the church because of the service.

'The Smiths, the Jones and Michael,' intoned Doris.

'Didn't he come back again?' said Joan all on one note.

'I think he came back again,' echoed Julie

31

'He went to University, and then came back again,' countered Elisabeth

'Yes he did. Yes he did. Yes he did….. ,' confirmed Jim, holding the last note like a good tenor.

Graham, uncertain as to when he should interrupt them, thought it sounded strangely musical, a kind of counterpoint conversation. He wondered whether it was because they had been together for so long that they did it automatically.

'Oh good' said Graham, 'the bishop and I think it's time we tried again.'

He thought bishop would have a greater effect than archdeacon and it was true in a sense.

The mention of the bishop was a masterstroke as it split the choir almost in two.

Elisabeth, Jim and Jane almost stood up at the mention of the bishop.

Elisabeth spoke for them.

'Some of us do think it would be nice to have some younger people with families in the congregation. We are not going to last forever. We used to have quite a few young people in the choir. It would be an opportunity to recruit a few. Which Sunday did you have in mind Vicar?'

'Well that's one of the things I'd like your views on. Not the communion services obviously, so it's the second, the fourth or the fifth that we could use. They would replace the current morning worship.'

'Are you saying there would be no morning worship at all?' asked John suspiciously.

'No No, the family service would contain many of the elements of morning worship. said Graham, and of course we would, still have the fifth Sunday.

'That won't please some; they'll feel pushed out to the margins. Why do we have to change it completely? Why can't we bring the children in at the beginning and then after something together, they go off into the hall for something separate? They do that in a lot of places.' John warmed to the task. He wasn't quite sure what the together bits and the separate bits would look like so he resorted to experience.

'Our grandchildren do that in Wimbledon. Don't they Doris?'

'Yes, then they meet up together at the end for coffee,' added Doris.

'Well, that's possible and we might do that eventually. The problem is that we don't have a wealth of people prepared to lead a Junior Church. So I am really looking at a different kind of service that would suit all ages, all of us worshipping together.'

As there was no immediate response, Graham decided to press on.

'I have managed to persuade a small group of musicians to play for these services.'

At that point he paused. It suddenly dawned on John what Graham had in mind.

'Not Happy Clappy! Graham, please tell me it's not going to be Happy Clappy'

'It's not a term I like, John, but I do hope the people who come will enjoy it.'

'Well it won't be me.' John laid down the first challenge somewhat sulkily,

Meanwhile Elisabeth was considering the implications.

'I, for one would not mind the musicians coming to choir practice on a Friday evening so that we could practice the songs and hymns.'

'It would be nice to have a bit of variety,' agreed Jane, 'do they have a drummer?'

'Yes, I believe so,' said Graham, 'but I think it may be rather difficult for them to be here on a Friday. They practice on a Tuesday.'

'Oh, that's a pity. It's my evening class. It's not easy to sing these modern pieces without practice, but I do like.....' Jane was interrupted by John.

'Don't be daft Jane.' There won't be a choir. Isn't that right, Graham? You've come here tonight to tell us we are surplus to requirements. I don't see how you can have a music group in the nave with a choir in the chancel and the organ on the other side. No one would see us, never mind hear us.'

'Well no, not really. I thought you might sing from the nave. I can let you have a CD with the music on so you can get to know the songs.

'Sing from the nave!' said Joan

'Sing from the nave!' echoed Julie

'Bloody near impossible for me,' said Fred Watson 'sorry about the bloody, vicar. I won't be able to see or hear anyone. The organ's in the wrong place for singing in the nave.'

'We won't need the organ if there's a music group playing.' John was getting warmed up.

Ok, let's leave it at that for the moment. I don't plan to start this until February, so we have time to sort the detail out. Thank you for your thoughts. I think we should pray about it. Goodnight!'

As Graham was almost, but not quite out of hearing range, John muttered. 'Typical ruddy Vicar, whenever they're losing an argument, we all have to pray about it.'

It was the fourth Sunday in February and one of those damp but bright mornings that prompt people with an aversion to exercise to go for long walks, or take up a hobby. Graham West had been up early as usual and served communion from the 1660 prayer book to that part of his flock who believed that the reformation had never happened.

As he stood at the high altar, he glanced around the church. Nothing much had changed in this church over the last six hundred years but today would be different. He was pleased to see the guitars resting on their stands and drums awaiting their drummer. He had worked very hard to prepare for the day. He had e-mailed all those who had their children christened in the last five years. He had leafleted the parents at the infant junior school. He had telephoned, visited, suggested and encouraged everyone he could think of who was a potential attendee, now he could only wait.

It was clear as ten thirty approached that his marketing strategy had worked. Unlike the usual reverential whispering at this time of day, the church echoed to the voices of young children and adults who didn't feel the need to be quiet in surroundings with which they were unfamiliar. The northwest corner of the nave had become a buggy park, a solid mass of blue and black giving off a faint smell of autumn dampness.

Graham made his way down the nave towards the vestry. This was largely out of habit. It was usual for him to meet with the choir before the start of the service for a short prayer of dedication and to dress appropriately for the service to come. They would then process into the church together and the congregation would stand until they were in position and ready to start.

Halfway down the nave isle, nodding and greeting the assembling congregation, he realised he didn't need to go to the vestry. He wasn't going to put on his robes and the choir were going to sit in the nave. He went straight to the platform in front of the chancel entrance and sat down to prepare his papers, prayer and hymn books. The musicians had taken their places and were beginning to tune up. Everything was ready and a strange silence gradually descended, punctuated by the occasional shrill voice or baby cry.

Unfortunately no one had told the choir that they were not to gown and that there would be no procession into the church as normal. All they knew was that they were going to sit in the nave. They waited patiently in the vestry, gowned as usual, waiting for Graham to appear. The thick oak door separating the church from the vestry prevented them from hearing speech, but they heard the guitars start playing with the dull throb of the base and the rattle of the drums.

'It's *Morning has broken*,' said Elisabeth, 'are they practising?'

'They can't be' said Jane, 'look at the time, it's gone half past.'

'They've started,' said John, 'it's the first hymn. They've forgotten about us!'

'They can't have done.'

'Surely not'

'What shall we do?'

They looked at each other.

Elisabeth took charge.

'We have two choices. We either stay here on the assumption that Graham will arrive or we go in because Graham has forgotten about us. My feeling is we have to go in. Just like normal, we process to our seats in the Nave. No one will think anything is out of the ordinary because we haven't done this service before anyway. Agreed? Come on then!'

No one actually said yes they agreed, but they shuffled into position with dumb consent. It was clear that if Elisabeth led the others would follow

The door was opened. The large iron handle turned noisily to lift the latch and clunked back to its position. The choir, heads held high with a look of medieval devotion, all filed through into the church. Graham heard the noise of the door handle before he saw the choir. At the same moment he noticed that the first two rows in the nave were empty and in a flash of realisation, he understood what had happened.

'What are they going to do?' he thought without any change of expression.

As Elisabeth led the choir in, two by two, she realised that the direct route from the choir vestry to the front of the nave was blocked by the music platform, so she turned right and set off for the back of the church.

'Where are we going?' sang Jim out of the corner of his mouth.

'We–e-e will go d-- own the c--entre aisle,' chorused Elisabeth being careful to stay in tune.

'Have wee-e the t--ime? I--t's the la-ast ve-erse,' continued Jim.

They turned left at the west door, and with a measured tread marched down the centre aisle, eventually arriving at the front on the nave. The congregation assumed it had been planned, and the bright blue gowns, in pairs and in rows had added a sense of awe to the proceedings.

As they stood and the last member of the choir slid into their seat someone thought it so special they started to clap, and like the starting of a cold engine, one or two gradually joined in, then gathered pace and before long the whole congregation was applauding.

Tension was released, and everyone smiled and relaxed. It started a trend. After the bible reading and the prayers of intercession there was other spontaneous rounds of applause. Not raucous, but approving, confirming, all of us joining together. The relative newcomers assumed it must be what always happened, the regulars assumed it was part of the new worship and joined in.

There were a few malcontents. John Panther kept his hands still throughout. For him this was dumbing down the essence of the church and its liturgy. Doris was on edge. She tried not to look in John's direction over her left shoulder, but she knew he was uncomfortable, and so therefore was she.

'Happy Clappy, I told you so,' he whispered in her direction, as Graham stood to announce the last hymn.

'And so we come to our final hymn *How great thou art*. Now we have at the front here a box of flags, some drums and tambourines, and I want all the children to come to the front, take what you like, a flag or a drum and while we are singing, bang the drums and wave the flags to celebrate the greatness of God'

As the band played the introduction, one by one, some keen, some shy, about twenty children of various ages assembled and selected their weapons. They turned and looked shyly at the congregation.

'Reminds me of a scene from *Lord of the Flies*,' muttered John.

'Any adults want to join in,' smiled Graham, 'there are one or two flags left.'

A young boy of around seven years old peered into the box and lifted out the two remaining flags. He had been brought up to share, and share he was going to do.

He looked around him and spotted John sitting at the end of the second row as the nearest adult. He walked forward until he was next to John and stretched out his arm to its fullest extent offering the flag. John sensed everyone was watching so he took the flag. The boy waved his flag with some energy, his eyes firmly fixed on John, who managed a restrained figure of eight.

As Doris sat drinking her coffee after the service she lost count of the number of regulars who commented on the fact that it was lovely to see John entering into the spirit of the service by waving a flag during the last hymn. Even Graham had noticed and he wryly suggested to John that they have a flag made especially for him. John kept quiet and just smiled.
'What could I do?' he confessed to Doris later, 'the lad was so determined I was going to wave the blasted flag.'
'Out of the mouths of babes and sucklings cometh forth wisdom,' said Doris.
John was determined to have the last word.
'I was right though. There were some who stayed away.'

For Goodness Sake

Chapter Three

Emails and Females

Wendy Stevenson was thirty six years old and had moved to the village of Random from London. A broken relationship at a time when she longed for a child had left her life strangely empty Her friends encouraged her to move to a new area and join dating sites, but it was alright for them, they had husbands and babies and jobs and homes. She increasingly felt like a maiden aunt, until she could bear it no longer. She needed a new start away from the city. Managing to arrange with her employers a deal which involved part time work at home with a fortnightly visit to the office in north London, was the catalyst she needed. Working for a publisher, she held a number of accounts with writers which could be organised from anywhere. Arriving in Random, she had bought a small cottage on the edge of the town, joined a number of groups, and quickly settled into a pleasant routine. In the morning she walked into the village to collect her newspaper from Singhs, and a croissant or a loaf from the bakers, depending what day it was. The route took her past St. Wulfstan's parish church at the top of the hill.

One spring morning in late March, she had paused to admire the church, the early sunshine illuminating the worn statues. Sitting on a seat in the sun thoughtfully placed there in someone's memory, she nibbled the end of her croissant and replaced it quickly in the white paper bag.

As she was getting up to return home she noticed a man walking up to the front door of the church, fiddling with lock, and then walking away without going in.

The realisation that the door was now open seemed to her an opportunity and she walked quickly across the green. She hesitated as if she was about to trespass then turned the handle and walked into the church. She stood for a moment and took in the height and length of the nave. The sunlight streamed in through the east window, coloured streams flecked with hovering dust. She had not been inside a church since she had left home at eighteen, and had never seemed able to find the time to go to one in London. None of her friends and acquaintances went to church, and her

Sundays had become filled with other more mundane things like shopping washing and housework.

As she glanced around she noticed the grand piano at the end of the north aisle. She had a keyboard herself, but it had not been used that much in London. She had found comfort in playing on it occasionally when she moved to Random, but the opportunity to try a grand piano, well…. she couldn't resist it.

She opened the lid, and toyed tunelessly with a key or two. There was no one around. She tried some chords…then some scales. Eventually, realising that no one was going to stop her, she sat on the stool and began to play. She slipped naturally into a Mozart sonata which had been one of her grade eight pieces, and soon she was lost in her music. She eventually stopped and sat looking at the keys.

'That was lovely, thank you very much.' said a man's voice from a seat at the back of the church.

'Oh I'm so sorry, there was no one here, I do hope you don't mind. I haven't disturbed you, have I?' Wendy closed the piano lid and got up. The man stood and came down the aisle towards her.

'Not in the least,' he said, 'it's lovely to hear that piano played at any time.' He stretched out his hand. A handsome man, a bit older than her, but with friendly blue eyes; she took his hand.

' Let me introduce myself. My name is Graham West and I'm the Vicar here. Do you live in Random or are you a visiting?'

'I live in Grange Close, the little cottage right at the end. Do you know it?'

'Oh, Granny Beatrice's old house.'

'Was she the old lady who lived there before me, Mrs Palmer I think her name was?'

'That's right. But everyone called her Granny Beatrice, not really sure why? Her first name was Lily but she never used it. The church was packed for her funeral. Lovely woman, ninety six she was.'

'Well thank you for letting me play, I must be getting back.'

'Be my guest, anytime you feel like it, it's not used a lot. It was used for the family service twice a month, but Sally our pianist left the village and we haven't found a replacement for her. What's your name by the way?'

'Wendy… Wendy Stevenson, and thanks again.'

'Nice to meet you Wendy, come in whenever you want. Let me give you a card before you go. It's got my details on it and times of church services. I do hope we see you again.'

'Cheerio,' said Wendy.

She wandered back up the aisle. The day seemed warmer as she opened the church door and she sauntered down the hill to Grange Close and home.

Graham moved toward the vestry to copy that weeks service order. He had been tempted of course, awfully tempted, but thought he'd done the right thing. It might have frightened her away if he'd suggested she might like to play for the family service. But you never know.

Later that morning, Wendy was working through a battery of e-mails, sitting at her makeshift desk of two bedside cabinets and a plank of marine ply. While searching for a tissue, she found the card from the church and punched in the details of the website and e-mail address. She had no real reason to do it, more a habit which came from the business she was in. Her networks were everything and you never knew when a contact would be useful, whoever they were.

That was the second Graham in her address list. Funny how she'd never known a Graham before and now there were two on her list

Some weeks later it was early May, the cherry blossom was still out and the daffodils were fading under the oak tree. Graham West was forty two years old and he sat at his desk looking out of his study window, wondering where the time had gone. It was neither his birthday nor any other special day. He was in the land of reverie that often came upon him on a Monday morning which he reserved for drafting the initial outline of the sermon that he would deliver the following Sunday. He had devised a method of construction which seemed to work. First the lectionary to determine the readings, and then a quick read through the three proscribed passages. This was followed by an initial choice of passage to study more closely, which often led to links with the others and a theme emerged. Research in his biblical commentaries then added to his thinking. Finally 'googling' the text often gave him additional material to bring the chosen passage to light. The process lasted something like two hours on a good day with no distractions. 'Ha. No distractions.'

He could list the distractions- coffee, making a second cup; e-mails, checking and answering; guardian newspaper; sudoku and crossword; telephone calls, non urgent;

internet browsing, wandering around the house looking for something he'd lost; general reverie.

Anyone of them could leap into the vacuum created by any difficulty incurred during the drafting process, or sometimes before the process even began. He tried to discipline himself by starting with the lectionary because that triggered everything else.

He placed it in the middle of the desk. It lay there, staring at him, the calf leather cover and the gold lettering, 'Common Worship' threatened him. Ignore me if you dare it said.

He dared. His forty two years stretched out in a long line before him, and he drifted across a range of random reflections that had constituted his life.

He contemplated his life. It was something he seemed to do more often these days. Perhaps it was having children that focused ones attention on time passing. They grew up so quickly. He had a daily blank sheet, to be filled by whatever he devised; self motivated and generally unstructured. There were services to prepare, weddings and funerals, some meetings during the day, school assemblies, diocesan clergy, the play group, the WI etc, but he was not bound to visit them every week. It was very different from his brief time as a teacher. Then the structure was the timetable to be followed; children appearing in a line outside the classroom door. In his early days, there was the school bell which echoed in empty corridors soon to be filled by the hordes pouring out towards their next dose of learning. What was it they used to say 'only teachers and fireman respond to bells?'

'And churches.' he mused.

His reverie was broken by a 'ding' from his computer indicating an email had arrived. He had resolved not to respond to individual e-mails immediately but in the end curiosity usually overcame him and he opened his inbox.

'Hi Graham,

Nice to speak to you last week. Hope it's not too early in the relationship but I've sketched out early thoughts (see attachment) as an example of what we might do together. I'll keep Tuesday afternoons free for you. Please see it as the beginning. I hope my thoughts accord with yours.

Best wishes
Wendy.

Graham read it two or three times to make sure he had grasped the content.
Wendy? Who on earth was Wendy? He didn't think he knew a Wendy. What was
the woman talking about? He read it again. Then he remembered Wendy. It was the
name of the woman who was playing the piano in church. He rehearsed the
conversation in his head. He had said she could play the piano at any time. It was a
genuine suggestion, she had played really well.

The attachment, which he opened, was a short paragraph.
'*Although it was the first time we met. My heart is still pounding, and that feeling of
passion as I imagined passion would be, fills me with longing for you. You can take
me anytime. My body is waiting and wanting .Cover my breasts with yoghurt and lick
it from me.*
What ideas do you have?
*I have planned in my mind our next meeting. I have booked us a room at the Moat
House Hotel for the first Tuesday in June. Can't wait. Wendy xx*

'My God,' he said to himself. 'My God' he said out loud, his mouth staying open, his
eyes staring at the screen. His first thought was to tell Judy; largely because she
would know what to do. His second thought was he probably wouldn't, as it might
worry her, especially as she would expect the full story and then assume he must be
to blame in some way.
How could this possibly have happened? He had heard stories from colleagues who
had been propositioned. It was something they laughed about at college, a fantasy.
He never thought of himself as a ladies' man. He'd never had trouble finding a
girlfriend when he was young, and because none had lasted, he'd assumed women
saw him as plain and rather conventional, even boring. There had been occasions
where members of his congregation had been, shall we say, a little over enthusiastic,
but nothing as direct as this. Judy had been the only woman he had loved and she
had stuck by him. Indeed they had discussed situations where she thought someone
might have a crush, and they devised strategies which meant he was never alone
with women in his study. But with this e-mail he was way out of his depth. However,

with a sermon still to write he tried to move on and was soon deep in Matthew chapter five trying to understand other wonders and mysteries.

The e-mail content never quite left him, but came back to him with a bump when two days later he was strolling across the green to the church to take his midweek communion service. As he approached the memorial bench, he was greeted with a cheery 'good morning.'
It was her, Wendy, standing in front of him, smiling, ready to talk.
His normally cheerful response got stuck in his throat. He half turned and at the same time continued on towards the church, crablike.
'Oh Ah. Good morning. Can't stop; midweek service; late already'
'I was wondering if I could play the piano this morning?' she shouted towards him.
He was by then walking backwards hoping she would not follow him.
'Oh Yes. Can you wait half an hour, after the service? Unless you want to join us?'
His laugh was rather feeble. He turned back towards the church and as an afterthought spoke over his shoulder.
'I'll introduce you to the verger.'
He didn't wait for her reply, but pleased and relieved by his last thought, he strode off.
She didn't sit with the congregation of four, but found a seat at the back of the nave where she could see the service going on in the Lady Chapel but far enough away not to be thought intrusive.
Graham conducted the service with a detachment that was not his normal style. Every time he looked up, she was in his eye-line. So he tried not to look up and read directly from the page. Even looking down he could feel her eyes upon him.

In the vestry after the service, he sat for a moment until Jim Walters, the verger, came in.
'Everything's put away, Graham, so I'll be going. There's a young lady waiting for you in the nave.'
'I know. She wants to play the piano, just moved in to the area apparently. She came in a few weeks ago and I said she could play if she wanted to. Thought perhaps she might be useful; we are a bit short on pianists. Can you introduce yourself to her and see what she wants to do?'

'Ok, it would be better for me if she had a regular slot, rather than any old time. I'll see what I can arrange. See you later.'

Graham disrobed and left the vestry by the outside door. He knew he was avoiding the inevitable. Sooner or later he would have to deal with it, but how? He would have to talk to Judy. He would do it that very evening when the children were in bed.

Later that morning, Wendy Stevenson had a lengthy and in depth discussion with her colleague Graham Jones on the content of the creative writing course she was organising. He was a newcomer to her list of authors, but had been very keen to lead a series of sessions. It was always fun creating activities for the keen amateurs who paid well to learn more about their art. For the company it was an opportunity to keep their authors active, was a good marketing tool, and one never knew, an opportunity to discover a new writing talent.

'Thank you Graham for your romantic fiction paragraph. It should give them a start, I think. I notice you didn't include the yoghurt. Did you think that went a little too far?'

'Yoghurt? What yoghurt?'

'Oh, didn't you see my e-mail? I just put a few ideas together myself.'

'Sorry no, when was that?'

'Oh, last week sometime, I guess.'

'Sorry, let me check my laptop's here. I don't remember anything. Let me see...no I can't see anything.'

'Oh well. Not to worry. I'm happy enough with your version. I included what I thought might be a fun element, that's all. No problem. Now I have your final draft I'll get the office to send out the workshop papers to our twelve participants. Thanks for sticking to the deadlines. It really does help. See you in July. Bye.'

With that, she replaced the handset and went back to her emails.

'Judy, I have a small problem I need to talk to you about.'

Graham had waited all evening to gain her attention. He had decided he must be totally honest. He had rehearsed his words and made notes so he'd remember them. Judy could be argumentative especially when she was tired, and a conversation could become like a game of chess, although she seems sometimes to have a logic of her own.

'Can I just finish my e-mails? I shouldn't be more than a few minutes, and then I can give you my full attention. OK?'

'Fine'

'You could go and settle the kids down and read them a story. We're halfway through 'Black Beauty.'

'Ugh! Not my favourite. Who chose that?'

'I did. I loved it when I was their age, and they are enjoying it. Don't put them off. We'll start supper when you come down. Sausages and mash with yoghurt for pudding.

'Yoghurt?'

'I thought you liked Yoghurt?'

'I do, I do 'er normally.' Graham disappeared up the stairs.

He found reading to the children more difficult than usual, and the idea of a black beauty covered in yoghurt sent shivers down his spine and certainly didn't help his concentration.

'Good Gracious, it's a bit fruity, even for me and I'm fairly broad minded.'
 Judy was reading the e-mail and its attachment.

'What have you done to deserve this I wonder? It's hardly an appropriate reward for time on the piano?' I know you like yoghurt, but as far as I am aware you tend to eat in from a dish! Have I missed out? Tuesdays not your day off now is it?'

'No it isn't. Oh Lord Judy, don't make it worse. I don't think it's something I can laugh about. It's terrible. What am I going do about it?'

'Have you replied?'

'No, I'm not sure what to say. I don't want to be rude or embarrassing. I don't want to frighten her away from the church either. I've been racking my brains to think whether I said or did something inadvertently. I'm sure I didn't '

'Well. I would take the view that she has made a mistake. Mistaken your friendly nature for something more; mistaken in forgetting you are a vicar; mistaken in thinking you are available, having a wife and two children. Mistaken in thinking that e-mail is a suitable means of communication for this sort of thing; it should under no circumstances be repeated. In short, mistaken! But be firm Graham!

'Yes that's best I'm sure. Thank you darling.'

The phone rang and Judy answered it and passed it to her husband.

'Jim Walters darling. Take it in the study would you?'

'Evening Jim, what can I do for you?'

'Hallo Vicar, I've agreed that Wendy Stevenson can play the piano on Friday mornings. Is that Ok with you?'

'Fine that should not be a problem. Oh hang on a minute, what about funerals?'

'I can let her know, we don't have that many do we?'

'No, OK then.'

'One more thing Vicar, She has agreed to play for us at the Family Service once a month in return for the use of the piano.'

'Goodness. That's a coup. Well done Jim that solves a real problem.'

The problem of the pianist for the Family service was a longstanding one and Graham had been unable to find a permanent replacement when the previous incumbent had moved. However he knew it would depend on resolving the issue of the e-mail.

The following Sunday, Wendy Stevenson had woken rather earlier than usual, and showered and breakfasted, she sat on her small sunlit terrace. When she had agreed to play at a church service in return for time on the grand piano, she hadn't anticipated what a change it would bring to her routines. Getting to church once a month by ten-thirty was going to take some doing. Buying the papers on the way to church and then reading them after lunch was one change. Cooking time would be needed after the service, unless she prepared her roast in advance and put it into the oven on a low heat.

'Other people do it, it can't be that hard,' she thought. She got up and cleared the small wooden table onto the tea tray and went inside.

'Oh well, I might as well start as I mean to go on.' And so saying she put her chicken in the oven with a large unpeeled potato

Ten minutes later, after changing her shoes and checking her hair in the hall mirror she was walking up the hill to buy her paper and go to church.

Hallo Wendy,

I was very surprised to receive your email and without wishing to upset you cannot think of any reason why you sent it to me. I am a vicar, and a happily married man with two children who prefers his yoghurt in a bowl.

I am going to delete the email and hope that you will not send others.

You seem to need help and I advise you in the first instance to consult your doctor

Reverend Graham West

It had been late Saturday evening when Graham had composed his e-mail, consulted Judy on the contents, and pressed the 'send' button. It was still on his mind throughout the morning service, but he went through the routines of worship which were very familiar to him and which he found reassuring.

The service finished, he walked down the aisle towards the west door as normal, ready to greet his congregation as they left the church. It was well attended and sometime before Wendy Stevenson stood in front of him, hand outstretched.

'Good morning Vicar.'

'Good morning Wendy. Welcome to St Wulfstans. Do I understand from Jim that you are going to play at a family service? That's very good of you.'

'I didn't have the courage to say no to Jim. He was very persuasive.'

They smiled. But in the gap that followed, Graham seized the opportunity and dived in.

'By the way I have replied to your e-mail and I hope we can draw a line under it.'

'I'm sorry?'

'The email.'

'What email?'

'You know, the email. I'd rather not go into detail.'

'I can't think...that is... I don't remember sending you an email...what was it about?'

The conversation was not going the way Graham had planned it in his head. She was supposed to lower her head, apologise and say it wouldn't happen again. He could then in a magnanimous show of compassion say everything would be OK. She didn't and he didn't.

'I think you know.'

'I don't.'

'Are you being deliberately evasive?'

'I beg your pardon, about what?'

'The email of course.'

'What email?' Wendy's voice had this time found an edge of irritation and Graham responded.

'OK, if you choose not to know what I am talking about.'

He turned on his heel and walked back into the church leaving a stunned Wendy standing in the porch.

'Well, she thought to herself, I didn't expect arms open wide but I thought that even the Church of England would be civil'.

Judy joined him for coffee in the church hall.

'How did it go?'

'Terrible.'

'Why? What happened?'

She denied everything, didn't know what I was talking about, and without wanting to go into the detail, I was stuck. I mean what could I say, 'what brand of yoghurt do you like?'

A loud voice interrupted them.

'What in God's name happened?' They were joined by a very red faced Jim Walters.

'One minute she's going to play for the family service, next minute she's never coming here again and we can do what we like with the grand piano.'

'Oh dear' said Graham, 'this was not supposed to happen.'

For Wendy Stevenson, Sunday had started badly and got worse. The Sunday papers did not include a magazine or the other extras, which included the television programmes; she had put the chicken in the oven but didn't turn it on; her mother had left a message on the answer phone complaining that she hadn't heard from her lately and would she please ring her.

She was not therefore in the best of moods as she opened her inbox towards the end of the day and saw the email from Graham West. What was the man dithering on about? Why did he keep on about some e-mail?

. Then suddenly a light switched on, reason broke through and all became clear.

'Oh no, oh dear. I couldn't have done. I didn't did I?

She found 'Sent' items, discovered the illusive email and re- read it. Her smile turned to a giggle, the giggle to a laugh, and eventually she was gasping for breadth and holding her sides when she realised that this was the email. The attachment came to life.

'Oh surely not. He didn't really think I meant him.... ha ha hoo ha.... with the yoghurt....hee hee hee. Oh he can't have done....could he? He did, he did.
Eventually her gasps for breath became more regulated and her calmer moments less interrupted by eruptions of more giggles.

'Oh Wendy you do get yourself into scrapes. How are you going to get out of this one?' she thought.

Jim Walters. That was it; she could telephone him. Not only was he the only other person from the church that she knew, perhaps if she confided in him he would be able to explain what had happened to the vicar. It might be a way of overcoming the embarrassment that the vicar clearly felt. But the meeting in the church porch still rankled. 'The Vicar obviously thought something of himself if he believed that of me,' she thought. 'What right had he got to judge me? Sod it.'

She pressed 'compose' wrote the e-mail and sent it.

Graham
I think I may have traced the e-mail you referred to on Sunday. The e-mail you received was not intended for you, but, by coincidence to another Graham. He is an author and we are working on a creative writing workshop for romantic fiction writers. We needed a specimen piece as a starting point since writing about sex well is often very difficult. (There are national awards for writing about sex poorly) This was clearly a misunderstanding on your part as well as a misdirection on mine. I am sorry you thought the worst of me.
Wendy Stevenson.

Graham West opened the email the following morning. Judy had left for work and he had returned from taking the children to school. The last line made him reflect. Had he thought the worst of her? He re-read the set of emails, trying to look at them with the alternative explanation in mind. It all made sense now of course. What a pompous idiot he'd been.

The following Friday, he went over to the church to use the photocopier completely forgetting that Friday was the day they had all agreed to Wendy playing the piano.

He heard the music as he opened the door and realised quickly who it was. He walked down the aisle and the playing stopped.

'Please go on, don't mind me. I'm so pleased you decided to carry on the arrangement.'

He sat on the front pew and she continued playing. After a couple of minutes he decided he'd better get back to work, and as he stood he noticed the brown paper bag on the chair next to him.. Wondering what it was, he reached for it.

Her voice carried over the music.

'Don't worry about that, it's my packed lunch. And it's alright, there's no yoghurt.'

For Goodness Sake

Chapter Four

Camelot

Choosing a set of numbers for a lottery draw can be an extraordinarily simple activity or very complex, ignoring or including whatever is inconvenient, at a whim. The list just has to convince the participant that he or she is in tune with the universe and that all things will conspire to produce the right result. The superstitious amongst us might well select numbers that have some intimate meaning; birthdates, lucky numbers, addresses, and so on. Should the numbers be spread across the range or focused at one end or the other? Maybe closing one's eyes in prayer with a finger poised above the grid and then descending like the Sword of Damocles, will suit some temperaments.

Jane Winters had tried that but she didn't like the result so she ignored it. She didn't like the number six, for no reason whatsoever, and it kept appearing. She had wondered for while whether it was sacrilege to ask God to tell her the numbers, so she tried it. Sitting quietly in her arm chair, eyes closed, but with pen and paper ready on her lap, she waited. But by that time she couldn't get the number six out of her head, so she gave that up, telling herself it was not a proper thing to do anyway. God had better things to do than worry about her lottery numbers. '

Then another thought struck her. What about the bible? She had heard of people using the bible for guidance. Closing their eyes, opening it at a random page and by tracing their finger across the page come to a sentence or a word which would help them. She tried it. The first time it read 'how beauteous are thy feet in sandals,' from the Song of Songs which didn't seem a great help. The second from I Samuel had 1,000, 6,000 and 30,000 in the same paragraph, and the lottery only went up to 50. What if she ignored the noughts? But again that felt like cheating. She tried birthdays with much the same result as all her family were born in years beyond 50 and days only went up to 31. It would have to be random; not inappropriate given she lived there.

So she started and put down the first four numbers that came into her head, 1 8 5 4. Then two more; 23 for her house number and finally 17 for no reason at all.

And so she settled on a set and she used that same set each week. Over the weeks months and years she had won nothing, and was often tempted to change. She had stopped watching the draw on television, and if she hadn't included the purchase of a ticket with her weekly paper bill, she would probably have given up altogether.

It was Sunday morning and Jane Winters was on her way to church, a ten minute walk from her cottage on the edge of the village. As she strode out in the autumn warmth she wondered how many times she had made the very same journey. It was a habit she had acquired from her father. Working things out in her head passed the time and gave her something to think about.

'Thirty years and well... let's say 45 weeks a year and on average twice a week; that's 1200 times two, 2,400 then.'

'Not as many as I thought,' she pondered.

'Oh the paper.' It was her custom to drop into the Singh's grocery for her 'Observer', if she remembered. Still she knew if she forgot, she could always get it on the way back.

As she stood in the queue for the checkout she looked around the store; not for any reason other than pass the time while her turn arrived. It was a shop that seemed to sell everything from lollipops to lottery tickets. She spotted a cardboard box on the bottom shelf, half open labelled 'British Mousetraps.' She could not honestly remember the last time she bought a mousetrap? Evidently someone still made them Over the counter by the till she noticed a blue sign with the lottery logo and a white square filled with the numbers from the previous nights draw, but without her glasses she couldn't see the detail.

'Good morning to you Ms Winter',' said Gulap Singh, taking the newspaper and pressing it against the small square of glass of the barcode reader, it is a lovely autumn morning is it not?'

'It certainly is Mr. Singh.' She handed over a five-pound note. He handed her the change,

'Have you checked your lottery ticket this week Ms Winter? We had a call from the marketing department of Camelot this morning. They have informed me that the Saturday jackpot ticket was bought here, and it has not been claimed yet. I think you are in it to win it are you not?'

'Oh how exciting, someone's going to have a good day. It won't be me though I can assure you of that. I never win anything.'

She didn't approve of gambling, but felt that her one pound a week was just a little bit of fun, nothing serious. However she felt it didn't quite suit her image. It was not something she was going to readily admit to. She convinced herself that her decision was in support of good causes, and although winning something occasionally crossed her mind, she never had.

She glanced again at the numbers above her, and folding her newspaper turned and squeezed through the lengthening queue. She paused briefly by the door, as if she had forgotten something and looked back through the shop, before making her way out across the road and over the green towards the church.

Jane had been a daughter of the vicarage, her father the vicar of Random for over 30 years. She believed it gave her some standing and some authority in the church and the community. When she spoke people listened. She had trained in agricultural management and married a wealthy farmer; had her children who had since moved away; was widowed in her early sixties and finally settled in a nice house on the edge of Random.

Her outdoor clothing of cloak and tweed skirt accentuated by her height and width reminded people of Miss Marple, with her mass of unruly white hair.

Inside the church the heating was on, Jane took her cloak off, was handed an order of service and hymnbook and made her way down the nave, nodding and smiling to friends.

She sat in her customary pew. Her twinset and tweed suit as well as the hat she habitually wore gave her an old fashioned air. No one could remember seeing her without the hat, as if it was the sole source of her inspiration and energy.

She bowed her head for a moment and tried to pray but she couldn't get it out of her head, someone local has won the lottery. Then upright again, she prepared herself for the service. Glasses in their case taken from her handbag, her sealed envelope for the collection, were place on the small narrow shelf in front of her. She put on her glasses, took up her hymnbook, and looked for the number of the first hymn from the notice board, 170. That's one of my lottery numbers, 17, she turned the pages, found the place and read the first line. She knew most of the hymns in 'Mission Praise', but this was not one they sang very often. She scanned it briefly to take in the sense; 'Give thanks with a grateful heart........let the poor say I am rich....let the poor say I am rich.'. Rich! Rich! Someone, probably someone she knew had won the lottery. She smiled to herself as she remembered Mr. Singh's words.

'It's not been claimed yet. It's not been claimed yet. And it's Number 17 as well.

She tried to concentrate on the familiar words of the liturgy without success.

'Our next hymn is number 615. "Stand up and bless the Lord, ye people of his choice."

Jane found the page and whilst the organist played the introduction she noticed the name of the composer. James Montgomery 1854-1,8,5,4, her first four lottery numbers. Now that was a strange coincidence.

After the hymn, Graham West, the Vicar began his sermon. 'My text this morning is from our reading from Isaiah the 49th chapter and the 23rd verse.'

'No one who waits for my help will be disappointed.'

Jane sat up so straight she was almost vertical. She was trembling. 49 was her number as well and now the text. But what about the 23rd? Of course, it's the 23rd today. It had to be a message for her. She was always afraid of wanting anything too much in case she was disappointed. This was just too much of a coincidence. God had to be telling her something. Perhaps it was her turn to be a winner.

The warmth of the church gave Jane ample scope for allowing her mind to wander further and wander it did, over hill and dale. How much would she get and what would she do with it? It was important to have a plan. She at first worked on the basis of a million pounds, which didn't seem Start at one hundred thousand. Then she counted down to first cousins and thought it was far too unreasonable. Money allocated to her family first. But how much should she give each of them?. Maybe she should only include the children? But at the same time it was important that the young stood on their own two feet and were not spoiled. Then money allocated for the church and for her favourite charities were next. What about her friends? How much should I leave for myself? At this rate she wouldn't have enough. So she doubled the winnings and began the process again. It soon became too difficult to hold the numbers in her head and she brought herself back into present. She was unsure which was worse, winning or not winning. She felt frightened of both. Winning would change her life which was scary, but she knew that if it turned out to be a false dawn, the disappointment would be overwhelming. Would God do that to her? But she kept coming back to the coincidences of having all her lottery numbers appearing in the service. What were the odds on that? It had to mean something. Isaiah seemed to know she was waiting for God's help; could it really be that she was the one who would not be disappointed.

She went through the routines in the rest of the service in something of a daze, and had not really recovered as people began to drift towards the door. She nodded and smiled, returning the greetings of friends and acquaintances, and walked down the aisle.

'Good morning Jane, how are you today?' Graham smiled and held out his hand. Jane took it and held on to it.

'Vicar, can I have a word with you?'

Jane had become almost tearful and Graham sensed it.

'Yes. Of course, Jane. Is there something wrong?'

'Yes, that is no, that is, I don't know. I think I may have won the lottery. I mean I haven't exactly won it but....' At this point she stopped. Graham was looking puzzled.

'I'm not explaining myself very well am I?'

The queue of people waiting to leave and shake Graham's hand was lengthening and the stationary Jane was being overtaken on the outside, with farewells and thank you launched on the run.

' Jane, why don't you go and get two cups of coffee in the hall, sit in a quiet corner, and I'll join you in a couple of minutes as soon as I've finished my goodbyes.'

Jane turned and made her way through the church to the hall.

As the congregation dispersed, Graham followed and with a 'I'm going to be a couple of minutes you carry on home' to his wife Judy, he joined Jane in the corner of the hall.

'I'm afraid your coffee won't be very warm vicar.'

'Never mind Jane, now whatever has upset you?'

'It's nothing really. I know I'm being very silly.' She reached for her pendant and twisted it around a finger.

'Why don't you let me be the judge of that? I know you don't normally let things get you down, so it must be important. Start at the beginning. Something about the lottery did I hear you say?'

'Can I ask you something first? Do you think God speaks to us? I mean through a service like this morning?'

Graham avoided the temptation of a theological discussion.

'Did something happen this morning that made you wonder?'

Jane explained that the numbers, 1, 4, 5, 8, 17 and 49 were her lottery numbers and that she knew that this week's jackpot winner was local.

There was a moment, a hiatus, as Graham thought what he might say. Jane sensed his hesitation.

'You think I'm being ridiculous, don't you. I know you do because I think I'm being ridiculous as well. But I didn't imagine it. They are my numbers. I'm just trying to stop myself wanting it to be true. Of course I know that there are hundreds and thousands of people every week hoping to win. For some it might mean their only opportunity of getting out of poverty, or of changing their lives for the better. They can't all win, can they? But somebody does, don't they?'

'You've just identified what I call the Camelot conundrum. It's very clever. The key to getting people to spend their hard earned money is to dangle before them hopes which can only be dashed for the majority. It's a stealth tax on the poor really. Of course they try to soften the hard edge by wrapping it up in charitable giving and banner headlines like *"you have to be in it to win it"* but in the end you can't live your life like that, can you? Money can't make you happy, and sadly Camelot is trying to make you believe the opposite. I fear there will be people who can't afford it buying lottery tickets instead of food.'

'It was a coincidence then; the numbers; Isaiah; riches; not being disappointed?'

'Truthfully I don't know Jane. I believe God speaks to us. Often we don't realise it until afterwards when we look back at events. At least you won't have long to wait. Did you buy your ticket at Singhs?'

'Yes.'

'Well why don't we wait until you find out? If you want to talk again after that, give me a ring and come up to the house for coffee?'

'Thank you Graham. I'm sorry I got so silly?'

'No problem Jane. Are you alright to get home?'

'Yes I'm fine now. I just needed to get things in proportion. Thank you.'

Jane walked across the green towards the shop. About halfway she stopped and stood for a moment; turned left to go down the hill; stopped again; looked back and finally strode purposefully away from the shop and in the direction of home. She could find out the lottery results on the television. She was pretty sure the BBC included them on the red button. It would be better that way if she had won something. She could keep it to herself. And anyway she hadn't got her ticket with her.

In the eight minutes it took her reach her front door, she had convinced herself that she could not have won. She began to feel rather ashamed of herself. If God was speaking to her, why on earth would he use such a strange way to do it? Numbers indeed. What had she been thinking of? How she was going to look Graham West in the face again, she was not sure. 'Oh well,' she sighed, putting her key in the lock. She took off her coat and went to put the kettle on.

While she was waiting for the water to boil, she went to look for her ticket. Wouldn't it be hilarious if she couldn't find it? She went to the small reproduction Georgian bureau in the dining room, pulled the hinged top towards her and sat, or rather perched, on the office chair. She reached across. The small drawer, surrounded by pigeon holes was closed and locked. She smiled to herself. Wouldn't it be funny if she couldn't find the key? But the key was in the key cupboard on the wall of the downstairs toilet and it took her seconds to find it and return to the desk. She unlocked the drawer and gently pulled it open. For a mini second she panicked, but the ticket was there, covered by her emergency fund of four twenty pound notes. She took it out and confirmed the numbers. 1, 4, 5, 8, 17 and 49, the same numbers; she hadn't changed a thing.

Ok so far so good, now for the television.

She had some difficulty in manipulating the controls as her hand was shaking; she took a deep breath and eventually negotiated a series of screens. It was rather surreal. 'Guinevere' had had a starring role with Ball set 5. Winning prize levels:- six balls- £1,663,502.00. Oh my God. There were the numbers, her numbers. She checked them several times. There was no mistake, She had won.

She got up and walked to the kitchen and then back again. It's over a million! What do I do now? *'Contact us'* seemed a good option and she found the number, went to the phone and dialled.

It was all pretty straight forward, serial numbers, name and address. The 'winning process' they had called it and it lasted no more than fifteen minutes. A 'winner advisor' would call and make an appointment. There was no need for her to contact Gulap Singh. As she put the phone down, she noticed she had stopped trembling, so she went back to the kettle and this time made a coffee.

She rang the children and her brother Tom and they all vowed to be there as soon as they could. By early evening, her sitting room was crowded. Jennifer and John had arrived with the grandchildren and Tom was due on Monday. Champagne had been opened and the conversation had slowly gone from celebratory to what are you going to do with the money.

Later that same evening Graham West was nodding off. Judy had a pile of papers around her, the children were in bed, and the television was coming to the end of *Songs of praise.'* The phone rang.

'Graham, can you get it. I can't put these down.'

'What. Oh yes. Hallo, the Vicarage, Graham West speaking.'

'Graham, its Jane Winter.'

'Hallo Jane, are you Ok? It sounds as if you're having a party.'

'Oh sorry can you hear me. Shush. No not you Graham, just the family. Listen, I need to talk to you urgently, can I pop in tomorrow, preferably in the morning?'

'Yes Jane can you come early, around 9.00? Would an hour be long enough? Good. Can you give me a clue as to the problem?'

No I'd prefer to wait until tomorrow if you don't mind? Thanks I'll see you then.

Jane put the phone down and redialled.

'Peter James speaking.'

'Peter, its Jane Winter.'

'Hallo Jane what's up?'

'Peter, I'm sorry to ring you at home, but it's urgent.'

'Go on. I'm listening.'

'I need your professional services. Tomorrow I have two meetings, one in the morning and one in the afternoon and I need you there for both. I'm sorry I couldn't give you any more notice and I can't tell you why until tomorrow, but when I tell you the background I think you'll understand.'

'How mysterious? What time are they?'

'The first is at nine, with the Vicar at the vicarage and the second is at four in the afternoon.'

'Well you're fortunate. I don't usually go into the office on Mondays. As it happens I'm playing golf at 10.30 tomorrow, so if you don't mind me turning up in my kit, I can join you. Will an hour be long enough? I say, no one's died have they?'

'No nothing like that and an hour is fine.'

'Ok I'll be there.'

'Thank you so much. I might sleep tonight now.'

'Good night then.'

Old School' summed up Peter James. Now in his early seventies, he had been, and actually still was, a chartered accountant. James and James had been in Ely for at least three generations. Curiously it was Peter's father and grandfather who were the original James and James, and it was rather convenient that over the generations the name had not needed to be changed. Indeed Peter's son Malcolm had also followed in his father's footsteps and actually did most of the work. 'Narrar,' fen folk would have called him. Over six foot in height, and long limbed, he weighed no more than eight or nine stone. Always formally dressed, he had once been described as man being eaten by his suit, as it seemed to dominate his increasingly fragile appearance. His white hair, long nose and slightly stooping stance, hands perpetually clasped behind his back gave him the appearance of a crane waiting to fly south. For Peter, things had to be done precisely and as the treasurer he saw the church accounts as his territory. In manner he erred on the side of pessimism, no risk and as little change to life as was possible.

He was just what Jane thought she needed.

In truth she slept badly. She woke early, made some black coffee, and tried to do some sums on a notepad. Her concern before she knew she had won was including everyone. Now it was about not wasting it.

'Hallo Peter. What brings you here?

Graham West stood in his doorway at the same height as Peter James, who was standing a step below him.

'Come in, I've got a meeting at nine'

'With Jane Winter?'

'Yes. She asked me to join you. No idea as to what it's about, but it's urgent apparently. Has someone died?'

'You know as much as do. She rang me yesterday. It's my day off actually but she said it was urgent.'

 I'm playing golf this morning, so I hope we won't be long. Are you joining us for the meeting at four o'clock?

'Not that I'm aware of.'

Jane Winter arrived five minutes later, and they were soon sitting in the study with mugs of coffee waiting for Jane to begin.

'I can't even begin to tell you how grateful I am. It is so good of you to drop everything at a moment's notice. I obviously owe you an explanation.' She paused for effect. 'Well, I heard yesterday that I have won one and a half million pounds on the National Lottery.'

There was silence.

'I do not want any publicity and outside my family, you are the only people I've told. I want it to stay that way. Peter, I want you to act for me in an advisory capacity and help me make sure I don't waste the opportunity.

'Good lord,' said Graham, the first to respond. I suppose I should have guessed after our conversation on Sunday morning, but I can honestly say it never occurred to me.'

'Congratulations Jane,' added Peter, 'I will be delighted to help.

'By the way, the meeting this afternoon is with Camelot. Their representative is coming to see me.'

'I'll be there, at your place I suppose.'

'Graham, I want your help as well. I want to do some good with this money. I want advice as to who needs help and how I might help them. Not just in the short term but over a longer period. I've always thought that if I ever won anything I would want to involve the church. Now it's happened I realise I haven't a clue how to do it. I don't want it to go on new hymn books or lectern with a brass plaque and one of my conditions is that nobody will know where it comes from. What do you think?'

'Ok. My initial reaction is that I'd like a little time to think about it. The method is more in Peter's department than mine, but I feel I must say at the beginning that I need to consider the principle. You both know that I think the lottery is a tax on the poor. Would it be hypocritical of me to accept money from a source that I am dubious about? Does the end justify the means? Jane, I don't mean this is as a criticism of you. Your heart is in the right place. Peter what do you think?'

'Can I just say to Jane that we have a booklet which sketches out the basic options on investment advice which we can discuss at another time and after this afternoons meeting which I guess will be a formality. You don't have to rush anything. As to the lottery, it so happens that it was discussed at the deanery finance committee a couple of months ago. I have to say I didn't see at the time why we were bothering with it. Someone asked whether the Church of England had a view. As usual the response from the Archdeacon was ambivalent.'

Peter opened his document case, turned a couple of pages and read. *'The church does not seek to benefit from the proceeds of gambling, and the stance it takes is on an individual basis and is up to the judgement of each parish priest. The Church of England has also received lottery money for the upkeep and maintenance of some of its buildings and the church gives advice to local churches on how to access lottery funds.'* For me as treasurer, I don't ask people who put their money in the collection plate where they got it from. For all I know they could have won it on the horses.'

'Graham placed his fist over his mouth as he was wont to do when he was thinking. 'Thank you Peter. Can I make it clear that we have not had any lottery funding and that I have no plans for this church to apply for any. Jane, I have no doubt of your sincerity and your generosity. Can you give me some time to think about it? Just a few days.'

'Of course Graham, but don't take too long about it.'

The next few days went very quickly and Peter and Jane constructed a budget. The meeting with the winner advisor had gone well. There had been much laughter when the man had introduced himself as Arthur King. Jane thought he was joking, a Camelot stage name perhaps .The money had been paid into her current account until Peter and Jane had agreed an investment package. The family gifts were agreed with a trust fund for her grandchildren.

Arthur King had given advice gleaned from other winners that one way to help the community was to set up a trust fund administered by local people that Jane trusted. It meant she did not have to make decisions herself. The remainder was invested giving her a sensible income from the interest.

In the meantime Jane had heard nothing from Graham. By the Friday it was irritating her, by Saturday she was annoyed. The man could have got back to her by now. But she was not going to chase him. If he didn't want the church involved she would do it without him.

It was as she was opening her collection envelope ready for the Sunday morning service that she had an idea.

She got out her chequebook and wrote out a cheque for ten thousand pounds in favour of St Wulstans Church, folded it and placed it in the envelope, pressing down the glued edge.

Counting the collection happened at the end of each service collection by a church warden. Envelopes were opened and the amount written on the outside. Including cash, the total amounts were recorded in the service ledger, bagged and put into a cloth bag, in the safe. Weekly, Peter James would collect the bag from the safe and visit the bank.

On this particular morning, no one noticed Jane in her usual seat and as the plate came round she dropped her envelope on the plate and smiled to herself. John Panther was on duty and he was an old friend.

After the service had ended he took the plates from the altar into the small vestry. He separated the cash from the envelopes and logged the total. The he worked his way through the envelopes, empting the amounts recording them on the outside and then adding up the total. It didn't take him long. The most common gift was a five pound note and he got used to retrieving and adding in his head. When he got to Jane's envelope, he unfolded the cheque pen in hand. Ten thousand pounds What What Ten thousand pounds!. He could feel himself overheating. Nothing like this had ever happened before. He must tell the Vicar. He left the vestry, and then stopped suddenly. Oh He better lock it up! He walked down the aisle towards the west door, almost running.

'Graham,' he hissed form ten yards away. No response.

 'Vicar' he yelled, decibels louder. Everyone turned towards him.

'Can you come to the vestry- now-please? We have a situation.'

'What is it John? You look flustered, a situation? Whatever has happened?'

'We've had a cheque for ten thousand pounds in an envelope in the collection. What do I do with it?'

Graham smiled. He looked round and saw Jane still sitting in her pew. He moved towards her and his smile turned into a giggle and then loud laughter. As Jane stood up, he grabbed her hands. Then they were both laughing.

People joined in without having the faintest idea what they were laughing at, but it was infectious.

Graham spluttered. 'You are a wicked woman Jane Winter and I thank God for it. OK you win, I give in.

John Panther just watched them. 'Is it me or has the world gone barmy?'

'Totally John,' said Jane. 'We'll have a round table in the church hall next, you wait and see.'

For Goodness Sake

Chapter Five

The Music Society

It was a Tuesday Elisabeth Walters looked out of her lounge window at her husband's silver Rover as it turned out of the drive and made its was eastwards down the Cambridge Road which ran past her house on its way through the village. She looked but did not see, not because the net curtains rendered the view virtually opaque, but because her mind was on other things. The white porcelain teacup in her right hand quivered slightly and the teaspoon gently rattled in the saucer in her left as she turned back towards the personal computer, and the screen reading Microsoft Word Document 1. It stood neatly and proudly in the corner, set in its mahogany case, which could be closed when work was finished, its appearance changed as if by magic into a Georgian bureau. Elisabeth liked that; technology had its place, but it was untidy and visually demanding and clashed with the chintz curtains and lace edged antimacassars. Her taste in furniture, fussy and pretty, was in stark contrast to her dress sense, which could only be described as plain; avoiding bright colour and distinguishing features. Her hair tightly framed around her face and arched to a complex tie-back held with pins, reflected her need for control.

She sat down, smoothed her hair, and began to tidy her desk. It was not untidy but had become part of the ritual in preparing to start the relationship with her computer .The fact that she often had failed to save her work to date indicated the level of her IT capability which might be judged basic. It was one of the reasons why she had taken early retirement; the onset of technology had reached the offices of *James and James Solicitors.* Though not beyond her intelligence, she had welcomed it at first and undertaken her training with some enthusiasm, but she came to realise that the world had changed and the things she regarded as important were under threat. Her view of the world of books and conversation and music were all active; computers were passive and sedentary. Computers changed time and everything became immediate. Her letters on computer had become more verbose and less precise, she thought.

However, the computer had served its purpose and she had been appointed chairperson of the Random music society largely because of it. She had written agendas and reports and now she had to produce a draft agenda for the Annual General Meeting.

She reread her effort so far but in reaching 'minutes of the last meeting', she had developed what she had heard was 'writers block' so she made some tea. The tea had served as a useful diversion, a device her father had used whenever a decision needed to be made which he wished to avoid. Since this seemed to happen several times a day, tea was a constant feature of her upbringing and her adult life. She had tried coffee but she felt it rather unpatriotic, un-British, more American or French. Tea was so much more civilised.

She must try again. It was difficult because she didn't have a solution to the problem, the consideration of which had been delegated to her at the last committee meeting. What to do about the AGM? Numbers at the AGM had been falling year by year so that it was becoming difficult to elect officers never mind the rest of the committee. Was there a way of arranging the meeting so that more people would attend? Early evening or later, Cheese and wine to accompany the business, were topics for consideration. Discussion had raged among the officers and a range of ideas for resurrecting the AGM had been put forward.

Bingo had been rejected as having no musical merit, despite one member's insistence that his recording of Des O'Connor singing 'Songs from the Musicals' would provide a suitable background. The same fate had befallen bridge, whist and a 'beetle drive' on the grounds that the music would be incidental and therefore not in keeping with the aims of the society. They could not afford a professional music group but music there should be.

An amateur concert performance from someone or other before or after the formal meeting was considered, and thought to be a possibility. Funds were short but the entrance fee could meet the total cost, including refreshments. Some local names had been suggested to the committee.

Lily Humble, Elizabeth recollected, a village resident and local teacher was in her day considered to be a fine mezzo-soprano and would be willing, but in her last attempt at 'the music of 'Tosca' she had changed octaves and her virtual bass vibrato somewhat dulled the sexual impact of that heroic role. Her claim that she had swallowed a fly was viewed with some suspicion by other members of the committee.

The village band was suggested but the committee but most believed this would be very much the last resort. Relationships with the band had not always been cordial, since the previous year when their annual concert had clashed with a performance of 'Stainer's Crucifixion' by the Ely Philharmonic choir. They both claimed they had booked the parish church and both had appeared on the same evening at the same time intending to perform. In a flash of genius, the Rector had persuaded the band to move to the church hall together with the three people who had bought their tickets in advance. It had been claimed that many more had come to see the band intending to purchase tickets on the door, but on hearing that the Philharmonic were performing decided to switch their allegiance. Unfortunately, neither the church nor the church hall was entirely sound proof and the distance between them was not sufficient to enable the audience to hear one performance exclusively. This gave rise to noticeable and apparently random juxtaposition. As the door between the two buildings was locked by the churchwarden, the choir opened with 'Fling wide the gates'. Later as the band had played the theme tune from Z-cars as part of its theme songs from the television, the choir began 'could you not watch with me one hour' and finally 'let the trumpet sound' had been accompanied by '76 trombones led the big parade'.
In the eyes of the music committee, the evening had been an unmitigated disaster despite the fact that many had left with tears rolling down their faces. 'Unforgettable', 'Amazing' was the summary judgement of the Huntingdon Post's arts critic.

Elisabeth, to polite applause from the meeting, had offered to give some thought to the issue of the AGM and come up with a suggestion that would be a more attractive proposition than those previously suggested.

The idea finally came to her as she settled down to watch her daily intake of Countdown on Channel 4- a quiz! That was it! A quiz of 40 questions set out on a sheet of A4 which could be filled in during the afternoon's proceedings and then perhaps a further 10 questions played on the piano. She almost ran to the telephone. to tell Jane.

Jane Winters had been a daughter of the vicarage, and had a deep sense of duty to the community. She had always wanted to be in the middle of things. She had always felt she was somebody who should be recognised as important to the village community even though the community never quite warmed to her. She was now labelled a lottery winner, so feelings of envy rather muddied that water.

She had been secretary of the music committee for five years and she felt it. She had become slightly weary of the pressure of expectation that she would always be the organiser.

Later that morning, the call from Elisabeth had been reassuring. A quiz would be popular, and would be something different. She rang round the rest of the committee with the idea. Elisabeth would be responsible for the 40 questions but since Doris Panther normally played 'Jerusalem' for the WI, it was resolved she be asked to come up with 10 questions that she could play on the piano.

The issue resolved, Jane had suggested to one and all that they concentrate on obtaining prizes for a raffle to cover the costs of refreshments.

She suggested the raffle with a slightly heavy heart. They had gone out of fashion in the village circles since a Spanish Rioja had been recycled several times and unwanted Christmas presents began to appear to the point where a giver might suspect the receiver of passing on a carefully chosen gift. It had been sometime since the last raffle so she hoped that the time span was sufficient to refresh the stock.

However it would be fair to say her expectations of a good turnout were rather low.

Graham West, the new Vicar of Random was sitting in his study, when the phone rang. He was stuck in the middle of his sermon and was rather grateful for the interruption.

'The Vicarage.'

'Hello Vicar. It's Elisabeth. Sorry to disturb you. I am ringing to ask a favour.'

'Hello Elisabeth, I'll do what I can.'

'Were you planning on being at the Music Society AGM in a couple of weeks; and if you were would you like to present the prize.'

'Let me look in the diary. It's a Saturday afternoon isn't it? It's there in black and white-but I think it was Judy who was planning to be there. I could be there as well, if you need me. What's the prize for?'

'The quiz- it's going to be a musical quiz.'

'Ok, it's in the diary. Thank you for asking me. Goodbye.'

Word had got round. The novelty of a quiz with tea and scones on a Saturday afternoon had struck a chord with the more elderly section of the village and as Graham and Judy approached the hall at 2.30 that afternoon in plenty of time, they could see what appeared to be a crowd gathering in the car park. He assumed it must be people coming to watch the football match on the sports field on the other side of the hall. As they both got nearer he realised the crowd was going into the hall and not around it as they first thought.

'I thought these events were poorly attended, they must have double booked' he said to Judy.

Inside the hall, Elisabeth was standing at the window looking at the queue, her mouth wide open and he hands raised to her cheeks. All these people had come for the AGM! She had been taught at school not to panic in a crisis, but to take a deep breath and prioritise. So she quickly took charge, divided up the tasks between the committee members and soon had tables and chairs arranged; jam, cream and scones prepared; packs of chocolate biscuits sent for from the local shop to supplement the scones; the scones cut in half to make them go further. She also produced more copies of the agenda and quiz from the photocopier in the church vestry.

120 people had come through the door and by 3.00 pm, they were now seated at tables in fives or sixes, emanating a low hum, the merging of numerous civilities from new or old acquaintances. Two copies of the list of forty questions had been placed on each table and as they became aware of it, groups had begun to fill in the answers, and the hum changed to more of a whisper.

The questions varied in difficulty, but the answers were all people or places. She also tried to include different genres from Victorian parlour to 60's pop. So 'who was invited into the garden?' would be relatively easy for those who remembered 78's, and 'who was asked to stay by me?' was from the late 50's, early 60's. 'Jesus loved her more than you will know' could be much more difficult. It was not always easy to determine the difficulty of a question. In the end Elisabeth supposed a difficult question is one which you cannot answer, so everything is relative.

As she gazed anxiously round the room she was pleased that most people were engaged in the task and seemed to be writing some answers down.

Elisabeth's way of organising the afternoon was intended to introduce variety. After the formal business of the AGM, Doris would play for her quiz, answers to both quizzes would be given out, tea and scones then served and finally the raffle held to bring proceedings to a close.

This way round would give more time for the refreshments to be laid out properly with no indication that the committee had been caught out.

Doris Panther, the 'h' being silent, thought of herself as a musician. She had also been a teacher. Her ability to play the piano has made her indispensible to primary school head teachers who had come and gone, but she had gone on forever. 30 years in the same school. She had eventually not been indispensible and had been dispensed with. Her current musical involvement was playing 'Jerusalem' at the monthly meeting of the WI, and was heavily involved in supporting the Ely Operatic Society where she was responsible for marketing. The music society was therefore not the only committee activity she had taken up after she had taken early retirement. The experience of being a committee member for the music society had been frustrating as they never seemed to discuss music. The programme was devised mostly by the officers and dates fixed by the officers. The rest of the committee discussed catering, made sandwiches and cakes, put out chairs and tables and packed them away again.

Doris owned a grand piano, the only one, as far as she could gather, in the entire county, certainly the village. It fitted her. She was a 'grand' woman, in width rather than height. She mostly dressed in dark colours, skirt and jumper, and rolled up her sleeves when playing, tackling the music with gusto.

She prided herself on her musical knowledge and made regular contributions to the church magazine. She had a wide general knowledge but was always irritated that in pubs and and Trivial Pursuit there was a sports round, about which she knew nothing and music sections that were usually about modern pop music which did not interest her at all.

Playing the piano for quiz questions enthused her and she began to plan her programme. She found the first the first four questions rather easy.

'Now question 5. Place or person...mmm?'

The pen dived and she began to draft in her best *Marion Richardson* handwriting-

'Who had buckles on his knee?'

She leaned back and head to one side examined her script as if it required artistic approval; and wrote Bobby Shaftoe. 'Mmm; perhaps a little too easy?'

She turned to page 4 of 'Songs from long Ago', and played the first couple of lines, in an operatic style. Her contralto voice rang across the sitting room.

'Bobby Shaftoe went to sea, silver buckles on his knee

He'll come back to marry me...Bobby ....

She slithered to a halt.

Some questions needed to be a little easy or people would get discouraged. Anyway most of the regulars were pretty thick and wouldn't know a suite from a symphony. She sought to make the next one really difficult........

'Mmmmm .....which English county would you associate with this music? That will test them' she thought. How old did you have to be to remember the 'Onedin Line'?

For a moment she forgot that she needed to be able to play it- then realised she had a CD which included the theme tune which had been taken from Khachaturian's '*Spartacus*'. The programme was set in Devon or was it Cornwall? She wondered whether this might be regarded as obscure. Not a question for the younger members anyway. Now she had to transfer the answers on to the answer sheet.

As she got to the point of writing the answer to question 6, the telephone rang.

By 3.30 the new committee had been elected and the officers appointed. Elisabeth had given her report and the AGM was closed.

Doris began her section of the quiz with great energy and served up a reasonable mix of questions. The audience were looking for things to amuse them. There was an impromptu humming for some questions, under the breath, with calls of 'shush don't give it away' from the more competitive. Before long the music questions had been completed and a round of applause had been forthcoming as Jane thanked Doris.

'Please make sure you put your name at the top of your answers sheet and swap it with a neighbouring group for marking.'

'Have you got the list of questions?' Jane asked Doris. Doris searched among her papers, finally extricated her own crib sheet and passed it to Elisabeth to begin giving the answers.

'Is there a prize?' A voice from the back rang out as the applause died down.

'Well no- not actually- we did consider….. but then felt the music was……

Before she could continue a second and third chimed in……'.I think there should be a prize.'

'A pity.'

'All this work and no reward?'

One voice was added to another and soon there was a general discussion taking place as to the rights and wrongs of the argument.

'I'm sure the reward of taking part is sufficient for most of us,' said Elisabeth, by this time shouting and trying to bring order.

The answers ritual for the ten questions was calm to begin with. The audience were looking for things to amuse them. There was an impromptu singing of Bobby Shaftoe, In a Monastery Garden, Yesterday and Blowing in the Wind.

Then Elisabeth misread the order and for question 5 she had the answer to question six. 'Surrey!' she announced.

Nooooo…….!! The response was almost choral in its singularity.

'Oh dear, have I get it wrong? It does say the answer is Surrey.'

Elisabeth checked the paper and then looked round to Doris for support.

'Surrey with a fringe on the top,' exclaimed several voices at once, that should be number six.

 'Oh dear, have I got them in the wrong order? 'What was the question again?' asked Elisabeth of Doris.

'Which county was associated with the music of Katchachurian?' said someone from the audience. 'The Onedin Line was not about Surrey', another equally determined voice came from the back.

Elisabeth turned to Doris. 'What should be the answer?'

'Oh dear, was it Cornwall?' she was flustered and her mind went blank.

Yeeeeeeessssssssss………..! A second chorus from points north and south brought spontaneous giggles, then raucous laughter and finally a continuous stream of conversation as those who hadn't quite followed were brought up to date.

The final 4 questions went by without any more mistakes and Elisabeth was able to say

'Lets have tea' and without too much delay scones jam and cream was winging its way to the tables. You have a further fifteen minutes over tea, to fill in the answers to the twenty questions, and then after tea we will give the answers.

Fifteen minutes later, Elisabeth intervened again.

'Let me give you the answers to the set of forty questions.' and without pausing began to read out the answers in order. All was well until she reached the end of question nineteen. Where she went wrong, as she listened to committee members later, was asking who had got the most right so far. This introduced a competitive element that she had previously been trying to avoid.

Two members of the audience claimed 18 out of nineteen for their group at the halfway point. One of them was Graham West. He and Judy had enjoyed the questions and despite having to make one of two educated guesses, he and Judy were going quite well until he overheard the conversation from the team at the next table.

'He's marking his own, how do we know he's not cheating?' claimed one.

'He is the Vicar, for Goodness sake,' someone retorted.

'I really think some of us are taking this a little too seriously', said Elisabeth, touching her pearls and smoothing her hair with the palm of her hand to a polite 'hear hear' from other committee members.

The scores were going to be close and it gradually became clear that the final result would depend on the last question.

'.......And now the final answer to question forty which I remind you was 'Who wrote the 'Pearl Fishers?'....'

Elisabeth paused for effect, 'and can I remind you we wanted his full name. The answer is,' she paused, 'Georges Bizet.'

There was for half a second a silence and then Judy shouted 'Hooray.' from one side of the room. Clearly the last question had decided things.

But before Elisabeth could continue, a loud voice exclaimed from the other side, 'I'm sorry but there is another answer to that question.'

'There is? Oh I mean is there?'

Elisabeth did not quite know what to say.

71

'Georges Bizet's original name was Alexandre Cezar Bizet? He changed it to Georges much later in his life.'

There was a buzz of conversation, clearly controversy was afoot.

'His friends just called him George then', someone quipped. Nobody calls him Alexandre-Cesar Bizet, for goodness sake.'

'I am right I assure you, I have a degree in French and studied Bizet for my dissertation.'

'If you knew that much you should have known he was normally called Georges.' Elisabeth fiddled with her pearls. A row was brewing.

Graham began to feel uncomfortable. He turned to Judy. 'I think we may have to withdraw, we can't be at the centre of this. I'll have a word with Elisabeth.'

Elisabeth was trying to look calm and as Graham walked toward her through the tables, she waved at Judy and the three of them met at the front of the room.

They turned their backs to the audience and Elisabeth whispered to Judy, 'Were you aware there could be two answers to this question? The man seems awfully sure.'

'No I had no idea- but common knowledge would say the answer was Georges wouldn't it?'

'Yes. But he is not wrong either! What shall we do?'

'It will have to be a tie.'

'Graham interrupted. 'No, Judy and I will withdraw. Give the prize to the other team. It's much better that way. We didn't expect to win, and I couldn't give the prize to myself could I?'

Elisabeth turned towards the audience and again touched the pearls by her throat. We were not aware of the possibility of another answer, but there clearly is. The Vicar and Judy his wife have agreed to withdraw, which is very generous of them.

'No.' A voice rang out from the now winning team. 'Why don't we share it?'

At this there was a spontaneous round of applause. Elisabeth gave Graham the box of chocolates and he asked for the team representatives to come and receive the prize?'

Judy looked at Graham, pointed to herself and mouthed 'Me?'

He nodded and the two champions weaved to the front. They stood, one on either side of Graham, like boxers waiting for their arm to be raised.. Graham held the box between them but neither seemed to want to be the first to take it.

'After you.'

'No! After you.'

In a low voice, Graham said to 'Alexandre Cesar, 'I'm sorry about the mix up, but you deserve the prize, can I suggest you take it, open it now and hand it round, to your teams first and then hand it to Judy if there are any left. This was never meant to be any more than fun.'

The two contenders shook hands and smiled, then laughed, and soon the whole audience began to see the funny side of things.

Elisabeth took over. 'Thank you to the Vicar for giving the prize, and thank you all for coming, it been quite invigorating and we hope to see you all in the new season'.

Elisabeth concluded the proceedings, to a polite round of applause, a scrape of chairs and a move for the exit.

Graham and Judy strolled home, arm in arm.

'Did you get a chocolate? Would you like one now?'

Judy handed him the box. It was nearly full.

'I think they were so embarrassed, they didn't take many.'

'At least everyone stayed friendly, just. I hadn't imagined that I would become the village referee.'

News of the AGM reverberated around the village for weeks and months to come, at home, at church and in the British Legion hall people recounted the events of that year's meeting, providing more laughter than perhaps the event itself had really deserved.

As Elisabeth herself commented to Jane after they had cleared away the plates, stacked the chairs and folded the tables. 'Well we won't forget that in a hurry.'

Doris was just glad it was all over.

It was the following Monday that Graham met Jacob Babcock coming out of the Post office.

'Greetings Vicar, I hear you had some trouble with the music quiz last week.'

'Not really Jack, it was just a bit of fun that people took too seriously.'

'They always do. No matter how much you tell people it's fun they get competitive. Human instinct I guess. We have two rules now for our monthly quiz, announced before we begin and pinned to the wall. There are only two rules.

Rule One - The Question master is always right.

Rule Two-In the event of the Question master being wrong, Rule One applies.

It saves a lot of argument.

'I bet it does. Thanks Jack, have a chocolate

For Goodness Sake

Chapter Six

The Bell Ringers

'For goodness sake,' said Graham West, incumbent vicar of Random Parish Church in the Archdeanery of March in the county of Cambridgeshire, 'there are no bells.'
He was walking from the vicarage towards the church, one Sunday morning in January, he was just passing the bank, when he first had the feeling that something was different, but he couldn't just put his finger on it. He raised his head and like a periscope searching the horizon he glanced to right and left. As the spire of the parish church came into the centre of his vision, he knew.
Where normally he would have heard the peal of the bells summoning the faithful to worship, there was a deafening silence.
He soon reached the west door and went in. Standing with hands in their pockets looking rather disconsolate, were two bell ringers.
'What's up? Are you locked out or has someone stolen the bells?' he said cheerfully.
Clearly merry quips were not going to be appreciated this morning and there was no reaction.
'They're all down with flu,' said George Wilson, the tower captain. 'I didn't get the phone calls until an hour ago and I just couldn't get any replacements at such short notice. There was only Danny and me fit to ring, and with the best will in the world we couldn't do much. It's a complete disaster. Did you know it's the first time since 1939 that these bells haven't rung on a Sunday morning? First the Nazis, now Asian flu! I am so sorry Vicar, what you must be thinking I can't imagine. Can you carry on without us?'
As it happened, Graham wasn't thinking of very much at all but George was clearly upset.
'Don't worry George, it's not the end of the world, I'm sure God will understand and give us the strength to carry on. I suppose we are a bit thinner on the ground than we used to be, when things are back to normal we better have a chat to see what we might do about it.

On weekdays, George Wilson was the village postmaster but from Friday evening to Monday morning he was transformed. No one would have guessed. He was a hearty well met sort of fellow, always ready with a cheerful word and the latest joke. His appearance didn't change at weekends. Grey faced, he wore grey trousers, grey shirt often with sleeves rolled up to the elbow, a sleeveless jumper, light green or light brown, and a waterproof jacket that he zipped up to his several chins at the slightest suggestion of wet weather. He was only five feet five inches tall, had a forty four inch waist and walked with a rolling swagger, shoulders and legs moving simultaneously. He smelt of stale tobacco which with his stained yellow fingers confirmed him as a forty- a- day man. He had lived in Random all his life, first with his parents in a cottage on the Cambridge Road, then for a short time in a council house on the estate. When his parents died, he went back to their house with his wife 'Em'. Largely because he smoked excessively he looked older than his fifty eight years. He had a standard response borrowed from George Burns when asked about his smoking habit, 'at my age I need something to hang on to and I've given up sex.' He would then roar with laughter shaking his whole body and coughing violently.

He stood outside his house to smoke in all weathers, either leaning on the front gate if it was fine or back pressed against the front door to take advantage of the eaves if it was wet. Em would not let him smoke indoors. This gave him the opportunity to chat to the people walking up and down the hill to and from the High Street and as a consequence he was known to all of the village residents who passed that way. Car drivers would press their horns or flash their lights and would receive the response of a raised arm as they sped past.

At a quarter to seven each Friday he made his way up the hill to the church, unlocked the tower door and climbed the spiral staircase to his second home with the bells of St. Wulfstans. Around the ringing chamber there were plaques recording various peals and photographs of the ringers going back to the beginnings of photography. They had a proud history. There were eight bells which had been cast by Taylors of Loughborough in 1919 as a memorial to those who had died in the first war. The tenor bell weighed 29 hundredweight, not for the faint-hearted and certainly too heavy for a beginner.

Not that Random had any beginners.

Generally, Random experienced very little turnover or movement in population over the years. You were born here and stayed here or you moved here and stayed.

With the bell ringers it had become a case of 'dead men's shoes.' There had been few vacancies as well as a decline in church attendance which meant a dearth of young people interested and these things combined meant that gradually numbers had dwindled and if the bell ringers had been wild animals they would have been identified as an endangered species.

But George Wilson had a plan.

Graham West was the antithesis of George Wilson. He was slim, and serious, a non smoker and had been in Random for under two years. If pressed, he would have acknowledged some doubt about the role of bell ringers in the Church of England. There was of course a long tradition of bell ringing going back to the very beginnings of the church itself, but bell ringers seemed to Graham to be something of a law unto themselves. In his experience few bell ringers attended the church services so they were a part of the church but also separate from it. He had never seen George at a church service, and it annoyed him that the beginning of the Sunday morning service was always interrupted by the tower door being closed and locked and the main door being opened and closed as the bell ringers left the church after their musical stint.
He was also acutely aware that it had become more difficult to offer the bells for weddings as he could not be sure that there would be enough people available. The bells were also becoming expensive. The tower steps had been in need of repair and had come up in the quinquennial review of the church fabric and some of the bell ropes had been renewed.
It was with all these things in his mind that later that week, he wandered through the SPCK bookshop in Cambridge. He was looking for some Easter resources for use in the family service. It was then that a colourful CD caught his eye. '*Bells for all Occasions.*' ran the yellow title set against a bright red background. He picked it up and turned it over to read the description on the back.
'25 peals of bells for all occasions- Sunday services, funerals, weddings etc.'
I wonder, he thought.
He read on.
'These recordings may be used to broadcast the sounds of bells from a PA system where real church bells are not available or usable.'
It would be fair to say that Graham had not thought through all the implications

of what came into his mind that morning in Cambridge, but he thought he had the beginnings of a plan.

'How much would it cost for a smallish advert in your paper this Friday?'
George, in his Tuesday lunch break, was ringing the *Fenland Citizen* small ads section.
'What is it you want to sell?' asked a young female voice.
There was a slight pause as George took in a response he was not expecting.
'I don't want to sell anything. Am I in the right section?'
' I'm not sure. Did you want to advertise something perhaps?'
'Yes that's it! I'm thinking of advertising an event.'
'Ah! How many words is it?'
'How many words is what?'
'What do you want to say?'
'I don't know, I haven't written it yet. I just want a price.'
It had seemed to George a very easy thing to do. You want to place an advert in your local paper. The only piece of information one needs to help decide whether to do it or not is the price. The young lady on the phone seemed determined not to give it to him.
'Of course you do. Let me explain!'

'The problem is,' she intoned and it seemed to George, she talked very slowly. He felt like a five year old and was starting to get very hot under his light cotton shirt.
'The price depends on what you want to say, which is related to how much room you require to say it. A newspaper you see sells space.'
There was silence from the other end of the telephone.
'When would this event be taking place?' she continued.
'I haven't decided on a date yet.' George was getting disheartened.
'Mmm. Ok. Well let's start from there. You go away and write what you want to say, decide on a date, come back to me and I'll give you a price.'
 Then to George's utter astonishment she added, 'Typically a single column of two centimetres will cost £30. Don't forget, all advertisements must be with us by Monday at twelve noon in order to meet our publishing deadlines. This newspaper is published weekly on a Wednesday. Thank you for calling the *Fenland Citizen*. Goodbye.'

George went back to his cheese and pickle sandwich. Why couldn't she have said that in the first place?' he thought. 'Why did we have to go through that rigmarole about counting the words?'

It gradually dawned on him that the young lady would be paid on how much space she was able to sell and of course salesmen try to persuade people to buy more than they think they want. He sat back in his armchair and mused. He would hate her job, being a salesman that is. Or in her case was it saleswoman or salesperson. He didn't particularly like telephones either, but he supposed they were necessary. His mind drifted back to the days when the newspaper had a small office in Random, where the hairdressers is now, and you used to be able to pop in, talk to someone, write your advert, pay for it and have the whole thing done and dusted in ten minutes.

It was supposed to be simpler now, but it seemed to George that it was actually more complicated and a hell of a lot more expensive; £30 for a small advert. Phew.

Two weeks later, on the Thursday afternoon, Graham West was sitting in his armchair. His wife Judy had just returned from a meeting in Cambridge. They sat with mugs of tea and shortbread biscuits, the calm before storm, when Graham would fetch the children from their after school piano lessons. Judy, picked up the weeks copy of the *Fenland Citizen*, and as she turned the pages, she talked about her day and Graham outlined his Sunday sermon which had been the substance of his day.

'Good lord! Have you seen this?, she said

Seen what? Graham felt a bit miffed at her interruption when he was trying to explain the meaning of the parable.

'It's an advert for bell ringers'.

Which church? Sounds enterprising!

'Yours,' Judy exclaimed handing him the paper.

What It can't be! Who in heaven's name?

ARE YOU LOOKING FOR A NEW HOBBY OR INTEREST? WHY NOT TRY BELL RINGING? RANDOM PARISH CHURCH BELL RINGERS INVITE YOU TO AN OPEN EVENING ON FRIDAY THE 20TH APRIL AT 7.00 PM-CALL GEORGE WILSON 01354 676675. COME AND HAVE A GO

George. He might have told me.

'I don't suppose he'll get many takers.' Judy reassured him grabbing back the paper from Grahams hands.

'I thought you said it was enterprising.'

'That was before I knew it was George.'

'I think you're being very mean. You were very critical when he wasn't doing anything. Well, now he is. You should give the man some credit.'

'I suppose you're right, but I had rather a different idea.'

Graham went into his study and came back with the CD, *Bells for All Occasions*. He opened the plastic case and put the disc into the CD player. In a few seconds, the room was resounding to the peal of bells. He handed Judy the case and pointed to the explanation on the back.

'This is what gave me the idea. You see, we could get a set of speakers put into the bell tower and simply use the system we have already got in church to play for whatever service we want. We wouldn't need bell ringers at every service. In the long run it would be much easier and more effective and if the flu struck or there was some other problem we simply put the CD on.'

He turned off the bells and extricated the CD.

'It's quite a good idea, don't you think?'

'Does George know what you are thinking of? Clearly not. Or has he put this in the paper out of sheer desperation?' Judy answered.

'Practical as ever my darling; but good lord, no. He and I had a conversation some weeks ago about the difficulty of attracting people to ring, but I thought it was hypothetical. George, you know the way he is, he doesn't always see problems until they're on top of him. Don't you remember, we had that morning service in January when we didn't have any bells. A couple of ringers cried off at the last minute with flu and George couldn't get a replacement. But we have been getting to the stage where we couldn't offer the bells for a wedding, and on some Sundays when we were very thin on the ground, George has usually been able to bring in ringers from other churches to fill the gaps, but that's not sustainable in the long run. We both said we would think about what could be done.'

'Well he certainly seems to have taken your conversation seriously If I were you I'd be very careful. Once you go down the road of no bell ringers, you can't go back. George won't thank you for trying to get rid of them.'

'But I wasn't thinking about getting rid of them, only for those occasions when we couldn't get anybody.'

'George might not see it that way.'

'No I suppose he might not.'

'He's thought of a different approach.'

'You do realise that it's the 20th tomorrow.'

'Ouch. He hasn't given people much notice has he?'

'Will you go?'

'No, I don't think so. Since he hasn't told me formally it's happening, I don't know about it officially, so I think I'll just let him get on with it.'

It was the Saturday morning when Graham caught up with the news of how the opening evening went. The children had gym and football, and Graham normally found himself standing on the touchline watching his son Peter play for the Random under 11's in the Ely and District league. There were a number of fathers who usually gathered on Saturday mornings and over the course of a season they got to know each other quite well by first names. David, whose surname Graham didn't know, was already in position just past the half-way line when Graham arrived.

'Morning Graham.'

'Morning David.'

'Nice morning for it.'

'Certainly is, who are we playing?'

'I think they are from Witchford; red shirts, black shorts.'

'Oh yes, we've already played them at their place, I think. We won didn't we?'

'I don't really remember, but I'm not sure Kevin was playing in the team then.'

'Although Jane says my memory is getting worse. You can't get dementia at my age can you?'

'I sincerely hope not. I'm much the same. There was an article in the telegraph about it a couple of months ago. It's something to do with as you get older you begin to distinguish between what's important and what isn't. Some things you need to remember so your do, others are not so essential so you don't. Common sense really, I suppose.'

There was a pause in the conversation as the teams ran out on to the field.

'Come on Random! Up the blues. Come on lads. Cries punctuated the sharp winter air.

'Freya had a great time at your place last night. She said it was really interesting. There's apparently a lot more to it than you think. She thinks she might give it go, but she's third on the waiting list so it might be awhile before she gets the chance.'

Graham for several moments hadn't a clue what David was talking about.

'Oh really. That's good. What event was that then?'

'It was some sort of open evening for the bells.

'Oh yes. Good gracious, I'd completely forgotten about it. See you're not the only one who can't remember things. George Wilson arranged it. Did it go well? Well it must have done if Freya wants to join.'

'She said there were a lot there and they had to line up around the ringing chamber. I think that's what it's called?'

Were there many there?'

'About twenty people,' she said.

'Come on Random… shoot…...oooooh. Good effort.'

'So what happened?' Graham was curious.

'Um let me see. I think she said that George, did you say his name was, gave an introduction to the bells and then they gave a demonstration and afterwards Freya had a go; sounded quite well organised.'

'And Freya enjoyed it. '

'Yes. She had to pull the rope down, release it at the bottom and hold it as it went back up again. I think that was something like that.'

'Did many join?'

'Freya said she was about seventh or eighth on the list, I think. She's been given a start date in April.'

'It was well organised then?....... Come on Random…Goal.'

The reply was drowned by the shouts of the crowd.

Should he offer them the bells? Graham West was sitting in his study talking through the wedding details with a young couple who had fixed their wedding for the end of April some months before and now they were going through Graham's checklist. Dates for the banns to be called, number and choice of hymns, date and time of rehearsal, choir or no choir, and the bells were on the list of decisions to be made. He decided he would offer them the bells. If George's new set of ringers were not in place by the end of April, he would go ahead with using the recording. He had a spare set of speakers that could be erected in the bell tower and he had the CD ready to play.

It meant of course he would have to speak to George.

'Would you like the church bells playing as you come out of the church into the sunshine, we hope for good weather anyway. It really creates a lovely atmosphere. We can offer you either the real bells, which some people find is a little expensive, or we can offer you a cheaper version from a CD played out through speakers in the tower. It can be just as effective. Would you like to think about it?'

They said they would let him know.

Of course Graham had never heard the CD through speakers from the tower and he did feel a little guilty that he might have been misleading the loving couple. He decided he couldn't wait and see what decision they came to before he did something about it. He needed a trial run.

George Wilson was finishing his pint of IPA in the Black Bull public house, when Jacob Babcock, announced that he liked the sound of church bells. The group of regulars gathered in the saloon bar were used to his idiosyncrasies and so no one immediately responded with a 'Do you Jack?' or Fancy that.' The noise of conversation in the bar that lunchtime was not excessively loud, but no one else, least of all George, heard what Jack had heard.

'Who is ringing today then George?' asked Jack.

'What?' Nobody! Why?'

'Well someone is. Listen.'

There was quiet for a moment, heads turned in the direction of the church. George broke the silence.

'What the hell is going on?' said George, already on his way to the door.' Some bugger is ringing my bells.'

He stopped as he reached the exit and returned for his coat and cap, swept them up and weaving between the tables at speed left the pub.

It was a five minute walk up the hill to the church and George was in a state of confusion. By this time the bells had stopped but George could still hear them.

'It sounded like it was a ringing team playing the wedding peal. Had he forgotten a booking? Was there a wedding that morning?'

'There can't be,' he said to himself. 'I checked the calendar, there was nothing on today. What if they did they not tell me? Perhaps they wanted to bring someone else in and didn't like to tell me.'

 The thought shocked him and he slowed and then stopped in the middle of the pavement, half turned, unsure of which direction he should now go in. Then he noticed there had been something not quite right about them but he couldn't quite put his finger on it. His hesitation did not last; he had to find out what was going on. He carried on up the hill. By the time he reached the church he knew what was wrong. It was not only too good, it was also a ten bell peal and Random only had eight bells.

'Somebody's playing silly beggars. It's that *Bells for All Occasions* CD Bloody Hell,' he muttered as he entered the church.

'My God Vicar, you nearly gave me a heart attack! I thought there was a wedding and I'd forgotten it. What's going on?'

'Oh, good afternoon George, I'm sorry to surprise you like that, I tried to ring you this morning, but 'Em said you'd already gone shopping and wouldn't be back until after two o'clock. I wanted to talk to you but I kept missing you on Sunday mornings and I was running out of time. I wanted to see if it would work and it did.

'*Bells for All Occasions* wasn't it?'

'Oh you know it then.'

'It's pretty well known. I just didn't expect to hear it from the Black Bull.'

 'Wow! That's marvellous! You could hear it as far as that. OK my suggestion is we give it a try.'

'Give what a try?'

'The recording; we've got a wedding at the end of April and I wanted to offer them bells, but I knew that even with your new recruits it would take time to get them trained and organised, so I thought we might use this as a temporary solution.'

George shook his head.

'It's the thin end of the wedge, Vicar. What's next? Robots pulling the bell ropes? How would you like it if we put a recorded sermon in the pulpit? It might be better than you, certainly cheaper, but that's not quite the point is it? If someone wants bells for their wedding, I'll do my best to provide them. What date did you say it was?'

'The twenty third I was in something of a quandary so I confess I did mention the recording alternative as well as live bells Of course, they may decide not to have either; they were going to think about it. I needed to know whether it would work before I see them next week.'

'Well it worked alright. And I bet you weren't going to charge them the same rate.'
'I couldn't really could I?'
'Just like Tesco!'
'Tesco?'
'Yes! I went this morning. When I was a lad they served you from behind a counter and the shop assistant would fetch what you asked for from the shelves. She would then add up the prices of the goods in her head and you paid by cash. Mother used to check it when I got home, but they were never wrong. Now you get things from the shelves and take them to the counter, where a girl puts them through a machine which adds them up. I notice they are even trying to get rid of the till girls. What's the reason we all go there? It's cheaper. Give people a cheaper option and they'll take it. Now none of the youngsters can add up in their head. We've lost the skill as well. That's what's happening here. Give people a choice of a cheaper wedding, they'll take it.
In twenty years, we'll still have the bells but there will be no one left who knows how to ring them.'
Graham West said nothing
'Well, Vicar, it's your church, and you can do pretty much what you want in it. But this time you're wrong. For the first time in a long time, the future of bell ringing in this church is looking good. There's a lot of enthusiasm from some youngsters and I think that if you want it you will have a good bell team for some years to come. They won't all stay of course, but enough of them will. I don't want to be the one to tell them that the church doesn't want them.'
George didn't wait for a response. He turned on his heel and with his customary swagger he left by the west door.

It was the following Sunday that Graham West walked up the pulpit steps and began his sermon.

'In our gospel reading this morning we heard the story of Martha and Mary, in which Martha forgot what was most important. It happens to us all from time to time, I wonder how many of you shop at Tesco's?'

About half an hour earlier, before the service had begun, the handle of the west door had turned to close and George Wilson and friends were walking across the green in the spring sunshine. He took the *Bells for All Occasions* CD out of his pocket and offered it to his newest recruit, 'Have a listen to this, it'll give you an idea of what bells should sound like. It's important we keep up to date and use the latest technology.'

Chapter 7

The Cricket Match

Random Cricket Club was situated on the edge of the village just off the Ely Road. The ground was shared with the football club, neither side achieving sufficient level of skill or league status to warrant their own place. Cricket, with its pavilion and tin hut, left there by the Home Guard after the war, were the furthest away from the road. The wicket, on a plateau, had from both ends run ups that ended with a slope uphill to the stumps. The two pitches, football and cricket, overlapped by several metres which made it a fielding nightmare in a section of the outfield From time to time the club had flirted with local leagues but eventually settled on playing a full season of friendly matches on Saturday afternoons.

As a result younger players had in recent seasons, come and then gone to seek a higher and more competitive standard, saying they were disappointed that they could not get sufficient support within the club for them to join a league.

The majority of the existing players were married men over thirty five who did not want to devote entire weekends to the game. So the picking of the team involved rotation enabling most people to play couple of times a month.. The process was complicated by a club rule.

The rule said that anybody who wanted to play on a Saturday had to turn out for net practice on the day before, Friday. This included preparing the pitch for the game by pulling the heavy stone roller up and down the wicket. It took four to pull it as a minimum, but the more there were, the easier it was.

The team was picked on a Tuesday evening for the Saturday after next by a triumvirate of the club president (non playing), the club captain and the vice captains, namely Jim Walters, Charlie Gray and Gulam Singh. They met in the Black Bull and gathered around a small table in the corner of the Lounge bar. It was not unknown for some on the edge of selection to ensure that they were seen by the selectors at some time during the evening by drifting between the smoke and the lounge bars

Charlie Gray, a local builder, was not happy.

'OK Chairman, what are we going to do about those people who don't turn up for practice?' said Charlie. 'These youngsters want to play but they don't want to share the load. We can't let them get away with it. In my day you were lucky to be invited to the club never mind play regularly.'

Gulam Singh agreed. 'It was the very same in Birmingham, Charlie. The problem is if you enforce the rule you have real trouble picking a team that's competitive. I can only bowl from one end my friend. In any case because we choose a team to play a week on Saturday, they always say they will be there for practice on Friday certainly.'

'And then they leave the ground after they have had a net, before we need them to roll the wicket. Or they claim they thought we were playing away, so we didn't need to prepare a wicket at all.' Charlie concluded.

There was a moment's pause as Jim Walters pondered. Eventually he cleared his throat and pronounced.

'I understand your frustration Charlie, but I'm not sure it's that simple. It's not just the youngsters is it? That rule was introduced just after the war when most people who played, lived and worked in Random. They finished work at five on Fridays and could have their tea, which would be ready on the table, and be out by six. Now, most of our players work in Ely or Cambridge or even Peterborough.

'Carl works in Bedford,' said Gulam.

'Nearly all work until five thirty and get home by six thirty if they are lucky,' continued Jim, 'wives are working and we can't expect tea to be on the table. If they get to us by seven they are doing really well. We have to be realistic.'

'My wife doesn't work and I still don't get tea on the table,' bemoaned Charlie.

'Give over Charlie, she has got the kids,' said Jim. 'Anyway we have to be practical. So let's make decisions on an individual basis. We know most of our people pretty well and in the main their hearts are in the right place. If we feel someone is not pulling their weight we have a quiet word with them. Charlie, as captain that's your job, and then if there is no improvement, we don't pick them until there is a change of attitude. How does that sound?'

There was a loud grunt from Charlie.

Jim took this to be assent. 'Charlie, one of the reasons I'm keen to avoid the issue is Graham West.'

'Good player, he's made quite a difference to our batting line up. I think number six is far too low and I want to try him at three.' Charlie said.

'Mmm.' Jim was non committal.

'Oh come on Jim, you know he's good and I don't think anyone would have their nose put out of joint if he was promoted a few places.'

'It's not that Charlie. Graham is thinking of giving up altogether. He had a word with me after service on Sunday.'

'But he's only just joined.'

'Is he not happy with his game?' asked Gulam, 'There does come a time when if you are not enjoying something… well you know.'

Jim shook his head. 'No I am sure it isn't that. He calls cricket the Church of England at play. Although he's 42, he still loves the game. It's just the pressure on him at weekends. Mainly weddings. He doesn't feel he can restrict the time of a Saturday wedding to finish by one thirty so he can get to his cricket match. That's hard for him when we play at home, but sometimes impossible if we are playing away and he has to travel.'

'But he knows a fair time in advance doesn't he?' said Charlie.' I mean the banns have to be called a few times, so that must be at least a month.'

'Of course that is true.' replied Jim. 'But he has a number of problems, the date and time of the wedding and the socialising afterwards. He can't play if the wedding is after twelve o'clock. Even then things get delayed. Brides are getting later. It's now the thing to be fifteen minutes late arriving.'

Gulam sympathised. 'You think you have problems, Indian weddings last several days and are getting longer. Cricket stands no chance.'

Jim continued. 'Then he can't always get away straight after the 'I do'. People want to speak to him, he has to socialise. He's getting to the stage where he can't guarantee that a wedding which has a start after midday allows him enough time to get to the ground.

Charlie mused, 'Can't think why people want to get married in the cricket season at all.'

Jim ignored the comment. 'Unfortunately for cricket Charlie, they do. It's not too bad if we're batting and he's late because the order could be adjusted. The trouble is that's not something we have control over. It's a toss of the coin. He's got to the stage where he's wearing his kit under his cassock at the wedding to save time changing.

'I don't suppose anyone notices,' said Charlie,' what the eye doesn't see, the heart doesn't grieve over.'

Jim continued. 'He feels that it is not fair on the rest of the team if he picks and chooses the games he plays, especially on those who are keen to play regularly and miss out if he is playing.

It also means when he has a wedding on a Saturday at any time, he can't get to net practice on a Friday night because that's the only time he has for a family rehearsal. He can't help but break the rule!'

Gulam looked puzzled. 'But we can't change the rule can we?. It needs a resolution at the AGM.'

'That's right Gulam. But I think we can turn a blind eye to it for now, can't we?'

Jim Walters ended the meeting and went to the toilet. By the time he returned Charlie had got another round of drinks and he and Gulam were chatting to a couple of chaps he thought he recognised. Of course he did. Pidley!

The last time they had met had been almost exactly a year ago in the 'friendly' match. Pidley was a village just a few miles from Random, had over the years developed a keen rivalry with Random on the cricket field. There had been occasions when players had come to blows and there had been serious discussions between the two clubs as to whether the fixture should continue. It had been agreed that it would be a pity to discontinue a local fixture and agreed to try and calm their players. The previous year, the Pidley players seemed to have tried their hand at sledging, an Australian imported tactic designed to wind up the other side and disturb their concentration. It had worked. A couple of Random players had lost their heads, tried to hit sixes off good length balls, and got out cheaply. Random had lost.

'Evening,' said Jim, reaching for his pint.

'Hi there' said the Pidley opening bowler and his captain in unison.

'Don't see you two in here very often; have they closed the pubs in Pidley then.'

The Captain smiled 'No but they're trying. We've lost two pubs in the last few years. Had a few things to pick up from a mate and thought we'd stop off for a quick one. I gather its selection night.'

'It is,' said Jim, 'and if you'll forgive me I need to put the teams on the notice board.' He reached across the table, picked up his papers and with a 'shan't be a minute' to his fellow selectors he went through to the other bar.

'Will you have a strong side out for a week on Saturday?' asked Charlie

We think so,' said the Captain, 'but we don't pick our sides until Sunday morning, I think we'll have most people available. What about you?'

Charlie smiled. 'We've managed to put a side together which we think might be competitive.'

'Any new players from last year?'

Charlie was non committal. 'One or two.'

The Captain pressed the point. 'Batters or bowlers?'

'Both really; a young chap to partner Gulam, George Wilson's boy. He's quite quick and is left arm over which gives us a bit of variety. And a new number three which strengthens the top order.'

'Is he local?'

'Yes. He's the new vicar.'

'You all have to behave yourselves then.'

'He's Ok. Just enjoys his cricket like the rest of us.'

Gulam joined the conversation. 'What about you guys? Are you having a good season?'

'Yes reasonable, Gulam, third in the league. We started a friendly side this year as well. It gives us a bit more flexibility. We can give more people a game obviously and if we're short in the league side we can bring people in.

'Good idea,' said Gulam. 'So your side on the Saturday week is the friendly side is it?

'The friendly side normally play on a Sunday afternoon, we've only made an exception for Random because it's such a long running fixture and it's at your ground. Yes it will be the Friendly side.' The Captain looked at his watch. 'Well we better be going. See you guys. Thanks Jacob, and with a wave to mine host they were gone.

They had hardly closed the door on their way out before Charlie was rubbing his hands together with a smile on his face.

'Did you hear that, we're going to be playing their friendly side, not the league side.'

'That should not be a problem for us,' agreed Gulam,' we had better tell Jim.

'I am really not sure what to do' Graham West confided in his wife. No one who knew Graham well would have described him as decisive. He was quiet and thoughtful. In any situation requiring choice, he would consider the consequences on all sides, carefully sift the evidence and eventually decide on his preference.

At that point, the other side of his character kicked in and he would see whatever it was through to the end. In fact there were times when he verged on the stubborn.

'Well you could make a cup of tea, darling.' said Judy with a smile.

Judy was the antithesis of her husband. As he was serious, she could be light hearted. As he troubled over decisions, she had an instinct for doing the right thing. As he was obstinate, she was flexible and open minded.

'Oh Judy you know what I mean. I have to put weddings at the top of my agenda and do what is necessary to make sure that everything goes well.'

'Of course you do, dear'

So I don't see how I can commit myself to the cricket team as well. It's just not possible.'

'Is that so dear?'

'Are you making fun of me?'

'Of course not, dear. I just don't see what the problem is. The team has said that they will accommodate you when you are able to play. You usually know when you have a wedding in plenty of time to let them know. If your wedding runs late, you just get there when you can. If they are batting that's fine. If they are fielding, one of the youngsters who like running around can field for you until you get there.

'I don't think that's legal.' mumbled Graham.

'Oh? Well can't you at least try it for a few weeks and if it doesn't work out, then you can quit.'

'Yes I suppose you're right.'

The Saturday of the next wedding, was by coincidence the day of the Pidley fixture, Graham West arrived at the church and nodding to early arrivals he made his way to the vestry. He opened the safe and found the marriage register and the book of certificates and took them to the Lady Chapel where he noticed that Jim Walters had placed the table and chairs ready for the signing of the register. The forms were already completed. He always did that after the rehearsal on the previous evening.

'Just the candles to light,' he thought to himself.

He looked at his watch; half past eleven; wedding at 12.00; a bit too early for the candles. As he looked down at his watch he saw the toe end of his white trainers standing out from the black of his cassock. He stood upright and pulled the cassock down as far as it would go and then slightly bending enabled the black edge to touch the floor. '

Goodness, I can't conduct a wedding looking like the hunchback of Notre Dame. I'd better get my black shoes, I've got plenty of time.'

He went quickly back up the nave out of the main door and was on his way back to the vicarage without a second thought.

As he approached his drive on the other side of the green, he began to feel for his door keys and not finding them immediately realised it was because he was not wearing his coat.

'Oh sugar. It's in the vestry!'

He turned and hurriedly retraced his steps.

He reached the vestry door and turned the handle. It was locked and his keys were on the other side with his coat. Jim will have locked it,' he assumed. He'll be here somewhere.

He checked the Church Hall. 'Jim are you there?' Jim wasn't.

'Good job I took the registers out,' he thought.

With a moments panic, he rushed back to the Lady Chapel.

'Phew! Everything is still there.'

He rechecked the registers. Everything was in order. He noticed the bridegroom and best man ambling down the aisle towards him. He glanced at his watch.

'Mmm. Ten minutes.'

'Hello gentlemen, how are you feeling? Everything Ok?

Come and sit down, you remember where? Good. I'll be with you in a few minutes.'

He took a deep breath and went back towards the vestry door. '

'I might as well light the candles now. It's another thing out of the way.

He felt for the matches behind the altar, lit one and the candles burst into life. Everything was ready.

'No it isn't, my notes; my surplice; my prayer book?'

Instinctively he returned to the vestry door, he could feel his heart pumping; he tried it again with his shoulder pressed against it. It was definitely locked.

He reached for his mobile, dialled and felt a moment of relief as Jim answered.

'Hallo, just a minute, I'm driving. Hang on, I'll pull over.'

Seconds seemed like minutes.

'Hello!'

'Jim, did you lock the vestry door. My keys are inside with my coat, my notes and..
Can you get back here? The wedding is due to start in five minutes. Panic flew to
his voice. Please Jim be quick!'

'No need Graham. Don't panic. I keep a spare set in the Church Hall on a hook
inside the cleaning cupboard. They are all on one ring.

'Thanks Jim, bye.'

He was through the door to the hall before he had rung off and quickly found the
keys. There were about thirty on a large metal ring. He grabbed them and as he
went back into church, it was beginning to fill. Now groups of people were standing
and sitting and waiting. He knew he had only a couple of minutes to spare. He
searched for the vestry key on the way but it did not immediately appear.

'Go through them systematically he said to himself. Don't panic. The bride will be
late. You've got more time than you think.'

After he had tried the first ten he was interrupted.

'Excuse me, Vicar, I think the brides here'

'What Er. thank you. Fred, keep playing for a bit. I'm locked out of the vestry. I'll go
and explain to the bride.'

The bride was not happy. 'But you said I shouldn't be late. I distinctly remember.
Rather impolite you said to keep everyone waiting.' The bride looked as if she was
about to burst into tears

'I know, I am very sorry, but I'm locked out of my vestry. I have the keys now and I'll
be with you in a minute.'

He did not wait for a response, went down the aisle, spoke to the bridegroom, 'be
with you in a minute' and began working through the keys. He had lost his place so
he started with the long brass key and hoped. Eventually the door was opened and
he rushed in, got dressed, picked up his papers and slowly and with dignity he
walked to the front of the nave.

'Good afternoon, ladies and gentlemen. I am so sorry to have kept you waiting.
Would you please be upstanding for the bride?'

Never has a vicar been so pleased to hear Mendelssohn as Graham was at that
moment.

The bride seemed to have regained her composure and she smiled at Graham as she made her way along the aisle on the arm of her father, twenty minutes later than she had intended.

By the time he had pronounced them man and wife, said the blessing, taken off his robes, locked the safe, closed the vestry, seen the last person off the premises and locked the door, it was just after two o'clock. He was late as he headed for his Car, parked in his drive on the other side of the green.

Meanwhile at the Random cricket ground, the two teams were assembling.
Jim Walters had been there since twelve, making sure everything was ready.
In the home dressing room they had already noticed that the majority of the Pidley players were first team regulars.
'Pidley? Friendly? Who do they think they're kidding?' At least eight of them play in the league side,' summed up the general conversation.
'Where's Charlie?' said Jim to no one in particular.
'Out in the middle tossing up,' said no one in particular.
'I don't suppose Graham's here yet.'
'Haven't seen him, is his car in the car park?'
'I don't know. Has Charlie given the umpires the team sheet?'
'Yes I have, and we're batting.
'Did you include.....'
'Yes I did. Is he here yet?'
'No I haven't seen him.'
'Well, let's hope we have a good opening partnership then.'
Charlie picked up his pads.
'Let's just hope he gets here. I put him down at number three.'
'I'll drive to the church to see if I can find him.'
It was just after two o'clock.

Graham got into the car, glanced over his shoulder to check he'd put his cricket bag on the back seat, started the engine and set off for Pidley. He'd put the note from Charlie on the passenger seat. He glanced at it again, 'Saturday, June 17th Pidley 2.00 pm.'

He did the five miles pretty quickly. He knew the ground; it could be seen from the main road. The players were out on the field as he drove through the entrance. He didn't recognise any of the fielders so he assumed Random must be batting. He headed for the away dressing room and rushed in.

'Sorry I'm late chaps.'

He glanced round and immediately knew something wasn't quite right. He didn't know anybody.

'Oh sorry, wrong dressing room.'

He crossed the pavilion corridor and tried again.

'Sorry I'm late chaps.'

The room was empty. He assumed the rest of the team would be sitting outside in the sunshine.

He was already changed, so he put his pads on, inserted his box, picked up his bat and gloves and strode purposefully out to wait his turn. He paused at the scorer's table.

'Hi there. What number am I?'

People turned and the scorer spoke for them.

'What's your name?'

'West, Graham West.'

'You're not on this list. You better talk to the skipper.'

'Where is Charlie?'

'Who?'

'Look mate. I don't know who you're looking for, but this is Pidley playing March seconds; Cambridge League.'

Jim arrived at the church and finding it locked ran across to the vicarage. Graham's car was not in the drive. He ran up the drive and rang the doorbell. No answer. As he turned to go back to his car, he caught a flash of white out of the corner of his eye, and saw a note stuck to the inside of the dining room window.

'CRICKET PIDLEY BACK AROUND 8.'

'Oh No ! He couldn't have. The dope's gone to the wrong ground.'

Jim glanced at his watch.

'Two thirty! Well if he's gone to Pidley, he'll find out soon enough it's wrong and then he'll drive back here. No point in following him. I better go back to the ground.'

Graham West finally drove into the Random cricket ground at two fifty, parked and headed for the pavilion. He was still wearing his pads and carrying his bat. Charlie saw him coming and got up from his chair. As he did so, there was great cry from the centre of the field.

'Howzaat Yesss'

Charlie turned to Graham, waved his arm and pointed to the middle and so Graham carried on, bending his knees and swinging his arms as he went. He took guard and with a deep breadth surveyed the fielders around him. Slip, silly mid off, short leg, square leg, mid off, mid on, and fine leg was moving up from the boundary. He then noticed the score 57 for 7 after 15 overs. Pidley had ripped through the top order, and despite a minor recovery in the middle, things looked grim. No wonder the field was clustered around the bat.

He took guard. 'Leg stump please.'

'That's it. Three to come,' said the umpire.

Strangely Graham did not feel panic. He'd used it all in the previous hour. It was such a relief to get to bat eventually that he felt quite calm.

'Right chaps, it's the bloke with his collar the wrong way round-no swearing now.'
Graham smiled and took guard. The fast bowler who had been doing all the damage was waiting at the end of his long run. In he came. The first ball was vicious, quick and on line with the off stump. It lifted off a length caught the outside of the bat and flew to the wicket-keeper who took it with ease. He was out. The Pidley team were ecstatic.

'No ball', said the umpire.

'The fast bowler turned, 'What?'

'No ball. You were over the line.'

'Bloody Hell. Oh sorry vicar'

Everyone laughed. As the bowler walked back to his mark, Gulam met Graham down the pitch.

'That was close' said Gulum. 'He's been bowling like that since the start, one good ball an over, then he tends to spray it around a bit.'

'Let's hope he continues like that.'

He didn't. The next ball was equally difficult, this time the ball flying to second slip at waist height.

'Howwwsaaa…oh no….the bugger's dropped it. Sorry vicar.

No one smiled.

The third ball was wide of the stumps and Graham went for a cut, got a top edge and the ball arced gracefully towards third man standing just inside the boundary. He raised his hands and at full stretch palmed the ball over the rope- six.

What the flaming 'eck. You lucky, lucky sod.'

This time there was no 'sorry vicar.'

'Over,' said the umpire.

The batsmen met again.

'We need to get a few, Gulam, if we're going to set them a target. Let's just try and push the field back first, that's if I can find the middle of my bat. We've got plenty of time, we just need a partnership.'

Gulam managed to find a single and Graham came down to the other end. The bowling at this end was much more medium pace and runs began to flow. The one hundred came and then the one fifty.

'Tea.' proclaimed the umpire and they all trooped off towards the pavilion.

In the dressing room, Charlie talked tactics. 'I think one seven five or more is a winning score this wicket, so I'll give you a few more overs after tea. Try and give Graham the strike if you can Gulam, it's obviously his lucky day.'

At that point the umpires entered the dressing room. The taller of the two began. 'Charlie, we've had a formal complaint.'

'What's that about then?'

'Pidley are saying that when you declared your team at just before two o'clock, one of your batsmen was not on the ground and as such should not have been allowed to play. It's the guy who's in now; West I think it is.'

'That's right, he got held up. What's the problem?'

'The rules actually say that a player has to be there when his team takes to the field.'

'He was, he got here in time to bat. That's the way we've always interpreted it.'

'Hmmm,' said the umpire looking at his colleague.

'OK You'd better come with me and we'll talk to the Pidley captain.'

They found him half way through a ham sandwich.

'Can we have a word skipper?' said the umpire.' We've had a think about it and after discussion we have made our mind up. The decision on who is eligible to play is the decision of the two captains at the beginning of the match. He turned to the Pidley Captain.

'Since you didn't have a conversation or make your point then, at the beginning of the match, it's too late to do anything about it now. West was on the team sheet.'

'Yes, but he was down as number three and he didn't come in then.'

'Sorry but there is nothing in the rules that says he has to bat at the number on the team sheet.'

Charlie had said nothing up to this point. 'Look here, this is a friendly fixture. That doesn't mean it's not competitive. It's been held as far back as anyone can remember. Graham did not intend to be late, but he got held up at a wedding and came as soon as he could. We had no intention of letting him field if he did not arrive in time to bat, and we were not trying to deceive anyone. I don't think we've broken any rules. If you insist, the game can be declared void, but what would be the point of that. I tell you if you do, it will be the end of this fixture, which would be a shame.'

'I'll talk to my lads,' said the Pidley captain and he walked back into the dressing room.'

The Pidley captain emerged ten minutes later.

'Ok, we'll say no more about it. Are you going to declare?'

' A few more overs, I think.'

At 194-7 Charlie declared the Random innings closed.

At five minutes to seven with the match due to end at seven, Pidley had scored 185-9 and the umpires announced one more over. Ten runs to win.. One more wicket to fall. It couldn't have been much closer. Given the events earlier in the day, it was inevitable that Graham West would be involved in the last over but no one could have predicted what actually happened. With four to win and one more ball to go, the Pidley batsman hit a fearsome lofted drive towards deep mid wicket, where Graham was fielding. The ball was in the air when it reached him and he stretched out his hands to take the catch. The ball hit his left hand, ricocheted onto his right arm and stuck somewhere in his armpit. At first it seemed that he had dropped the catch and it was only when he retrieved the ball from his armpit and held up his arm to indicate the catch, that the Pidley Team Captain knew the game was lost. He came across to Graham with a rueful smile on his face.

'Well played Vicar; dropped twice, a lucky no ball and the winning innings and a catch in your armpit. It seems in Random at least, the Lord looks after his own. I'm glad you were late though. What the hell you'd have done if you'd got here on time I dread to think.

For Goodness Sake

Chapter Eight

The Archdeacon

It was a warm summer's morning as Archdeacon Bruce Bailey drove his silver Mazda 5, top down, along the A14 towards Newmarket. He smiled to himself as the wind streamed over the windscreen and   tossed his greying hair. It made him feel younger than his fifty years. The car had been his treat to himself as a reward for his promotion. He had hesitated about the personal number plate, AD 15 ERE, but it had made people laugh and that was a good thing and it hadn't cost as much as he'd expected.

The call from Bishop David to become an Archdeacon had come as something of a surprise. He knew there was a vacancy of course, but had not imagined in his wildest dreams that he would be asked. He had been quite content in his Cambridge parish, whose link to Gonville and Caius College had given him access to the academic community, where he had earned something of a reputation for his pastoral work with students. He wouldn't be leaving that, but the offer of a curate to help him manage the extra responsibilities pleased him. To this point he really had not thought of himself as ambitious, but the step up had changed his image of himself. Perhaps it's the first of many? Perhaps one day it might even be.... he dismissed the thought and then found himself trying it out for size. 'Bishop Bailey.' His smile widened to a laugh as the road became three lanes, and his humming of 'Shine Jesus shine' drifted away on the wind. It was going to be a really good day.

As he turned off on to the Newmarket –Ely road he noticed a young lady standing on the grass verge just before the lay-by, her arm, hand and thumb waving in traditional pose. In normal circumstances he wouldn't have given her a second thought, but the beautiful morning, his sense of personal contentment and the opportunity to help what he thought must be a student, and an attractive one at that, got the better of him. The company would be nice. He pulled into the lay-by and looking in the rear view mirror waited for her to reach him.

Out of the corner of his eye he noticed a young man running across the lay-by towards him and. before Bruce he could protest the passenger door was opened and the young man jumped in, pulling the girl onto his lap and closing the door in one movement.

'Thank you so much, I'm sure we can both squeeze in, Linda can sit on my here with the rucksack on her knee.'

'I'm not sure about that; can you get the seatbelt around you both? It's going to be too tight isn't it.? And I can't reach the handbrake.'

No one moved or said anything.

'Perhaps if you put the rucksack in the boot we might be better off.

No one moved or said anything.

'Oh give it to me.'

Tugging the rucksack behind him he got out, lifted it over the back of the car, opened the boot and breathing heavily managed to stuff it in.

As he reached to close the boot lid, the engine roared and the car accelerated on to the road in the direction of Ely, the young man at the wheel. His futile attempt to grab the boot lid pulled him over and left him face down in the dust.

'I suppose I was a bit naive, officer, I thought she was a student you see, and in my work I do meet...' At this his voice gave way and the remaining 'quite a few students' was barely audible. In truth he wanted to cry with frustration.

'You see, everything was in the car, my mobile, my wallet, my briefcase and all my papers. It was only because the lorry driver over there saw what happened and kindly helped me to get in touch with you.'

'Ok sir, we've put out an alert for them. I don't think they'll get very far. There won't be many young couples driving a silver coloured Mazda 5 across the fens. Now, I've got all the details we need, so we'll be getting along. Can we give you a lift somewhere? There are buses and trains in Newmarket. Where were you headed?'

'I was going to Random. It's a village west of Ely.'

'I do know that, sir. Well, we're going in that direction I think we could drop you off.'

'Oh God bless you, that's very kind.'

100

'Let us hope he does then Sir, let us hope he does. Jump in.' With that they sped off in the same direction as the silver Mazda.

Half an hour later, the dishevelled Bruce walked up the Random Vicarage drive and rang the doorbell.

'Archdeacon, Good Lord! What on earth has happened to you?'

Bruce stretched out his hand in greeting but a car horn gained their attention and they both turned to watch the patrol car move away. Bruce turned to wave.

'Come in, come in! We thought you must have got lost. Your secretary said you'd left two hours ago. What were the police doing here? Has something happened? Come on through to the study. Take the comfy chair. You look as though you need a gin and tonic.'

'That would be nice, but I'm a little shaken and I'd quite like to tidy myself up a bit first. Would you mind?'

'Mind? It's the least I can do. Let me get you a clean towel. I think I might be able to find you a clean shirt, if you'd like one? We're much the same size I should think. Come down when you are ready.'.

'Thank you dear boy.'

Fifteen minutes later, the Archdeacon came down the stairs and quietly shuffled into the study. The gin and tonic was waiting for him on the coffee table and as he lowered himself into the armchair he raised it to his lips.

'Ah that's better dear boy, I needed that.'

A second gin and tonic saw him through the telling of the morning's events.

'I am so sorry to have caused you so much trouble.'

'No trouble at all. Can I get you another, Archdeacon?'

'I shouldn't really. I think I'm still suffering from the shock of everything but perhaps this once. Oh and please call me Bruce. I'm still at the stage when I hear the word Archdeacon I'm looking round to see who it refers to. I'm just beginning to come round and another gin would complete the revival. Are you alright for time by the way, we can always rearrange our business if I am imposing on your good nature or the pressure of your diary commitments?'

'No I'm fine, I have to go over to the church just before lunch for a moment or two, other than that I have the rest of the day. I wasn't sure how long we needed so I've kept the day free just in case.'

'I wonder if you have a copy of your review papers handy, mine were in the briefcase in the car, and I think I will need my memory refreshing on the detail? Contrary to popular opinion I don't carry Mission Action Plans and targets around in my head.'

'No problem,' said Graham, the photocopier is over in the vestry, so I can easily get a copy while I'm there.

'Splendid, so let me finish this admirable gin, Bombay sapphire unless I miss my guess, and I'll walk across to the church with you. I think it will help me to see your place of work.'

Revived by the gin, the Archdeacon uncertainly strolled with the Vicar across the green to the church.

'I'm meeting Pam Smith my deputy treasurer.. She needs access to the safe so she can take the collections to the post office. It was decided before my time that there should be two keys to the safe, both kept in the vicarage for ease of access. And since the post office is just across the road...'

'Very sensible Graham.'

As they reached the west door, they met Pam and after introductions the Archdeacon was left to look around the church. It was not long before the Vicar emerged from the vestry.

'She needs to count it so she'll need a few minutes. Let me show you round while we're waiting.'

In the few minutes that it took to walk around the building the conversation was what you might expect from two practitioners. How was the building used? How flexible was it in accommodating the range of services needed these days? Was the pulpit used for preaching or did he speak from the lectern? What was attendance like?

'My Cambridge church is late Victorian, and I envy you the history of this place. And it's not as flexible as you might think, the Victorians had very fixed ideas about what a church should look like. I still use the pulpit, I like to be six foot above criticism if you get my drift.'

Sharing the joke, they made their way to the west door. Pam was waiting. 'I'll say cheerio then, Vicar, Archdeacon, nice to meet you.'

'Bye Pam,' they chorused.

'Bruce, I'll go and do the photocopying, shan't be a minute. Do you want to walk back to the vicarage and make yourself comfortable? I'll be as quick as I can.'

'Certainly dear boy! I'll escort the lovely Pamela as far as the post office, and see you in two ticks. Now Pamela, can I help you with those money bags, they must be frightfully heavy.'

So saying, with the money evenly distributed between them, they walked out into the sunshine and made their way across the green.

The direct route to the post office, less than a hundred yards, led them past a row of parked cars, somewhat obscured by the shade from the horse chestnuts. The Archdeacon was one moment deep in conversation, then the next he stopped and turned in one movement, money bag in hand he pointed to a silver Mazda 5.

'Good God, it's my car. Is it?' He checked the number plate at the front. 'Yes it is."

The lovely Pamela had not heard of the morning events so could only contribute a puzzled, 'Is it?'

'Yes, it was stolen this morning on my way here by two young hitchhikers.'

He looked up and down the road. 'There's no sign of them, unless they're in the post office.'

'The keys are still in the ignition,' contributed the helpful Pamela.

'Wait there Pamela I won't be a minute.'

With that he ran across the road and with movements resembling a peacocks mating ritual, bobbed up and down in front of the post office window, turned back across the road and jumped into the driver's seat of the Mazda.

'Quick get in, they're in the queue in there, I need to move this before they come back.'

'But.......'

'I can't leave you here, when they see the car is missing there's no guessing what they might do and I can't tackle them on my own. Get in!'

The Archdeacon backed the car out of the parking bay and accelerated down the hill. The tenseness of the situation seemed to grab hold of him. He just wanted to get as far away as possible.

'We should call the police, archdeacon,' Pamela said.

'Yes, yes, oh please call me Bruce. Yes of course, you're right, you're absolutely right,' he said, seeing her panic stricken face. 'Have you a mobile phone Pamela?'

No 'I don't have one, don't you?'

'Yes, but it was stolen this morning. Oh look in the glove box, that's where I left it.'

She leaned forward and rummaged. 'Nothing in here.'

'Is there a phone box nearby?' asked the Archdeacon with a degree of panic in his voice.

'Not one that's working.'

'Where is the nearest police station, then?'

'I'm not sure, Ely? But I can't go to Ely; I can't carry all this money around with me.'

'Don't worry, if we see a post office, I'll stop.'

This conversation was punctuated by periods of silence from them both; The Archdeacon felt Pamela's eyes on him from time to time, as if checking that he was concentrating on his driving. He assumed she was anxious. He was concentrating on driving and after three gin and tonics the world began to look rosier, sunny and warm. He was enjoying the ride. He rejected the idea of the going back to the Vicarage because he would have to go past the post office, and as Pam said she lived on the same road on the other side of the village he didn't want to go there. By the time they concluded a police station was the best option they were approaching Witchford, and without a second thought, the Archdeacon turned off the main road towards the village.

'There must be a phone box here,' he explained.

As they reached the small row of shops in the centre of the village, the Archdeacon noticed the post office. He pulled into a space on the opposite side of the road.

'I'll find a place to phone the police. Why don't you get rid of the money while I do that?'

'Ok, good idea, I shan't be long.'

As she was crossing the road and the Archdeacon was looking around the car to see if any of his other valuables were there, a police patrol car came up the road and stopped some fifty yards away from them in front of a bakery which was advertising homemade sandwiches.

As they came to a halt, PC Doug Sanders noticed the lovely Pamela crossing the road and then the silver Mazda.

'Dave, didn't we have a call about a Mazda earlier on? He said looking Pamela up and down.

'Yup.' He consulted his notebook. 'Stolen near the A14 at nine- twenty. Can you read the number from here?'

'Alpha Delta one five, Echo, Romeo, Echo'.

'I'll call in. Alpha one, this is Foxtrot 4. Come in please.'

'Yes Dave'.

'Just sighted the reported stolen silver Mazda 5 parked in Witchford High Street. Two occupants; driver white Male accompanied by a younger female.'

'That's them, fits the description. Car owned by a Reverend Bruce Bailey. Bring 'em in Dave.'

'It's them', Dave confirmed to Doug, 'let's do it.' They strolled over to the Mazda.

'Good afternoon sir. Is this your car?' Dave asked the archdeacon

' Ah the police, thank goodness. Yes officer it is.'

'Would you mind getting out of the car for me, sir?'

Graham West came out of the church armed with his photocopying and strode off towards the vicarage. As he passed the Post Office, he noticed a young couple standing by the row of cars, looking up and down the road as if searching for something or someone.

He stopped.

'Hello. Have you lost something?'

'Well yes, said the young man, 'Our car actually. We're sure we parked it here ten minutes ago, but it's gone. I can't understand it.'

'Oh dear, you are sure are you? You couldn't have put it in the car park over there,' he said pointing across the street?

'No we're sure.'

'You'd better ring the police,' said Graham.

 'Our mobiles are out of credit,' said the young woman.

'OK let's think. Come and use my phone in the vicarage, it's just over there. Follow me'

Graham led them into the house and through to the study.

'You can use the phone in here. Would you like some tea? Yes? I'll put the kettle on, back in a minute.'

As he passed the sitting room he thought he ought just to explain to the Archdeacon what the delay was, and was surprised to find it empty. He thought he must be in the bathroom.

Wanting to turn the oven on for lunch as well as make the tea, he went straight to the kitchen. Five minutes later, he carried the tray of tea back to the study, glancing into the sitting room on the way. Still no sign of the Archdeacon! Where had he got to? 'Here we are,' he said, as he carefully manoeuvred his way through the study door. to find, or rather not to find, that the young couple he had left there ten minutes before were not where he had left them.

He put the tray down, and thinking they might be visiting the downstairs cloakroom, he went out into the hall and listened at the door. Nothing. Had they made a mistake and realised where they had left the car? He opened the front door and looked out.. There was no one in the street. He turned to close it, when he noticed something was wrong. His red Peugot 107 was not in the drive. It took a millisecond for him to check his memory. He had left it there; his wife had not used it; he hadn't moved it. It was gone. He reacted by reaching for his pockets. The keys were not there. With an 'oh no!' he rushed to the study as the truth dawned. The keys were not on his desk. The window was open; the couple had fled with his car. So where was the archdeacon?

The Archdeacon was so intent on finding his possessions, and relieved his briefcase was still where he had left it, that he didn't notice the patrol car arrive, and was slightly startled to find what he had been seeking for the last half an hour standing at his shoulder asking him to get out of the car.

'Oh yes officer, oh yes thank goodness. Am I glad to see you?'

'We're quite glad to see you sir, aren't we Doug? Is this your car, sir? He repeated.

'Yes it is.'

'The car is registered to a Reverend Bruce Bailey. Would that be you, sir?'

'Yes it is.'

'Do you have any means of confirming that for us, sir? Driving licence, insurance for example?

The Archdeacon instinctively reached into his jacket pocket.

'Yes I mean No. I mean I did have, but they were stolen. I was looking for them just now.'

'We have a report of a silver Mazda being stolen this morning. He paused in mid sentence and looked at Doug, then back to the Archdeacon.

'Have you been drinking sir?'

'No! Well yes! Well I mean I just a pre-prandial gin and tonic, you know, largely for medicinal purposes. Well actually it was two, I mean three,' he confessed.

'Would you mind getting out of the car sir?'

'Oh dear!'

At that point Pamela came out of the post office as the Archdeacon was being breathalysed.

'And who would you be madam?' asked Doug.

'My name is Pam Smith. We were just on our way to the police station.'

'Well perhaps we can help you there' said Doug.'

Dave examined the breathalyser. 'I'm sorry sir, but you are over the limit. I must ask you to accompany us to the station.'

Doug took over, 'Now let's get a few things straight. Start at the beginning.. Your car, this car, was stolen. Its that right?'

The Archdeacon told the officers the full story from the time he left the house and arrived in Witchford. It all seemed so unlikely, but much of it was confirmed by Pamela. Doug at least seemed inclined to believe them but there was still the issue of driving while under the influence.

The car was left in Witchford, Pam was to be picked up by her husband, and the Archdeacon was seated in the back of the patrol car.

The effect of the gin and tonic and the warmth of the car made the Archdeacon feel sleepy and he felt his eyelids begin to droop.

The patrol car steadily made its way out of the village and towards Ely. As it stopped at the traffic lights on the Witchford road, the Archdeacon opened his eyes and glanced out of the window. He was suddenly wide awake. A young woman was looking at him from the next lane through the passenger window of a red Peugot 107.

'It's her. It's the car thieves. In that red car.' said the Archdeacon now very wide awake and pointing.

The lights changed and the red car turned right towards Kings School.

'Quick follow them,' said Bruce.

'Ok sir, don't get excited. Take the next right Doug, said Dave, 'let's see if we can catch them. They might be headed for the A14 again.'

'Come in Alpha One.'

Yes Dave.'

'Alpha One, we have just spotted a red Peugot 107, which we think may be driven by this morning's car thieves. Registration number Foxtrot Tango zero eight Foxtrot, Mike, Uniform, heading west towards Ely station. We'll try to follow.
'OK Dave, let us know if you need backup.'

Past Kings School and down the hill towards the station they drove. Bruce saw no sign of the Peugot.
The communications radio came on, Foxtrot 4 this is Alpha One. Dave responded, 'Come in Alpha One.
Foxtrot 4, a Red Peugot 107, number foxtrot, tango, zero eight, foxtrot, mike uniform, reported stolen from Random about an hour ago.'
Alpha One, I think we have lost them. Heading towards Ely station. We'll check there and then return to base.'
As they turned into the station car park, the Archdeacon shouted, 'There they are. Look you can just see the red roof.'
 Doug raced the car across the forecourt and skidded to a halt in front of the small red car. Dave got out, put on his cap and approached the car. After a few minutes, he returned. A middle aged lady waiting for her husband's train was not very amused at being thought that a car thief.. Dave was not pleased.
'Hmm! Waste of time. It was not even the right registration number. Let's get back.'

He turned towards the back seat. 'Sir,' he said to the Archdeacon, I would be very grateful if you would sit quietly in the back there and not try and be so helpful.'
The Archdeacon stifled his apology and sat quietly.

At the police station, the Archdeacon phoned Graham West.
'Graham, it's me, Bruce.'
'Where on earth are you?'
'Ely police station.'
'What are you doing there?'
'It's a long story. Can you come and pick me up?'
'Well no, I can't, I haven't got my car. It's been stolen.'
'What. You as well. Has the world gone mad? Wait a minute!'
 He rewound the previous hour in his mind.
'Not a small red car?'

'Yes, my Peugot 107 from outside the vicarage. Have you seen it?'

'No. Well yes, well not lately.'

'Oh. I reported it! I thought since you were at the police station you might know something.'

I don't know where it is now. Anyway, I'm stuck here for the time being. Sorry to say I got breathalysed. Too many gin and tonics before lunch! Not that I had lunch', he said ruefully.

It was two hours later when Graham learned the full story as he and Judy drove a sleeping Archdeacon back to the vicarage.

Judy tried to appear optimistic. 'It could have been a lot worse Archdeacon...a lot worse.'

'Bruce dear boy, Bruce,' mumbled the Archdeacon

'Sorry Bruce. At least your results at the police station were marginal, and they found your car.'

'Actually I found my car. It might have been better if I hadn't. But there is a chance they may not prosecute. You're right, the breath tests were marginal, or so they told me, but I shall have to wait for the results of the blood test.'

. 'Well at least they have found both cars and you are all in one piece, thank God?' said Judy.

'Did they catch the thieves?'James asked

'No. Apparently the car was abandoned in Cambridge. They are bringing it to Ely tomorrow.

We can pick them up then. Judy Could you drop us off there in the morning?'

'Certainly darling.'

The Archdeacon had by this time sunk into the rear seat, asleep again. Judy glanced in the rear view mirror.

'Arch...Bruce you had better stay the night with us. Things will look a lot better after a good night's sleep.'

There was no response from the back and there was a period of quiet. It didn't last long. Graham looked at his watch and unusually for him swore. All three of them were suddenly upright and awake. As swear words go, 'Damn it' was not really excessive but it was nevertheless surprising as it came from Graham.

'What is the matter?' puzzled Judy.

'Damn it, damn it!' said Graham again, 'we've got the prayer meeting in half an hour. Sorry Bruce, I completely forgot all about it. It's our monthly meeting. We meet in the study, but you don't have to join us. Stay with Judy in the kitchen while she gets the supper.'

In truth, Bruce would have liked to do just that. The words that he actually used were more about his sense of remorse for his part in the day's chaos and his pastoral duty as Archdeacon.

'Certainly not, he said. 'My duty is to support you. I shall join you in prayer, it's the least I can do in the circumstances.'

As they parked, one or two of the prayerful had gathered in the drive awaiting their arrival, and were soon seated in the study bringing a range of matters to the Lord's attention. The Archdeacon, asked to open proceedings, raised a few eyebrows.

'Lord we have come apart, please knit us together,' he began. After which he thanked God for the parish of Random, for its Vicar, for the diocese and the bishop and then withdrew from the fray, allowing others to unburden themselves.

Having done his duty, he closed his eyes as others prayed, and unable to resist drifting towards a light sleep, he was grateful for the lengthy periods of silence which came between each intercession. He came to as each member of the group had their opportunity to raise something specific. Finally, Graham, summing up, asked them all to pray for those who have lost their way.'

The archdeacon added with feeling, 'And for those who find it in someone else's car.'

For Goodness Sake

Chapter Nine

The Cider harvest

At the end of September the chestnut trees that frame the village green in Random begin to drop their leaves. The morning dampness is in the air and the colours of autumn spread across the trees and bushes that surround the village. The Vicar, Graham West, made his way across the green towards the church, dressed in shirt, jumper and jeans, his normal garb for a Saturday morning. He had no meetings, no services and sermons were written.. As he walked he pushed his feet through the piles of fallen leaves. Judy was having her lie-in and all was right with the world. He raised his head to feel the light breeze as it swept across the open ground. His two children Stuart and Sally, aged ten and eight ran on ahead and threw leaves at one another

'Come on you two, we're late, and they will have run out of breakfast.' He called to them, and rubbed his hands at the thought of the bacon butty waiting for him in the church hall

It was a typical Saturday morning for him in Random. The Church hall breakfasts had become a popular autumn event for most of the churchgoers and others who are not regulars, but who find time to fit it into their routine. Graham tries to be there at eleven. It's a kind of changeover time. The early risers have done their shopping and call in on the way back from the supermarket in Ely or Huntingdon. For those who like to lie in, coffee and bacon are a tempting attraction before engaging with the trolley and bent wheels.

The children having caught up with him grab a hand each, and swing on his arms with their morning energy.

In the church hall with its small kitchen annexe, the tables were mostly occupied. Colonel Jeremy Pringle and his wife Sarah were busy toasting and frying to supply the hungry shoppers with their mid morning sustenance. Each Saturday morning in October and November, the Pringles ran the coffee mornings. He cooks; she serves. It was their idea; a contribution to the life and work of the church. It raised a considerable amount of money each year and had become a focus for fellowship.

They also attended church on Sunday mornings for the eight o'clock communion and that was their total involvement. They do not 'do' meetings.

'Spent my life in meetings-most of them a waste of time' summed up Jeremy's philosophy of life. Offers of help on Saturdays were politely turned down. 'No offence, but I like to run my own ship, saves time and effort in the long run.'

Sarah, a small, quiet, neat woman had followed her husband to numerous postings over his career and seemed to be revelling in having her own house and garden for the first time in her life. She moved around the hall with a smile on her face, quickly and carefully clearing the used cups and plates in time to serve the next group of waiting customers.

Graham opened the door of the church hall and the warm air greeted them. The sound of conversation and laughter echoed through the building. The children having left their coats behind pushed the glass doors open, and ran into the hall narrowly avoiding Sarah Pringle and a tray full of crockery going back towards the kitchen.

'Morning Graham, your usual is it?' said Jeremy without looking up from a large frying pan of eggs and a grill loaded with bacon. 'Can I tempt you to an egg as well?'

'Thank you Jeremy, gosh, that bacon looks good. I could almost smell it from the vicarage.'

Sarah squeezed through the queue, delicately turning her tray of clean crockery sideways to avoid collision..

'Good morning Sarah, how are you?'

'Morning Graham; do you want your usual?'

'Yes please, but with the addition of an egg please, and two small ones for the children.'

'Certainly, they won't be a second.'

'Good turnout this morning Jeremy; when the morning is fine, people seem to get the urge to leave the house.

'Yes looks that way. Oh, by the way Graham, can we leave the takings in the safe before we finish today. I don't like the idea of money hanging around over the weekend.'

'It would be best I suppose. I've got the keys on me, take them now and pop them through the vicarage letterbox when you've finished.

As the children found friends to run around with, Graham sat with a group of his oldest parishioners. The conversation, as often with the elderly, was nostalgic as they recalled past events in their lives and the life of the church. Graham picked up the conversation as Annie Smith and her friends reminisced. Annie now in her late seventies, had lived in Random all her life and was the source of remembered history for a all of that time.

'Course Harvest Festivals were a lot earlier in them days than it is now, always the third Sunday in September in church. Nowadays we don't seem to get round to it until October. We'd spend the week making our corn dollies, and bring 'em to the church to decorate on the Saturday afternoon.'

Richard, Annie's twin brother joined in. 'Our parents would be in here getting the veggies ready for the evening supper. All the produce was from our own gardens or the allotments of course. Us young'uns would be given the cutlery to put out; three long tables right down the hall.'

'You always used to try and race me to finish a table. Course you was bigger than me then, said Annie. Ah we won't see those days again.'

'Well,' said Graham, I've a mind to try and do it again. I know it's a bit later than in your day but I'm planning a supper nevertheless on the third Saturday, two weeks time, and then a special service the following day. And am I right in thinking that you had a barn dance on the Saturday as well?'

'Cor yes!' Annie's eyes lit up with the memory. 'It was so exciting for us kids. We didn't have television then of course. Them autumns and winters could seem long and dark. It were a chance to put our best frocks on and meet the boys.' Annie giggled.

'I don't remember you needing much excuse to meet boys Annie Smith, added Richard.'

'Talk about pot and kettle black, Richard Smith. Vicar, I could tell you a tale or two. They used to keep the cutlery in that cupboard over there.' She waved her hand and pointed behind her to the small walk-in pantry. 'Richard always seemed to run short of knives just when May Brown was in there.'

Richard looked out into the distance as if trying to remember. 'I wonder what ever happened to May Brown?' he mused.

'Emigrated I think,' said Annie.

This rather killed the conversation so Graham mentioned the 'Ceilidh.'

'The what? Kaylie? We used to have that in sherbet dips, with a stick o' liquorice like a straw. That were Kaylie weren't it Annie?' Richard licked his lips.

'No no Richard,' said Graham, 'it's the name for Irish dancing, bit like your barn dance. They have a caller and dance reels and things. Anyway I've booked a local group, so we can dance after we've had our supper. What do you think?'

'Well we might manage an odd dance Annie, might we? Sounds like a good idea.' Annie smiled and then frowned. 'Ow much are you going to charge then if you're going to cover the costs of the meal and the band.'

'Always careful with the pennies is Annie,' said Richard.

'£10 per ticket and we need 30 people to break even. I'm going to announce it in church tomorrow and there is a list for helpers to sign at the back of the church.'

By the following Sunday evening Graham has announced the Harvest Supper and Ceilidh in church. The response was positive, 10 people had signed the helpers list and it looked as though they would have a good attendance.

'I just need to send out the circular e-mail. I've booked the band and ordered the food from the Farm Shop. I bought pieces of chicken, cauliflower and leeks and they are giving us the potatoes; so everything is booked and paid for.

'Well done darling, said his wife Judy, it sounds wonderful. What are we going to drink?'

' Well I thought people could bring their own. It wouldn't cost us anything.'

'Good idea, make sure you include it in the e-mails and on the posters.'

It was later that week when Graham called in to see Jeremy and Sarah.. He was a tall man in his middle fifties. He had a neatly trimmed grizzled beard and in most situations, he wore a bowtie and a waistcoat. He always looked smart. He and Sarah lived on the edge of Random in a large rambling house which over the years had been extended. As each extension had been added, some single and some two storey in height, and each had its separate roof. The only time Graham could remember seeing something similar was in an illustrated book of fairy stories in which the 'the old woman who lived in a shoe' had such a house for all her children. It was set in its own grounds; a smallholding of several acres, at the rear of which was a large apple orchard.

Graham parked in the gravel drive and rang the front door bell.

'Good morning Vicar, how are things with you?'

Jeremy Pringle appeared around the side of the house, dressed in blue serge overalls and carrying a large wooden rake. 'What can we do for you?'

'I just popped by to tell you that I've banked the takings from the coffee morning. You did really well again; two hundred and sixty pounds this time. We are very grateful, you know. It isn't just the money. The event has become part of the village calendar. People look forward to it, put it in their diaries.'

'Oh thanks for that. It was a good morning, wasn't it? Anyway, do come in, have you time for a coffee? Sarah's in the orchard, I'll give her a ring.'

'That's efficient. Does she have her mobile on when she's in the orchard?'

Jeremy chuckled as he walked down the side of the house, grabbed a thick length of rope and yanked it. A rather high tinkling sounding bell rang out from one of the roofs across the garden.

'We think it might have been a school at some time,' explained Jeremy.

After a couple of minutes Sarah joined them.

'Good morning Sarah, "Summoned by bells" were you?'

'Yes, I'm sure Betjeman would have approved.'

They sat at the well scrubbed table at one end of kitchen and soon had large mugs of hot coffee in their hands.

'Jeremy, this is really excellent coffee. I hope I haven't interrupted anything important?'

'No, we're just harvesting the apples in the far orchard. Only we found this old apple press at the back of the old barn and thought we'd try pressing them for their juice. We weren't sure what it was at first. Then we saw one being used on 'Country File,' so we thought we'd try it and see what happened.

'It's our first time at anything like this, you know, but it seems a shame not to use all those apples.'

'It must be very satisfying to make your own drinks like that. Is it cider?'

'Not immediately,' Sarah intervened, 'it's simply apple juice with no additives. Mind you we're not experts; but I've managed to find some instructions on the net. Apparently if you leave it as it is, the natural yeasts in the apple skins will ferment it; or you can add yeast yourself and then leave it about six months in the barrel.

'You've got all the equipment then?'

'We think so. It was all these under a pile of sacks in the barn, the press and a few barrels. It looks like the previous owners made a lot of cider. We've even got a rather large bottle rack, full of cider bottles.'

'Empty ones?'

'No full. Finish your coffee and I'll show you.'

A couple of minutes later they were walking down the path towards an old stone barn surrounded by apple trees. The tall arched pair of old, wood doors were pulled open, Jeremy needing both hands, and they went in. As well as the entrance, the barn was lit by glassless windows high in the walls, and there was just enough light to see the array of bottles stacked in a wooden structure which ran the whole length of the wall at something like six foot high.

'Good gracious, I don't think I've ever seen anything like it. How many are there? Have you counted them?'

' It is extraordinary isn't it. We think about 250 bottles?'

'How old is it? Have you tasted it?'

'They're not labelled but we opened one bottle, just to see what it was like. It was really quite nice. No idea how old it is but judging by the layer of dust, I wouldn't have thought too old. We've been here nine months now, so they could only be a couple of years old. Sarah's quite pleased as she's quite fond of cider, aren't you dear?'

'Yes it was quite nice; not too sweet. We were wondering Graham, whether you might like some for the Harvest supper? How many are coming? Do you know yet?'

'Not sure. My guess is between 40 and 60.'

'Ok, said Jeremy, let's assume 4 to a bottle. There's bound to be some who don't drink. So say 60 maximum, that's only 15 bottles. So let's say 20 bottles. That should be enough, no problem at all.'

'That's very generous of you both. I must say it will add to the feeling of harvest. And cider is the sort of drink that appeals to men and women. It'll be a wonderful surprise for people.'

'That's a deal then. We'll bring them along on the night. They'll need a bit of a clean first.'

As the diners gathered in the church hall, there was a feeling of excitement in the air. The white table cloths stretching down the length of the hall, the sparkle of the cutlery and the smell of the cooking wafting from the kitchen added an edge to their hunger.

'God I'm starving,' muttered Fred Watson to no-one in particular, rubbing his hands in anticipation of the feast to come. He turned to his twin sisters, Julie and Joan. 'Where shall we sit? We're early, take your pick. Do you think they'll serve from this end first or the other?'

'Oh Fred, do be patient, no one's sitting down yet,' said June.

'Bloody Hell, what difference does that make, someone's got to be first.'

Behind them, Elisabeth and Jim Walters were deep in conversation. 'Now please Jim, we said we would sit with Doris and John,' she reminded him.' She looked around and continued,' they're not here yet and you know what Doris is like, she'd be late for her own funeral. Now if it comes to it we may have to sit down ourselves and save seats for them. I don't like to do that, I always think it's rather a common thing to do. So let's wait a bit before we move. I cannot spend an entire evening sitting next to someone I don't like.'

At that she touched her ever present pearls and smiled generally at others who were gradually filing into the hall.

Jeremy and Sarah Pringle arrived with three carrier bags containing the cider and began to put them out on the tables

So reluctant were people to be the first to sit down it was getting to the point where the space between the entrance and the door was filling up and people were spilling out into the foyer.

Graham West acted with unaccustomed decisiveness, 'Ladies and gentlemen, please take a seat.'

The crush eased as one or two moved forward.

Eventually Elisabeth and Jim decided they could sit down now and not look too conspicuous. They placed coats on two chairs fto reserve them. Doris and Jim eventually arrived, not quite last, and as Graham said grace, forty four out of the forty five diners had arrived. There was a single seat remaining at the end of the third long table nearest the door.

'Who's missing?' asked Graham.

He decided to try and take a register using the list of people who had bought tickets. Unfortunately he had no list of who was supposed to be there as there had been no requirement of someone who had bought four tickets to say who the individuals were.

.'Does anyone know who is missing?' He raised his voice above the general chatter. Then the door to the hall opened and in came a breathless Jane Winter. 'Sorry Graham. Sorry everyone Have you been waiting for me?'

'Good evening Jane, we haven't quite started yet.'

'Sorry, my dog sitter got the time wrong and turned up half an hour late. So I got here as soon as I could.'

'Not too worry, come and sit down. Look there's a seat here next to Richard and Annie.'

By this time the pate and salad starter was being passed round, and conversation conceded to the serious business of eating.

'What's in the bottles Jeremy?' asked John Panther.

'It's Cider, John. We found it in our barn when we moved in. Tastes ok. Have a glass.'

The bottles were sealed with a clip mechanism reminiscent of some fizzy drinks in the 1950's that were delivered to your house in the 'Corona' van. This prompted a whole new discussion led by Annie, of the pleasures of cream soda and dandelion and burdock. The top came away with a satisfying pop and Jeremy poured it into the glasses of those around him.

'Please help yourself, he said generally, just say if you need help opening them.'

'Is it alcoholic?' asked Annie Smith.

'Just a little Annie, we think, but it's mostly just healthy apple juice.'

'Thank you, Jeremy,' said Elisabeth, as her glass was filled, 'just a little would be nice, I am rather thirsty. Mmm, that's really nice, not too sweet. It does remind me of the pop we used to drink as kids.'

Jane Winter agreed. 'It really does remind me of cream soda. Do you remember Elisabeth, we used to go round our Aunt Laura's in Queen Street after church on Sunday mornings. It was always cream soda. It looked a bit like this as well, a light golden colour, if I remember. Of course she wasn't really my aunt. No relation at all. We just used to call everyone who was old, aunt and uncle, in those days '

The chicken main course arrived and glasses were recharged more than once.

'I didn't know that.' Elisabeth's voice was becoming a little louder and her face a little redder

The group looked at her and waited.

'Jane. Are you listening?'

'What's that Elisabeth?' replied Jane, with a mouthful of chicken.

'I didn't know that.'

'Didn't know what?'

'Laura wasn't your aunt.'

'Course you did. I must have told you every Sunday morning for five or six years.'

'You didn't. I'd have remembered…I know I would. You didn't.' Her voice slurred.

'Did you know Jim?'

'Yes I think so, if it's the one I'm thinking of. She always wore an apron and a hairnet?'

'Yeeesss,' cheered Jane. 'That's her. You and your mates were always hanging about outside, waiting for us to come out.'

Elisabeth was not pleased. 'Well isn't that just typical, I'm always the last person to be told anything. Is there any more cider?' She filled her own glass.

'Well it was a long time ago Elisabeth,' said Jim, 'It doesn't matter now. Just forget it.'

'Matter, matter, of course it matters. I've spent most of my life trying to forget the lies that I was told as a child and this is just another one.'

Her voice was becoming louder and she began to attract attention.

' Do you know...do..you ...know, I can remember my father told me there was no Father Christmas and there were boys who said they loved me. They didn't mean it at all, and there was no such people as Adam and Eve. Now there was no Aunt in Laura. It's just the last straw, the end.'

'Try not to let it upset yourself, darling,' said Jim, 'have some black forest gateau.'

The conversation stopped and everyone who spoke at all tried to be ultra polite and as non offensive as possible. The coffee was served and the band began to arrive and set up their instruments ready for the Ceilidh.

Then Jane, who was by this time finishing her fourth glass of cider and clearly dwelling on the earlier conversation, entered the fray.

'Anyway, I don't know why you're feeling so sorry for yourself, Elisabeth Walters. You didn't do so badly. You didn't do so badly' The second 'badly' was reinforced with a pointed finger.

Elisabeth didn't even pause for breath. 'Oh here we go again, poor old Jane, one of life's victims. Winter comes early this year. Ha! Ha ha ha! Get it! Winters come early, mind you she's usually late,' and with that Elisabeth convulsed into a fit of giggles.

'You can laugh, Elisabeth Walters, you can laugh, but we all know how got your husband. You stole him, that's what you did, you stole him.'

Jim blanched and the room went quiet. In a low voice he tried to sound firm. 'Jane Not now. Not here. It's a long time ago for goodness sake. Come on Elisabeth, I think I need to get you home.'

'Oh no nooo, I want to dance an Irish reel. Can't we stay for one teeny weeny little dance?'

'Let's see shall we, come and get some fresh air, it'll make you feel better. We can come back.'

At that, he tried to get Elisabeth on her feet and with some assistance from Graham and Judy he made his way to the foyer and outside.

Elisabeth's dress was a loose fitting wrap around and due to the energy used to get back on her feet, the tied bow at the front came loose. With her right arm leading in a sweeping arc, she turned, and as she slurred 'G'dnight every... one, the front of her dress flew open, revealing her pink knickers to everyone in the room. The room went quiet.

'Woops,' she said, trying to bring the two parts of the dress together to cover her embarrassment. Jim took off his overcoat, wrapped it around his wife and without another word, he steered her through the door.

Soon the dishes were cleared to the kitchen, the tables were pushed to the side and the band took centre stage. The Panthers, Pringles and Jane Winter found themselves on the same table in the corner of the hall. It was assumed that as the Walters did not return they must have gone home.

'Perhaps for the best,' said Doris, 'that cider of yours must have been quite strong Jeremy.'

'Seems so, but Sarah and I have drunk as much as Elisabeth did and we're alright. Is she not used to alcohol?'

'Don't expect so, bar an odd glass of dry sherry at Christmas. I think they put too much salt in the chicken that's all.'

'Your Sarah enjoys her dancing, don't she?'

They sat and watched with some amazement as Sarah Pringle, whooped and wound her way through tricky manoeuvres in an eightsome reel.

The dances were a mixture of Scottish and Irish country as well as Old Time and people stopped worrying whether they knew what to do as the caller managed the progress through a succession of energetic twirls.

Jan Winter though, on a table of five, seemed reluctant to participate. Doris nudged John.

'Ask Jane to dance or she'll be sitting there all night.'

'Do I have to?' whispered John.

'It won't do you any harm; give the poor girl a bit of pleasure.'

John waited for the next dance to be announced and stood up. 'Jane, would you like to dance?'

'That's very kind of you John. Are you sure?'

They wandered onto the floor, and were soon wheeling in and out and under with the best of them. Jane began to smile. At the end of the 'dashing white sergeant' they returned to the table, passing the others as they went to join in.

'Thank you John, that was very kind of you. I do hope Elisabeth isn't too ill. I don't know what got into her. I've never seen her like that before. She always so.......'

'Repressed? Well she certainly let herself go tonight. She'll be sorry for it in the morning.'

'I expect she will. The four of us have been friends for a long time now. Did you enjoy those days?'

'I found them mostly pretty confusing. Who fancied who? Who was going out with who? I was never sure what I felt never mind what anyone else thought.'

'I always thought you'd end up with Elisabeth, you know.'

'Really? What made you think that?'

'Well I had Jim then, we were a couple and Elisabeth fancied you, well actually we all did. So it seemed logical somehow.'

'I had no idea.'

'You were quite a looker then you know. You still are actually.'

'Jane Winters, I'm an old married man.'

'Old is as old does, John Panther. Let me know if you get tired of Doris.'

'I think you've had too much to drink, young lady.'

'I have.'

The Ceilidh complete, Graham and Judy finally dried the last plate and put away the last glass. Jeremy took off his apron and dried his hands on a tea towel.

'Come over and have a coffee with us in the vicarage,' said Judy, 'I think you've earned it. I'm not sure what we would have done without you?'

'You three carry on,' said Graham, 'I'll just look round before I lock up, make sure everything is secure.'

Over the next day the story of the Ceilidh was retold, though not everyone had quite understood why Elisabeth had left early.

The next morning being Sunday, Graham slipped into his normal routine of the eight o'clock service, followed by breakfast, then the ten thirty morning worship.

Over breakfast Graham pondered. 'Interesting at the service, no Jeremy and Sarah, and Elisabeth Walters was wearing sunglasses. But everyone seemed to have enjoyed themselves last night. Shall we do it again next year?'

'Let's get Christmas over first shall we, and then think about it.'

On the following Monday morning, as he was checking the gospel reading for the following Sunday, the phone rang.

'The Vicarage, Graham West speaking, how can I help you?'

'Oh, good morning Vicar, my name is Colin Bassthwaite, I'm the editor of the Ely Recorder.'

'Oh hello, what can I do for you?'

'We are about to publish a story about an event in Random last Friday evening, and we would like to give you the opportunity to comment.'

'Oh good, the church doesn't get a lot of publicity these days, so that will be good for us to help.

'I think I should tell you that the headline we've got at the moment reads "Church holds drunken sex orgy."

'Goodness gracious, which church was that then?'

'We have been told it was your church Vicar.'

Graham swallowed. 'Mine? Are you sure you've got the right number?'

'You are Reverend Graham West, Vicar of Random Parish church.'

'Well yes, but I don't know anything about a drunken sex orgy on Friday night.'

'It was in the Church hall on Friday night we've been told.'

'Really? I was there in the church hall on Friday night but i don't remember...any...

'Oh thank you we didn't know that... so we can add "vicar was present but remembers nothing... I take it there was alcohol being drunk "

'Oh No...well yes... well .. I don't know'

'You don't remember that either.'

'Hang on just a minute. When did you say you were publishing this story?'

'Thursdays edition.'

'Ok give me time to make some enquiries and I'll come back to you. When's your deadline?'

'Tomorrow lunchtime, say one o'clock?'

'Ok I'll give you a comment before one o'clock tomorrow.'

With that he put the phone down.

He was unsure what to do next. Had something happened that he had not seen?. Were there young people playing around in the foyer who might have drunk too much? He was pretty sure there hadn't been. But he'd better check that first. But where had the paper got the information from? He rang Jim Walters.

'Jim it's Graham. Look I need some information fairly quickly. The Ely Recorder is about to publish a story that there was a sex orgy in the Church hall on Friday night'.

'Good God, was there? Why do I always miss the exciting things?'

'You didn't see anything then.'

'No, I left early if you remember, Elisabeth wasn't well.'

'Oh yes.'

'That apple juice made her ill. So I took her home.'

'But Graham, you were there all evening, weren't you? You would have noticed a sex orgy I'd have thought.'

'The editor wanted to imply that we were all drunk so naturally we wouldn't remember anything.'

'Can't you just ignore it?'

'I don't think so, first I said I'd comment by one o'clock tomorrow, second I remember someone saying never ignore a newspaper, good or bad, because that means the paper can say what it likes whether it's true or not.'

Graham decided what his approach was going to be and had the opportunity to talk to Judy about it. She'd been on a media course once and would know what to do.

Supper was finished, the children were in bed and they finally managed to relax with time to themselves.

'OK Judy here is what I am going to do. I will respond to the editor in a firm but friendly way. I've written it as a statement for them. Here it is.'

' "On Friday evening, (add date) to celebrate harvest time and Gods gifts to us, around 60 people of all ages sat down in the church hall to a meal of salad, chicken and black forest gateau accompanied by soft drinks and apple juice This was followed by a Ceilidh led by the Michael Clark trio. The evening was very enjoyable and raised money for church funds."

So that's the factual bit which I think is important to state. Now here's the tricky bit. "Having checked with a number of people who attended the dinner dance, there is no evidence of a sex orgy and no one could be described as drunk. The headline is patently untrue and besmirches the good name of the church without just cause".'

Judy thought for a moment. 'Mmmm, that's pretty good I think. I'm not sure I'd use their words "sex orgy" or drunk. Why don't you say "nothing happened to justify the headline." Otherwise it's fine.'

'What about Elisabeth?' said Graham, was she drunk?'

'No. She certainly wasn't well and not her normal self, but there is no objective evidence for her being drunk. She went over the top for a moment or two and then left. Perfectly normal.'

The next morning Graham rang the editor and read his statement to the editor.

'I don't know where you got the story from, and I don't expect you to tell me, but it simply isn't true.'

'What about the alcohol?' said the editor.

'Apple juice with a meal hardly justifies your headline, and no one got drunk. You could change your headline of course to "No sex or drunkenness at harvest supper," or "Christians behave well"

'Ok Vicar thank you for that, I'll quote you, if we decide to run it. Good bye.'

It was Wednesday morning as Graham bumped into Fred Watson as he was leaving the SPAR grocery shop.

'Morning Fred.'

' Morning Vicar nice morning. Bloody good do on Friday night. by the way'

'Glad you enjoyed it.'

'Never knew Elisabeth Walters would wear pink knickers, and she'd nice legs for her age,' said Fred striding away, leaving Graham standing open mouthed

Chapter Ten

Churches Together

There happened to be three places of worship in Random; the Parish Church which is of course Church of England; a Methodist church in the Wesleyan tradition and a branch of the Salvation Army. However, Graham West was the only full-time clergyman to live in Random, so one of his early tasks on arriving in the village had been to get in touch with the representatives from the other churches and suggest that they meet occasionally.

The Methodist church services were supplied with preachers from the Ely Circuit, and the Methodist superintendent, Reverend Gail Parsons was nominally in charge of the small Random congregation and its chapel. The nearest minister of the Salvation Army, Lieutenant Michael Rogers, was based in Huntingdon and he had oversight of a number of churches across the county.

It had become traditional for these three churches, whilst maintaining their independence and their individual emphases, to work together on three occasions during the year; Christmas morning, the week of prayer for Christian unity, and Good Friday. They met once a quarter at the Random vicarage to plan the events.

As they sat in the Vicarage study one November morning, revelling in the smell of fresh coffee and doughnuts, the contrast between the three ministers could not be starker.

 The Reverend Michael Rogers, the Methodist, was the youngest of the three, six foot four and eighteen stone, he wedged himself into the leather chair in the corner of the study. He was married with three children under five, and possessed the strained and unkempt look of a man who needed a good night's sleep. Before his call to ordination, he had been a chef, and the plate of homemade sugary jam doughnuts on the coffee table in front of him, was his contribution to the meeting.

Captain Gail Parsons was Salvation Army and the eldest of the group, in her early fifties; slim to the point of thinness; short sighted; unmarried and unattached. She was tea total, and fanatically feminist. To be totally tea total may sound tautological, but often those who claimed to be tea total could be found accepting the offer of a small sherry at Christmas, or not objecting to the brandy in a Christmas Cake. Gail Parsons was not of that ilk, she believed that alcohol was a completely unnecessary feature of human life, with no compromises. She brought the same no surrender approach to her feminism and religious minorities, and was prepared to veto any suggestions which did not allow her and her church equal standing with the two younger men in the group. Fuelled by enthusiasm, it sometimes got the better of her. The doughnuts this particular morning tested her New Year resolution to give up sugar as she perched on the edge of the stiff-backed chair sipping her unsweetened coffee. Her resolve was further provoked by the Methodist minister.

'Go on Gail, have a doughnut. It'll do you good. Gives you energy.'

'Get thee behind me Satan, Michael Rogers, it's hard enough as it is, without you adding to my temptation. My energy levels are fine thank you very much.'

Captain Gail brought a further resource to the table. The 'Sally Anners' in Random, though small in number and aging, managed to produce the basic players for a brass band; two cornets, one trombone, one euphonium and a tuba, leaving five others to make up the regular congregation.

Graham West, the Vicar of Random, in his early forties and married with two children was neither large nor thin. Being resident in Random and of the Church of England gave him the opportunity to be magnanimous. Though he tried not to show it, he represented the status quo; his congregation was by far the largest and demonstrated that he was working with the others out of principle rather than necessity. It gave him an edge. He chaired the morning meeting and retained a degree of formality as he waited for an appropriate moment to begin.

The terms of reference of the group indicated not merely a common purpose, but a willingness to ensure that the use of buildings was also fairly shared. This leads on occasion to some curious outcomes. The Sunday morning during the week for Christian Unity had developed what the three of them call a 'safari'. This involved the congregation moving from one church to another, stopping at each for a part of the service. This might in principle demonstrate unity but it had unintended consequences. It was a sad fact of history that enthusiastic attempts to bring about unity often had the reverse effect. Last year, when it began in the Parish church, several C of E members went home after their section had finished, several Methodists joined in for their part only, and the Salvation Army band, who played at every centre, found that their ability to carry their instruments around the streets rather too much for their aging limbs. At first, the tuba was discarded, then the euphonium, so the climax to the service in the Wesleyan chapel was somewhat muted.

'Good morning everyone, shall we begin the formalities? Michael, it's your turn to lead us in prayer.'

Unfortunately, at the word formalities, Michael Rogers decided he ought to finish the half doughnut still on his plate, and before Graham had finished the sentence he stuffed into his mouth. His attempts to swallow, followed by pushing it to one side of his mouth with his tongue, prevented him from breathing, never mind speaking, and with his cheeks bulging, he ventriloquised, 'Let us pray.'

The silence which followed might have been mistaken for a meditative pause, except for the sounds of him clearing his mouth. However, after a quick plea for God's blessing and wisdom and guidance in their decision making, the collective 'Amen' led Graham to begin the agenda.

'We better deal with Christmas morning first. Time is getting on. Are we going to do the same as last year?' He looked at Michael for a response.

'I think so,' said Michael on cue, 'just a matter of who does what. I preached last year, so it must be Gail's turn. Graham it's your turn to lead and that leaves the intercessions for me. Is that alright?'

Gail's yes was rather drawn out, which carried the implication that she was not entirely happy with the suggestion.

Graham picked up the hint. 'You have another view, Gail?'

'Well yes and no. I have no problem with Michael's suggestion as to roles, but I would like to do something slightly different.'

Graham and Michael both smile and raise their heads in a knowing fashion. When Gail uses the words 'slightly different', they both knew that what followed was 'very different.' For example the time she had introduced real animals, a sheep and a donkey, to the morning service two years before, still had Jim Walters, the Church caretaker, waking up in the middle of the night. Ever since, he had kept a large shovel and bucket in his cupboard in case it happened again. The first time he had been totally unprepared for the large pile of dung that sat in the middle of the central aisle.

'How different is slightly different?' asked Graham.

'Well, it's something I've been thinking about for some time, but I've not been able to find the right time to use it. This may not be the right time, but let's leave it at that. I'd

127

rather not go into detail in case you think it is silly. Let's just leave it that. I will preach.'

'Very well, we will leave it with you. Next then is the week of prayer for Christian Unity which this year is the third week of January. In the last two years we have had the 'safari,' which my PCC thinks was not entirely successful. There is a view that people come to their own church and a lot drop out on the way. Perhaps we can think again.'

Gail was the first to respond. 'The band would prefer to be in their own building, they tell me. They are all getting on and it's just too difficult to lug the instruments around. I think we have to be practical.'

'The other thing, said Michael, 'is that the Parish Church is the only place big enough to hold everybody if we have the band as well.'

It was difficult for Graham. He was happy both to be Anglican and the largest and he accepted the reality. 'You are of course always welcome to use St. Wulfstans, but it is a sad fact that our people support the idea of unity as long as it's on their terms. How about if we provide transport for the instruments? Would that help? At least your players won't have to lug them around?'

'Will you be there this year Michael?' laughed Gail

This was not the innocent question it perhaps appeared, evidenced by the sigh from Michael who had overslept on the morning of the service and missed it altogether. The others had covered for him.

'Oh dear. I'm so sorry I hoped it might have been forgotten by now. I still have nightmares about it you know. Every time I answer the telephone I wonder if I have forgotten something important. I don't think I shall ever forget it.'

'There but for the grace of God go us all, Michael,' said Graham sympathetically.

'Yes but you didn't, Graham. I was the one who overslept. I'm sure my congregation have never forgiven me. I haven't forgiven myself. I still remember my secretary saying '"where were you?" and that sense of confusion quickly followed by the feeling in the pit of my stomach that I had forgotten something really important. Alison was away, you see; the alarm didn't go off.'

Gail rushed to withdraw the barb and stem the tide of self criticism.

'Oh Michael I never dreamed it had upset you so much. It just wasn't that serious. I wouldn't have mentioned it; we understood. As Graham said, it could happen to anyone, especially when our family is away. I know, let's settle for a single service in the parish church with the band, I'll take on the transporting of the instruments. We've got a van. Michael you can take the service and Graham, will you preach?' Michael's smile was more like a grimace. Gail continued.

'Ok, I'll talk to the band after Christmas. If you don't hear from me, assume it's alright for them to play, and I'll deliver the instruments.'

'We can serve coffee after the service in St Wulfstan's hall if you like,' suggested Graham.

Gail could not resist returning to equality as a prerequisite to unity.

'It's not your turn to do refreshments, Graham, it's ours. I think I need the Salvation Army to be involved in something which gives them responsibility, besides the band that is. Otherwise we might as well all join you and become Anglicans.'

Michael smiled 'Of course you'd be very welcome and there is an historical precedent. The Salvation Army came out of Methodism, the founder of which was John Wesley, who was of course an Anglican. In fact only the other day I was reading about a church in Northamptonshire that is a combined Methodist-Anglican church. We could be a first and combine the three of us.'

As the laughter died away the meeting was brought to a close with prayers and pleasantries and they went their separate ways.

Christmas morning duly arrived, and at nine o'clock a rather weary Graham West glanced out of the landing window and noted the flurry of snow that had begun to settle on the green. He shivered and felt the soreness in his throat brought on by excessive carol singing. There were years when the Christmas workload of the priest seemed endless. It had been almost two o'clock by the time he had finished midnight mass the previous evening and crawled into bed. 'Last lap,' he thought as he buttoned his cassock and made his way down the stairs.

Stuart and Sally, his children, had woken at seven o'clock, rushed into their parents room, and undid their stocking presents. Next they would charge down the stairs to see what other goodies had been left by Father Christmas under the tree. Not to be opened yet of course. This was a house with Christmas traditions, one of which was that presents under the tree were opened after lunch. Their Daddy was working this morning.

'It's snowing Judy,' he called back up the stairs. His response was the cheers of excitement from his two children, who passed him on the stairs, pausing only to check the facts of the situation through the window by the front door.

'Yippee,' cheered Stuart, 'Christmas and snow. Can we play in the snow daddy?'

'Not before church you can't.'

'Come on Sally; let's see what Father Christmas brought us.' Sally needed little encouragement and they skidded into the sitting room along the parquet floor. Graham followed them. 'No peeping you two; breakfast first.'

He stood in the doorway with an arm pointing towards the kitchen, only lowering it when the children had passed him.

The family eventually assembled in the kitchen. Graham was checking through his order of service and the readings in Common Worship indicated by the multicoloured silk ribbon book marks. He glanced at his watch.

'I'd better be getting across,' he said, standing and emptying his coffee mug all in one movement. I said I'd open up today to give Jim a bit of a lie in. With his last piece of toast held between his teeth, he donned his large black cape, and with a 'see you all later,' he strode across the green towards St. Wulfstans, leaving a set of dark footmarks in his wake.

The east wind was blowing directly into his face as he neared the church, so he bent forward to keep the snow flurries out of his eyes. It was only when he reached the porch that he noticed what appeared to be a rolled up carpet across the west door of the church.

The porch was quite large by country church standards; fifteenth century; square in dressed sandstone; windowed on both sides; with an original tiled floor and an open entrance about three metres wide. As such it provided some shelter against the prevailing east wind, though not a place to linger on a cold winter morning.

As Graham entered the porch he realised it was not a carpet, and he could not help his gasp of incredulity when the parcel moved and groaned. The smell of alcohol seemed everywhere. The idea of a tramp's shelter has been discussed by the diocese at one of its clergy meetings, and occasionally the vicarage had had a knock at the door and a request for food and water, but this was pretty rare even in harsh economic conditions. He had a small hardship fund agreed by the Church Council that he could use in such situations. But a man sleeping rough in the porch. On Christmas morning. What desperate straits resulted in such things. He knelt and tapped the bundle somewhere near where a shoulder ought to be.

'Hallo, are you alright?' Why don't you come into the church, my friend, and I'll make you a hot drink.

'Mmmmmm.. go away ....' muttered the bundle, 'let me be, I'll come in later.'

'You would be so much warmer inside. Would you like me to find you an extra blanket?'

'No. Leave me alone, Graham.'

This time the face was just visible among the wrappings.

'I'm sorry, do I know you? Have we met before? Can I help at all?'

This time the response is clearer.

'For goodness sake, leave me alone.'

'OK, OK, sorry, the door will be open. Come in when you want to. It'll be a lot warmer inside.'

With that he took the large ornate door key from his pocket, stepped over the bundle, unlocked the door and walked down the aisle to the vestry. A kettle and tea bags were kept in a small cupboard, and he prepared to make the promised cup of tea. What else could he do? Was this someone who had sought his help and he had let them down? Well he jolly well wouldn't let them down this time, and he rehearsed a conversation with Judy in his head, explaining why there would be an extra guest for Christmas dinner. He knew his wife to be a sympathetic and generous woman, but Christmas dinner? What was the world coming to? Nowhere to go at Christmas-not even a stable he thought to himself.

The next to arrive was Jim Walters, the churchwarden. Jim had a brusque approach to life, his bark being worse than his bite. He enjoyed two things, apart from his family and the church of course, a tweed suit and single malt. Today being Christmas, he worn the green tweed with a red fleck.

'Graham, I take it you've seen the new doormat. What are we going to do? He can't stay there; people will be arriving soon. I nearly fell over him. What are we going to do?'

'What do you suggest Jim? We can't throw him out and he shows no inclination to leave of his own accord. I've made a mug of tea and found a spare blanket in your store. It would be better if we got him into the warm. If he's still here at the end of the service, we'll have to invite him for lunch.'

'Does Judy know?'

'Not yet. Anyway I'll take him the tea, and try to persuade him to come in. Can I leave you to get the altar ready for the Eucharist? Who is on welcome duty?'

'Jane Winters and John Panther.'

'Are they here yet?'

'Jane is, she came on her bike for goodness sake.'

'Good Lord! Ok I'll talk to her about how we are going to handle this, so they can explain to the congregation as they arrive.'

With that Graham headed for the west door with a mug of tea in his hand, said hallo to Jane Winters who was in a corner, shaking the snow from her coat.

'Jane! About the bundle, just tell people we are dealing with it and not to worry.'

By the time he had left the tea and muttered words of encouragement to the bundle, one or two had begun to arrive and were stepping carefully over it. Inside there was only one topic of conversation.

'Graham.'

'Yes Jane.'

'Can we really just go ahead with the service as if nothing has happened?'

'I think we have to. Ah here's Michael.'

Michael Rogers smiled as he strode into the church,

'Good morning Graham. Who's your friend? 'he said, using his eyebrows to indicate who he was referring to. There was no need, everyone know who he meant.

'Come to the vestry,' said Graham and they went down the aisle.

In the vestry, Graham brought Michael up to date and they began to put on their gowns and prepare for the service. Minutes later, Jim Walters joined them.

'Everything's ready Graham.'

'Thank you Jim, any sign of Gail Parsons?'

'Not as yet. It's not quite time, I make it another five minutes.

They could hear the Salvation Army band warming up. The deep thump of the tuba, scales from the euphonium which joined by the trombone and cornets all playing different notes produced an odd cacophony of sound.

'OK it's about time. If Gail doesn't arrive by the time of the sermon, I'll fill in with something. They said a prayer and walked into the church. The attendance was excellent, and all three churches were well represented. The service began.

After half an hour there was only a hymn left before the sermon, and Graham sat down and made a few notes on his service sheet. He knew he didn't need to speak for long. Most people were looking forward to their Christmas lunch, and no one would judge him harshly if he was brief. As the congregation began the last verse of the hymn, he headed for the pulpit and waited.

Just as the band stopped, and the congregation sat down, the large metal door handle clanged and the west door opened. All heads turned and there was a single communal gasp. The tramp had chosen that moment to come into the warm. No one moved. It was customary for any latecomer to be greeted by a member of the welcome team, to ensure they found a seat, had a hymn book and service sheet. Not on this occasion. The tramp shuffled to the top of the aisle. Heads turned. The tramp slowly began to walk down the central aisle of the nave towards the pulpit. As he did so, he unwound a blanket and let it drop to the floor, and then a second blanket was discarded. As he, rather now more obviously a she, reached the end of the aisle she removed a red woolly hat and overcoat, and the full uniform of a captain in the Salvation Army was revealed. Gail Parsons had arrived.

Graham came down from the pulpit and shook Gail by the hand, 'Welcome,' he said, smiled and returned to his seat. She climbed the steps herself and had what every preacher hopes for, the full attention of the congregation. She reminded them of the real meaning of Christmas and asked them for their prayers for all those alone and destitute.

There was only one topic of conversation after the service, but since the majority were anxious to return to their home, families and turkeys in the oven, nothing was prolonged.

In the days that followed there seemed to be a number of points of view. There were those who said they knew it was a put up job right from the beginning. Then there were those who were totally surprised by the whole thing and thought it hilarious. The last group were those who wondered what they would have done if it had been real, and remembered the feeling of discomfort and worry as to what they would have really done about it when the service ended. Among this latter group was Graham West, who rehearsed in his dreams that night the conversation with Judy, as he escorted a tramp to his family's Christmas dinner.

With Christmas a distant memory, and January in its third week, Graham West sat down at his desk in the study, intending to pen an outline for the service of the Week of Christian Unity. John chapter 17 verse 21, 'I pray that they may be one,' was the normal text for such occasions. He had not heard anything from Gail since her Christmas escapade. People were still talking about it. However he needed to think about his theme so that he could steer Michael in the direction of appropriate hymns and readings. Then he remembered the band. There had been some doubt in Gail's mind as to whether the Salvation Army band were going to be there and Gail was going to let him know. They had played at the Christmas morning service without any fuss. The instruments had been brought by van. Perhaps there was another reason. He recalled the minor outburst about venues. Did the others feel left out because the united services needed to be held in the largest church? Were they in revolt? In his head he saw the band parading outside the parish church with banners saying things like, 'Save the Sally Anners,' and 'Down with the C of E.' He tried to ring Gail, but her answer machine cut in. He left a message.

By the end of the week, he had finished his sermon, chosen the hymns and readings and emailed them to Michael and Gail. In return Michael sent his order of service, his choice of readers, one from each denomination. On the Friday afternoon he got an email from Gail which read,

 'Problem with band- may be short on numbers. Corps meeting is discussing possible solutions this evening. Best wishes Gail.'

That was still the position at 10.00 on Sunday morning. On the Saturday, Graham had briefed Fred Watson, the organist and choirmaster, that he may be needed to play.

'Bloody hell. Sorry Vicar. No not really a problem Graham, I was going out, but it's not urgent; I can be there. The missus can go on her own, its 'er cousin.'

Graham thought best not to explore the missus or the cousin and left it at that.

'Good morning Fred,' he said as they met in the nave the next morning.

'Mornin' Vicar.'

'No sign of the band then.'

'Not that I've seen. I've put out three chairs for them, which is the least we can get away with I reckon.'

Graham went to the west door to greet arrivals. Michael Rogers was on time, exchanged pleasantries and with a 'you know the way to the vestry' from Graham, headed off to prepare.

Jim Walters, the churchwarden, joined him at the door, and they both stood as people began arriving. In was very pleasant in the weak January sunshine greeting not only his own flock, but people from the other churches.

It was almost twenty-five past ten, when a white minibus pulled up at the end of the drive, disgorged its contents, and Gail rushed up the path, breathless.

'Sorry, had to hire a van and it didn't turn up, puncture, but six players though. Sorry.

'No matter you're here now. We better go in. It's almost time.'

As he and Jim went through the west door, Graham suddenly realised they had only put three chairs out and there were going to be six band players.

'Quick Jim, get three chairs for the salvation Army,' he said pointing to the area In front of the chancel arch.

Jim Walters looked a touch surprised, but being used to Vicars and their strange ways, he took it in his stride, marched slowly down the central aisle, turned and faced the congregation. And as the band players entered the church, his deep voice rang out

'Ladies and gentlemen, three cheers for the Salvation Army. Hip Hip, Hoorah! Hip Hip, Hoorah!, Hip Hip Hoorah. '

For Goodness Sake

Chapter Eleven

A Night at the Opera

E Ely Operatic Society had something of a reputation for producing robust and enthusiastic shows. Doris Panther (the 'h' is silent) epitomised the spirit of the group with her robust and enthusiastic contralto. Over the years she had appeared in countless productions and her whole family, two daughters and husband John had provided loyal support in roles front and backstage. In her earlier days, her strong alto had been heard in parts of some significance. Indeed her performance as 'Cherubino' in 'The Marriage of Figaro' was still talked about. In recent years she had faded back into the chorus but it would be difficult for those who had regularly attended the annual performance to think of a production without her. She also provided the communication link between the Operatic and other local music groups including Random music society. It was her custom, as soon as the years offering had been agreed, to ring round her contacts and try for an early commitment to the opera in their programmes.

'We're going for Madame Butterfly again this year, Elisabeth, it's been about ten years since we last did it, which is a reasonable time.'

She looked at herself in the hall mirror as Elisabeth responded and checked the line of her lipstick with her finger and then she continued.

'It was either that or the Queen of Spades, Tchaikovsky you know, but I do think that is not as well known and when we choose the obscure our audience numbers go down. Of course there were some on the committee, you know who I mean, who always choose the least popular because they think it makes them look intellectual. Silly I call it Will you do your usual coach load? Mmm yes, mmm I'm so glad.'

'Of course', Doris continued 'I know you haven't put your annual programme together, so I hope I'm in good time. Yes, of course I know I'm on your committee...but I'm on a lot of committees.'

She licked her finger and drew it along her eyebrow.

'Ok the prices Yes. Can I say I think the prices will be much the same as last year. We have decided to continue to focus on November; we think it's the best month. It gives us enough time after the holidays to rehearse properly. Does that suit?

It does good.'

Now I know you are going to ask about who the leads are this year, and I can tell you we are more or less settled. Susan, Heather and George have been pencilled in.' She paused.

'Oh What about John? Mmm, yes...I understand. I thought you might ask, and I have to say there has been some debate. He may win the day of course because at the moment we have a shortage of tenors. Ah well I must go, see you next week Bye, bye.'

The debate surrounded Doris's husband John, who had been a member of the operatic society for over 10 years. In his day he had been a fine tenor. That was undisputed. He had appeared from time to time as a soloist on the morning service for Radio 4, but that had been some years ago.

Now it is well known in opera that the romantic lead is for the most part a tenor. It is also well known that Father Time catches up with tenors just like everyone else. Therein lay the contradiction; that an elderly, rotund tenor challenges an audience's disbelief, however far it may be suspended.

It remained a fact that John's waistline had expanded in direct proportion to his receding hairline. He had tried to disguise his shape by the cunning use of the cummerbund, belts and loose fitting shirts which had extended his opera life for two or three years.

It was his performance in Tosca the year before that had caused controversy, and was the reason for Elisabeth's question.

He had decided to wear a toupee. He had received much advice from friends and fellow performers about the use of false hair, and many felt that the role of Mario Cavarodossi, the painter, could justify a wig . The opera was set in Rome in the 1800's and it did not seem unreasonable for a painter to have long hair at that time. But a toupee?

Despite advice to the contrary, he went ahead. It is fair to say that for the first two acts on the opening night the audience were enthralled by the unfolding tragedy. The singing was lively and Susan Banks was acting her socks off as Tosca.

In the third act the mood changed. As the shots of the execution ring out, Mario is killed and John Panther duly fell on his back and lay still. In almost all respects he gave his best imitation of death, eyes wide open, head lolling to one side, artificial blood spilling from the bag secreted in his shirt. At this point in the plot Tosca realises that this is not a mock execution and that her beloved Mario is dead. She flings herself across the dead body.

Susan had not found this an easy move in rehearsal, and on this particular night she was rather too enthusiastic, and as she fell, her arm brushed across the top of Johns head.

The toupee slowly, but inevitably, fell to the stage.

The drama of the moment was recognised by the faint 'aah' of the audience and all was still.

Then miracle of miracles, the dead was raised to life, as John Panther's left arm lifted slowly into the air, searched the stage behind his head, found the toupee, and placed it firmly back into position.

After a moment, there was a noticeable titter from some around the audience which gradually combined to produce raucous laughter across the whole theatre

His action quite diverted attention and thus undermined the dramatic ending as Susan Banks flung herself off the bridge.

John's ability to turn tragedy into comedy was unsurpassed and the curtain eventually fell to a chorus of partially suppressed sniggers overtaken by sympathetic applause.

Elisabeth resolved to put the decision to the committee as to where they would go for their annual trip to live opera. Doris would be there of course, so she could make her points directly. No guesses as to where her loyalty would rest. Their decision might depend not only who had the tenor role, but whether there was anything else on in the region to compete with it', Elisabeth concluded that she should do her usual trawl of theatres and see what else there was.

The committee met at Jane Winters house, 2.30 pm on the following Tuesday afternoon about a week after Doris's phone call to Elisabeth. It was a fairly typical late August afternoon, where the threat of sunshine seemed equally balanced with the threat of rain. The air was humid and close, but with French windows open to the garden the slight breeze was pleasant. Tea and biscuits were on the coffee table in the centre of the room around which Jane had circled both comfy and straight back chairs.

There was not a great deal of room as one end of the room was taken up entirely by the grand piano.

Jane recorded in her note book from which she would draft the minutes those who were present.

Elisabeth Walters (Chair)

Jane Winters (secretary)

 Doris Panther

Graham West

Jeremy Pringle

Sarah Pringle

Graham West looked around the room. It was his first meeting and he was feeling a little out of place, and unsure how he had got here. He had been in post over a year and was in that corridor of uncertainty which often seemed to define him. To begin with he was uncertain whether he was getting involved in enough things and the following day could be equally certain he was doing too much. He had enough planning issues with the church, so he wasn't quite sure what he was doing . His wife, still working, wanted to make sure he used his time profitably or at least usefully, and had been chatting to anyone she thought would listen. When Elisabeth has been chatting to his wife, he overheard the offer to join the committee, but assumed it was his wife who was being asked. So when he commented, 'Jolly good idea, I think that would be a lot of fun', he felt them both turn to look at him and it slowly dawned on him that the object of the conversation was him. He couldn't instantly think of a way of getting out of it, and he was hooked. 'We'll look forward to seeing you on Tuesday next then John,' Elisabeth smiled at him, hand on her pearls. 'Really my dear,' he said to Judy, 'I do have enough on my plate without the music society'.

'But you said how important it was being part of the community outside the church.'

'I know I did, but I do wish you'd ask me first before any commitment is made.'

 As the preliminaries got underway, Graham glanced around the room. He noticed particularly the spread of small paintings across the long wall. They reminded him of the display at the end of an evening course, 'Oils for beginners', a step up from painting by numbers, but not a big step. They all had the initials JW in the bottom right hand corner. They must stand for Jane Winter. It reminded him of the time when the elementary scribbles of their own children had adorned the walls uncritically. He wondered what Jane really thought of them. His reverie was interrupted.

'And welcome to Graham for his first meeting, we are really delighted he agreed to join us......'

'but we would rather have had his wife,' Graham mentally completed the sentence,

'And we are sure his organising skills will be of special use to us,' Elisabeth concluded.

'The main item on this afternoon's agenda is the next phase of our programme which runs up to the AGM in January.' Elisabeth continued. This has in previous years typically featured a home based concert, probably in the village hall, and a trip. Just to fill in the newcomers.....' They all as one turned and smiled in Graham's direction.

'We have had trips to London, a touch expensive for some. Bedford, which we all know is the provincial base of the Philharmonia orchestra and of course Ely for the opera'. They turned as one and smiled at Doris.

It was obvious to Graham before the discussion had even began, that the others knew what each other's preferences were. They didn't know what his preferences were, but then he didn't know what his preference was either. As each member established their traditional territory, he mused over the options that were being presented to him.

A trip to London was clearly where Jane stood. She was all for raising standards, seeing the best, the Albert Hall and all that. Sarah's second cousin twice removed had once played in the Philharmonia and family tradition was good enough for her to vote for Bedford. Jeremy supported Sarah. It was obvious where Doris's allegiance lay.

This left Elisabeth.

'This year I'm really torn between London and Ely opera. I have looked around to see if Opera North is touring in our area this year, but sadly they are staying closer to home and we must bear in mind, as Jeremy often reminds us, that many of our members are pensioners so we must be careful not to put too much pressure on them. So I'm going to suggest we support Ely for a second year. Is everyone in agreement?' Elisabeth paused and looked around the committee.

That this scenario had been rehearsed so many times before was obvious, and where Elisabeth led, the others tended to follow. They had their preferences of course, which they expressed, but they were not natural rebels, and were not prepared to stand up and be counted.

'Obviously not' The short silence was broken by Graham

His response came out of instinct rather than firm opinion. He had been assessing the mixture of opinions wondering what the outcome was going to be, two for Bedford, one for London, and now two for opera, that he simply reported what he had heard. He did not gauge or take into account the depth of opinion, only the numbers.

'Please forgive me Elisabeth, but unless I've miscounted we've a tie, two each between Ely and Bedford, with one vote for London and I haven't voted yet.'

If the truth be known, Elisabeth was almost at a loss for words because nothing like this had happened to her before. She straightened her back,smoothed her hair with the palm of her hand and touched her pearls. Like many long standing chairs she knew her committee, and took for granted what its response was likely to be. Her short cuts did not originate from a lack of thought, more from habit and custom.

'Graham. Thank you for reminding us' she said, so tight-lipped it was as if she was in pain. She looked at the ceiling no doubt seeking divine help and smoothed her hair again.

'Yes that's very helpful, please we really would like a contribution from you, fresh thinking is always welcome'.

'Well now, my problem is that I don't think I, that is we, have enough information to make a final decision. I for one, would like to know what we might see in London, a concert? a musical? What are the Philharmonia playing? Could we take a little more time before we decide? Graham had clearly decided to play the role of thoughtful newcomer'

He stopped and there was a pause in proceedings.

Then Elisabeth stepped into the fray once more, her right hand shifting from hair to pearls.

'Of course Graham, we could do that. However when you have been here a little longer you will realise that the programme for the year gives us further opportunities. We can go to London in the spring when the nights are bit lighter. The Philharmonia are doing a summer series next year, so we can pick that up then. The local opera is a once a year opportunity and I feel we should not let them down. Jane Can you make the necessary arrangements with the coach company and e-mail our members, and Doris can you arrange our block booking. OK? Date of next meeting.'

'How did it go?' asked Judy as they sat down for supper
'Which particular it did you have in mind, my dearest.'
'The music society meeting of course, did you enjoy it?'
'The whole thing was a foregone conclusion- waste of time really. Elisabeth had decided, no one wanted to cross her, so we are going to Ely to support the local group. God knows why they wanted me there?'
'Oh well, I expect we'll be going won't we? I do enjoy a night out at the theatre. I'm looking forward to it already.'

Random was twelve miles from Ely, and the only means of travel was by road. The railways had not been kind over the years, and March and Ely had always taken precedence. Random villagers, the poor and the young, were used to a poor and expensive bus service with an air of resignation. It had always been like that and probably would always be so. The young aspired to own a car, the poor did not aspire to anything except winning the lottery.
The coach company, *Random Coaches was a* misnomer as there was only one coach and it was owned by Jacob Babcock of the Black Bull who usually drove the evening bookings. Evenings were better for Jacob as they were usually shorter journeys and it gave him the chance to get out of the pub for a change. The journey to Ely Community College, where the operatic usually performed, normally took around twenty-five minutes. Time enough for him to entertain his passengers He was jolly, they said, and could keep a coach load entertained with his 'off the wall' humour. He loved innuendo and could keep it going so long as he got a response and mostly he did from the pink and blue rinsed ladies who sat near the front of the bus.

Elisabeth, having checked that Jane had counted the numbers seated, would normally address the assembled throng before they started the journey. She took a deep breath, was about to stand, but got no farther.

'Nice to see you' Jacob boomed through the microphone, and a somewhat feeble 'to see you nice' came back to him. 'Where are we off to then, Ely Casino?'

'Oooh!' came the response

'Been saving up the house keeping?'

'Ooooh!'

'I like a bit o' opera meself, that Nessum Dorma 'specially, and he began to hum the tune in a gravelly baritone.

Elisabeth gave up and sank back in the chair, clicked into her seat belt and closed her eyes. They would have to manage without her introduction to the opera and hope that the programme would contain a resume of the plot.

Jacob went through his preparations and slowly gathered speed through the village. As he went along and passed the various landmarks he went through what was obviously a well rehearsed routine. The manor house became the home of the Random Royal Family and Prince Charles (Charlie Gray the builder lived there); the church, where he got married to 'er indoors, never 'ad a cross word in twenty five years, because she'd stopped speaking to 'im; the cemetery was the 'dead centre' of the village, and so on until the outskirts were left behind and Ely beckoned. They were soon drawing up in the Ely Community College car park.

'Now Jacob, you will be here when we come out. I expect it to be somewhere around ten o'clock, but it might be a little later as they have been known to overrun occasionally' said Elisabeth.

'Yes maam, I'll be 'ere,' said Joe touching his forelock.

And with that they all disembarked, went into the main hall of the school, found their seats, and sat waiting for the show to begin in eager anticipation.

The interval came after Acts One and Two. The audience were not disappointed by what they had seen. The scenery incorporating the church, which turned into an apartment looked very professional and brought a gasp and a spontaneous round of applause at the beginning of Act Two. The tension surrounding John Panthers toupee was quickly relieved when Cavaradossi entered wearing a proper blond wig which seemed secure throughout the first two acts. Susan's singing was excellent and the love duet in the first act was very moving. There had been the occasional wobble of the scenery as an eager member of the cast hurried to his place, but nothing serious. And as the curtain came down for the interval, everyone was feeling very positive.

'I'd better go and check on Jacob,' said Elisabeth to no one in particular. 'It looks as though we will be out after ten o'clock,'

'Would you like me to come with you Elisabeth, it is rather dark now?' said Graham, responding quickly to his wife's elbow in his ribs.

'That's very thoughtful of you, Graham, thank you.'

The two of them squeezed down the aisle to the exit, through the main school entrance and out into the car park. Jacob had parked the bus on the school side of the car park, and it was lit by the lights of the school hall.

Behind the stage curtain, decisions were being made. The dry ice machine was being wheeled into place in the wings.

'I think we'll go with it,' said the producer, 'it will give atmosphere to the scene. Switch it on now, as it will take about five minutes to create the fog, but it will stay around for much longer. We'll use the higher setting,' he said, pointing to the ratchet lever on the side of the machine As he switched on and moved the lever upwards smoke began to pour out of the nozzle laying across the stage. It quickly took on a snake like appearance zigzagging from side to side. The technician moved swiftly, grabbed the end of the hose and began to move it around to try and get an even spread of smoke across the stage. The area behind the stage began to fill with smoke.

As the curtains were closed air was drawn down onto the smoke so that when they were pulled open at the beginning of the next act the dry ice was sucked out into the auditorium and over the audience.

Elisabeth and Graham were about to return having assured themselves that Joe knew the timing of events, when Graham noticed the smoke coming out of a small window at the back of the hall. He turned to Elisabeth and they walked towards it.

'My God. Look the schools on fire. Have you got your mobile? Quick, ring the fire brigade.'

Without waiting for a reply, he ran towards the hall.

He banged on the misted windows to try and attract attention and get a fire door open, but his banging went unheard, so he ran along the side of the building to the main doors, and rushed into the foyer.

He knew he could not simply run in and shout fire. That might cause a panic. He went quickly down the short corridor that led to the hall. There were a couple of stewards sitting at the entrance table.

'I don't want to worry you, but I have seen smoke coming out of a window, at the back of the stage.'

'That'll be the dry ice then. We haven't used it before'.

'What do you mean?'

'They are going to use a dry ice machine in the next act to create the impression of early morning. First time we've used it. We were just joking that someone was bound to think there was a fire.'

'But...Oh dear, we thought it was a fire and we've called the fire brigade, or my friend has, on her mobile.'

'Oh no. We'd better go and meet them. Leave it with us.' They walked out towards the car park, as Elisabeth came rushing into the foyer.

'What's happening?' Why isn't anyone moving?' she asked.

'It's dry ice', the embarrassed Graham explained, 'let's go and sit down.'

As they made their way down the aisle, the curtains were flung back to a rousing introduction from the orchestra, and the smoke from the machine blew across the stage and out over the audience. The first few rows were quickly enveloped and the coughing and spluttering began. On stage, Butterfly tried to sing her lullaby but was being overcome by dry ice which was not sinking fast enough. She tried waving her arms using the long sleeves to disperse the smoke to little effect and gave an effective rendering of a frenetic windmill.

In the front rows one or two began to make their escape down the hall.

As those towards the back of the hall commented on the proceedings, the noise began to overpower the voices on stage.

At that point the fire brigade arrived. A tall rather officious, helmeted fireman marched unannounced to the front of the hall, up the steps across the front of the stage and behind the curtain. A hundred and fifty eyes followed him. A moment later he reappeared. The smoke began to disperse.

'Ladies and Gentlemen, there is no need to panic, but I would be grateful if you could quietly leave the hall in an orderly manner by the nearest exit.'

145

As his arms indicated the direction, the glass fire escape doors down the side of the hall were flung open and within a few minutes the hall was cleared and everyone was standing in the car park.

As they gathered in groups, those with experience of the stage recounted their own stories of dry ice and how you really did need to know what you are doing, completely unaware of the true state of things.

No one noticed that the ladders and hoses in use by the small window at the back of the hall were focused on an electrical fire which was being efficiently dealt with by the firemen and women..

The tall helmeted fireman approached Elisabeth.

'Excuse me, Madam; I understand that you were the person responsible for calling us out'.

Elisabeth coloured from her pearls upward, the darkness of the car park covering her embarrassment.

'Oh dear, yes,' said Elisabeth, 'I'm so sorry. It wasn't really me. Well I know it was my mobile, but it was the Vicar who was really responsible. He was the one who thought there was a fire and he told me to phone. I, of course, did realise it was probably the dry ice. I have some experience of the stage you know, but I didn't want to argue.'

'Where is he? I'd like to talk to him.'

'He's there, look, helping our group on to the coach.'

He turned and walked over to the coach.

'Excuse me sir, can I have a word.'

'Certainly officer.'

'I just wanted to say thank you; but for your prompt action this could have been really serious. The fire was right at the back of the stage and unfortunately the use of dry ice camouflaged the initial effect. Any further delay might have had serious consequences. It's under control now. Thanks very much. Could I have your name sir; for my report you understand.'

'Oh... yes of course......West. Reverend Graham West.'

The following week, Elisabeth picked up the local paper from her front doormat and glanced at the headline:

'RANDOM VICAR SAVES THE DAY AND PLAY'

There was no mention of her phone call. As she smoothed her hair with the palm of her hand and touched her pearls she sighed,' Oh dear, it's not really fair, it was my mobile after all.'

It was an hour later that Judy and Graham West sat down for supper. Judy picked up the paper.

'Have you seen this?' You're a hero.'

She read the rest of the story.

'It says here that you were the only one who could tell it wasn't the dry ice. Did you really know there was a fire?'

'Darling, as we often say, you should not always believe everything you read in the newspaper.'

For Goodness Sake

Chapter Twelve

Jingle Bells

No one could remember when it started; they just knew it had always been there. They looked forward to it because it had become a tradition of a Random Christmas. The whole town was involved, both prominent individuals and local groups contributed to the annual festival. Large and small, themed and plain, lit and unlit, the Christmas tree festival was part of the life of Random. It lasted for about two weeks before Christmas, and every window and floor space around the walls of the church was filled with trees. The centrepiece was always a large tree, beautifully decorated and lit and set up at the junction of the nave and lady chapel.

History would suggest it was the Victorian worshippers at St.Wulfstans who had first introduced the idea of a Christmas Tree into the church. As far as anyone knew Prince Albert had not been to Random and it was he who introduced Christmas trees to England. Cambridge was as close as he got, to visit Prince Edward who was studying at Trinity College, after which he caught typhoid and died.

In happier times perhaps they read the Illustrated London news which pictured the royal pair with their Christmas tree at Windsor from which their popularity spread-the trees that is.

One can imagine the eager gentry discussing the prospect and wealthy landowners searching their estates for a good specimen for the home and the church. Size appeared to be everything. The bigger the tree the greater the position in society was deemed to be.

It was Sunday lunchtime at the beginning of December. Charlie Gray, Prince Charles to some, and a member of the 'tree' brigade; and a local builder and resident of the manor house, sat at the saloon bar in the Black Bull public house. He was halfway through his first pint, perched on a bar stool, half turned into the room, with his back to the wall. The bar has been decorated for Christmas with coloured paper chains, not new, across the ceiling and a small tree in one corner with flashing lights. The window panes have been frosted in the corners to give the effect of snow.

'All ready for Christmas then Charlie boy.' George Wilson, village postman, assistant postmaster and bellringer breezed into the bar around the wooden scrubbed tables and chairs scattered in a somewhat random fashion. He rubbed his hands to bring the feeling back, and prepare them for his lunchtime pint. He had walked the four hundred yards from the church and the December wind was bringing cold air in from Russia.

'Pint of best, please Jack,' George called to Jacob Bocock who was about to serve a customer in the lounge bar, but stopped to please one of his regulars.

Charlie and George were regulars at Sunday lunchtimes.

'Busiest time of the year for you, George isn't it? said Charlie, 'I shouldn't think you get much time to do your own shopping.'

'Not like it used to be, Charlie. Presents on the internet now, and there's more delivery companies each year. Not to mention the boy scouts. You'd think they had better things to do than take business away from your working man. The trouble is everybody tries to earn an extra bob or two at Christmas.

'Gin and Tonic, Em?' He called to his wife as she came through the door.

'Please George.' She took her coat off and hung it on the row of pegs beside the door and placed her carrier bag on the floor below the coats. She took out her *Sunday Mail* and joined her husband at the bar.

'Have you seen the advert on the counter at Singh's?' she announced to no one in particular.

'What advert?' George and Charlie both respond.

'The poster on the counter about ordering Christmas Trees.You can order a Christmas tree from Mr. Singh- you simply say what size you want and it will be delivered to your door the week before Christmas. You have to leave a deposit. I said to him that I didn't think his lot went in for Christmas.'

Charlie laughed. 'Cheeky! What did he say?'

'Business is business Mrs.W. We have to make sure we meet the needs of our customers. If we don't someone else will.'

Charlie continued. 'He's a good man is Gulam, a lot of people in this village would miss him if he closed. Do you know he gave old Miss Graveney some bread and milk last week because someone told him she'd run out before pension day? Told her he'd put it on the slate-but I bet he didn't.'

'It's little things like that that make such a difference to a village,' says George, 'shall we order a tree Em?'

'Oh shit.' said Charlie, before Em could reply, banging his hand noisily on the bar, and grabbing the attention of everyone in it. There is moment of silence. Charlie is not in the habit of banging the bar so everyone is waiting for the explanation.

'I forgot to order the Church Christmas Tree.'

'Oh is that all, I thought it was something serious for a minute,' says George.

'It is serious, George, you can't get a fifteen foot tree at a moment's notice.' He looks at his watch. It's the 3rd today, for goodness' sake.

'Who is your normal supplier?'

'I get it through a nursery the other side of Ely. I've got a mate who's the manager there. He won't have remembered without me asking - he does it at cost for me as well.'

'You can always try Gulam,' laughed George. 'It must be my round, same again Jack please.'

On Tuesday afternoon, the phone rang in Gulam Singh's SPAR shop in Random High Street.

'Singh's grocery.' Mr. Singh answered the call, 'how can we be of service?'

'Hallo Gulam, it's Charlie Gray. I wonder if you could do me a favour?'

'What is the problem Charlie? I will help if I can.'

'I don't expect you'd know 'cos I don't shout about it, but every year I give the church a Christmas Tree. You know the fifteen foot job that usually stands at the front of the church.'

'No Charlie, I didn't know.'

'No reason why you should my friend, no reason at all. Well this year I just forgot, and I went to my usual contact and he's not doing big trees this year. He's had trouble with his supplier or something. Anyway I'm up the creek without a paddle. Then I remembered that you were advertising trees in your shop and I wondered whether you had a supplier that could help me. I really need to get it early next week, though I don't expect a day or two will make a difference.'

150

'Ok, Charlie, leave it with me. I'll see what I can do. I don't know whether my supplier can deliver that quickly and whether he has access to bigger trees. Does it have to be fifteen feet?'

'I don't think the vicar will mind if it's a bit smaller, but if it's too small it gets lost among all the others. It's a big building. I can get it picked up if it's fairly local. Where is your supplier?'

'Lincolnshire, Charlie, near a town called Louth, I think. It's my wife's brother-in- law's sister's cousin. He owns some land up there full of fir trees and thought he'd see if there was a market for his small trees. So he offered it round the family. I am planning a bulk order to make it worthwhile him delivering. I've had quite a few orders already, but we were thinking of one delivery to Random on the 15th.'

'That's a bit late for me. Still, see what you can do. Thanks Gulam. Bye.'

In the Vicarage, Graham West was looking out of the front window from his study, hands in pockets, swaying toe to heel, watching members of the prayer group trying to get out of his semi circular drive. They had entered and parked on the left hand side of the drive, while the Verger, Jim Walters was facing them on the right hand side. The left entrance was now blocked, probably by some unknown person visiting the bank. All the other parking bays were full and as was often the case, cars tended to be left wherever the driver saw space. While Jim had been delayed by a last minute discussion with the vicar, Julie and Joan Watson had reversed in the hope that the unknown person would return and move their car. Julie looked as if she was trying to squeeze past Jim's car, tried and became entangled with the small box hedge which lined the drive. She came forward again, looking as if she was in the process of a three point turn. She got her angles wrong, and she ended up across the drive. It would have been a twenty point turn if she had continued. At that point Jim came out and reversed down his part of the drive. He stopped at the end as the unknown person who had returned to her car, saw she was blocking one entrance, and moved it forward, only to block his exit.. She then went across the road to the Post Office. Eventually, Joan and Julie got out and cleared the way for Jim.

Graham had other more pressing concerns. The Christmas arrangements discussed in the planning meeting seemed to be a long way behind schedule. They did not know whether a Christmas Tree would be provided from the usual sources and Lily

Bennett, who normally organised the Christmas Tree festival has gone off to stay with her sister in Sheringham because her brother in law had died. She had left a file of papers with Jim Walters who had agreed to act as stand- in until she returned. No one was quite sure when that would be. He had also agreed to talk to Charlie Gray about the Tree.

Graham was not sure about the Christmas Tree festival. It seemed more pagan than Christian, but it had been going for a long time, it involved the whole community and the church looked splendid for the Christmas period. It also brought people into the church to look at it. For that reason alone he thought it was worth keeping. Still he could leave everything to Jim.

.Jim Walters chief responsibilities as verger were for the maintenance of the fabric of the church and supporting the vicar for wedding and funerals. It included Christmas Trees. He had got home after the prayer meeting and his chat with the Vicar with two things on his mind. Would Charlie be donating the tree this year and when would it arrive? Secondly had the people who usually take part in the festival have this year's details?

So when he got home Jim rang Charlie.

'Charlie Gray speaking'

'Charlie, it's Jim Walters. I'm just checking up on progress with the Christmas Tree.'

'Hi Jim, I hope to have some news for you later in the week. I think I've found an alternative supplier. My usual source let me down, you know.'

'OK! Keep me posted. I've got the lights ready, so we can get it organised for the tree festival weekend, just as soon as you say the word.'

As soon as he put the phone down it rang again

'Hello Charlie ,it's Gulam. Can you get one of your trucks to Louth on Thursday? My brother-in law sister's cousin has found you a tree that he thinks will do.'

'Excellent Gulam, I'll arrange for the lorry. What do I owe you?'

'Nothing Charlie; that part of the family owes me a favour so there is no charge.'

'Very generous of you, shall we call it joint sponsorship, your tree and my lorry?' Then Charlie rang Jim.

'Hallo Jim, it's Charlie. We are picking the tree up on Thursday from Louth. Gulam Singh at the SPAR grocery has found a supplier from one of his relatives. So he and I are joint sponsors.'

'That's really splendid, Charlie, thank you so much. We will put a card by the tree saying who the sponsors are, if that's alright with you?'

'That's nice, Jim. I'm sure Gulam wouldn't mind the publicity. As he often says, 'business is business.'

By Friday lunchtime, the tree had been erected, and by teatime it had been decorated with lights.
A small notice was placed in a prominent position.
'This tree has been generously provided by Gulam Singh, SPAR grocery, and Charles Gray, Builder.

On Friday evening, Mr Gulam Singh was cashing up. His wife Manjit was filling shelves.
'Does a Christmas Tree count as Sadh Sangat, giving as the Guru commanded us, my husband?'
'I believe so, my wife! Did Guru Nanak not say, 'A place in God's court can only be obtained if we do service to others?'
'Did he also not say, 'business is business, my husband?'

The following Thursday had been designated by the planning team as the setting up day for the Christmas Tree festival, and when Jim Walters, the Verger, arrived at 8 am there was already a queue at the door, mostly from those businesses, shops etc who liked to participate, or from people who worked in them and needed to use the time before work to prepare their stand.
'Where would you like us to go?' they asked Jim. 'Shall we use our usual places?'
'Yes, that'll be fine.'
In fact Jim hadn't envisaged having to organise anything. He assumed that Lily Bennett had made the necessary arrangements. He was a fraction concerned at the initial response of the first to arrive but if it came to it, it would be first come, first served.
Lily, it turned out had assumed that because there were no new groups, everybody must have done it before and would know exactly where to go.
They were both wrong. Lily had not made the necessary arrangements and although it was the same groups who were taking part in the festival as in previous years, the individuals putting up the tree were different.

Jim Winters was busy with extension leads when Mandy James, representing the British Legion came into the church. They traditionally had the first window on the right. Mandy James was the treasurers daughter, and had been briefed thoroughly by her mother who was temporarily indisposed with a heavy cold. Mandy had entered the church via the church hall where the play group met, as she was dropping off her daughter. Without checking with Jim, she went straight up to the first window on the right and began to unpack the decorations from the basket that had been provided by her mother.

As Jim eventually discovered, she had entered the church through the west door, which meant the first window on the right was on the other side and at the other end of the church.

Jim was blissfully ensuring that his extension leads were covered, unaware of the disaster that was beginning to unfold. What he did not know was that this was the window that traditionally belonged to the Music Society. Who was responsible for the society tree? Jim's wife, Elisabeth.

Elisabeth arrived rather later in the day, by which time most of the work had been done. There were trees in half the windows, some lit and some unlit; some had flashing lights, some coloured lights. The majority had tried to link the tree to their group or society. 'Random in Bloom' had flowers around the base and artificial roses on the tree. The 'Little Imps' playgroup tree was decorated with garden gnomes and their eyes lit up in a rather ghoulish fashion. The British Legion tree was covered with poppies as one would expect but the usual star or fairy at the top had been replaced by a Union Jack. At the bottom of the tree was a doll dressed as Father Christmas which played 'Jingle Bells' if touched. However she was slightly puzzled that standing around the west doorway were six or seven trees which had not found a window or floor space.

As she moved towards her window at the end of the north aisle, she couldn't help feeling that the festival had quite lost its purpose and become rather vulgar. It was going to take a lot of work to make it successful. She would talk to Graham West about it. But thoughts about the value of the festival went quite out of her mind when she saw that the British Legion had occupied her space. She stood open mouthed and without taking her eyes off the Union Jack, she raised her voice. 'Jim'....JIM....JIIIIIM....in a rising crescendo.

'What's the matter, Elisabeth?' Jim was in the choir vestry but came rushing out as he recognised his wife's cry.

'What's the matter? What's the matter?' Have you seen this? How could you let this happen? What were you thinking of? You surely must have known? When did it happen? Who did it?

Jim did not see the problem. 'What?' Is it in the wrong place?'

'Is it in the wrong place? Is it in the wrong place?

It quickly occurred to Jim that when his wife went into repetition mode he was in trouble. 'It must have happened first thing this morning. Mandy put it up I think.'

'Jim where is your plan? 'What does your plan say?'

'Er..I haven't got a plan.'

'You haven't got a plan! You haven't got a plan. Well you will have to move it. This window belongs to the Music Society.'

'Does it? OK dear, where should I put it?'

'The first window over there,' she said, pointing angrily across the church. That's where the British Legion goes.'

Jim picked up the doll and the tree and made his way across the church to a melodic accompaniment.

'Jingle Bells, Jingle Bells, Jingle all the way,' sang Father Christmas.'

'Oh shut up,' said Jim.

He tried to stop the device by pressing the stomach, the arms and the legs, but only succeeded in starting it from the beginning again. It took him some time to find out that there was a button on the back of its head which switched it off.

After Elisabeth had finished setting up her tree, it became clear to her and then by osmosis to Jim, that a number of the trees were in the wrong place and that was the reason for the group of trees around the west door. They needed to be sorted out before other contributors realised their space had been taken by someone else.

'First things first Jim, has Lily left you a list of those taking part?' Elisabeth went into management mode, smoothing back her hair and touching her pearls.

'I think so. I counted twenty groups on a paper in her file.'

'Ok. Good. But there is no plan?'

'No.'

Elisabeth rather snatched the file from her husband's hand, took a biro from her bag and after penning a quick diagram of the church and the spaces available, began to fill in the ones she was pretty sure of. After about ten or so minutes with a little help from Jim who went dashing round the church noting which had to be moved, they had completed the rearrangement, including the group of trees by the west door. The diagram was then pinned to the notice board for those who hadn't already set up.

Unfortunately, most of those who had not finished decorating their tree returned the next morning to find that their trees had been moved. There was no sign of the Verger who had unlocked the church at the normal time and gone home for breakfast. They gathered at the west door, discussing what they should do.

'Well I'm on the floor and I understood I was going to have a window,' said one.

'I had a lovely spot in the window,' said another, 'but I've been moved to the floor and some of the decorations have fallen off. Is it vandals?'

'My label's gone missing,' said a third.

It was at that point that Graham West, the Vicar arrived.

He was in something of turmoil. He had left his reading glasses somewhere and since he had a funeral at three o'clock that afternoon, finding them had become his priority.

He was not by instinct a brave man and as soon as he saw the group he hesitated.

They gathered around him, respectfully, with distance between them. But if someone had called for an eight-some reel they would have been ready.

'Good morning all. How are we this morning?' he said cheerfully.'

The barrage that followed made Graham wish he hadn't put his head round the door. However it is at times like these he decided, that vicars earn their keep and while the tree decorators complained about their individual situations, Graham was thinking about his spectacles. He only half listened.

'Ok! I think I understand. Since yesterday when you came to set up, someone has moved your trees, is that the problem?'

'Yes!'

Did you not get instructions from Lily Bennett?'

'No. Only the date and times for setting up.'

'Oh Ok. I would have thought there should be a plan of some sort somewhere. Let me have a look round.'

He strode off murmuring to himself 'Now where would Jim put a plan?'

'On the door? No not there.'

'Vestry? Not there.'

'Notice board?'

'Ah What's this?'

'Yes we have a plan?' he said with an air of triumph.

'Here we are,' he called, 'this should do the trick.'

He laid the paper on the side table by the west door.

'This wasn't here yesterday when we came to set up, and some of us have had to take time off from work to come back again today.'

'I'm so sorry, Lily Bennett normally organises things, but her brother–in–law died so she has gone to be with her sister. I am sure you understand. Now if you'll forgive me I must get on.'

With that he shuffled sideways crab like towards the door and escaped back to the vicarage.

It was nine o'clock on Sunday morning when Graham West had time to think about Christmas Trees. Eight o'clock communion was over; plates and chalice were back in the safe; and as he made for the door he was thinking as much about his coming breakfast than anything else. He was pleased to note that everything appeared to be in place. The big tree looked splendid in the corner, tastefully decorated and lit with twinkling stars. He looked round as he went down the nave. He noticed that gnomes of different shapes and sizes seemed to be popular this year and some of the signs indicating the donor seemed to him a little large in some cases. He made a mental note to put together some guidelines for next year. On balance he was quite pleased with the effect and there was no doubt that the tree festival added to the feeling of well being that came with Christmas.

As he reached the door, a head appeared.

'Good morning Graham, are we interrupting? We thought you might be open today, it being Sunday. We just thought we'd have a look at the tree now it's in place, if that's alright?'

The 'we' turned out to be Charlie Gray and Gulum Singh.

'Of course, do come in, I've just finished the first service of the day and then I'm back again for the 10.30 family service.'

'We assumed it would be your busy day, didn't we Gulam?'

'Oh yes, Charlie. I thought as I was sorting the newspapers it would be good to see the tree and when Charlie came in for his paper, we thought we'd just come across the road. I can't be very long, it's my busy morning too.'

They stood, hands on hips looking back down the church towards the tree.

'Let me switch the tree lights on for you, so you can see it properly. There you are, what do you think?'

'Excellent! Excellent!' said the donors.

'Thank you for your generosity gentlemen. I want you to know how much it is appreciated.'

'Well, if you'll forgive me, I must get back to my newspapers, Manjit will not be pleased with me.'

'I must get home for my breakfast,' said Graham.

As the three of them strolled down the aisle towards the west door, Charlie turned to Gulam.

'It's the Carol Service next Sunday, you know, why don't we all go together. You could bring Manjit and the children. They'd love it. The whole church will be candle lit. Come to us for supper afterwards.'

'Would there be a problem if we came Graham, we are Sikhs?'

Good gracious no. We'd be absolutely delighted to see you.'

Later that evening as the family sat down for their evening meal. Gulam raised the issue. 'So what do you think Manjit? said Gulam. Susan and Charlie would like to take the children to the Carol Service on Sunday evening and they have asked us if we would like to go with them.'

'Oh yes daddy, can we go, please can we go' chorused the children.

'You see Gulam, the children have talked about it at school apparently, and they obviously want to go. Do you think we should?'

'I can see no reason why we should not go. It is not forbidden, Are we not each and every one of us, making our own way up the mountain? Where then is the harm?'

And so it was that a week later, they were all sitting towards the back of the church, singing carols with the rest of the congregation. Everyone was delighted to see the turban and the sari adding great colour to the proceedings. Candles had been lit and 'Silent Night' sung.

158

As the service came to a close and the last verse of 'O come all ye faithful' was in full flow, Aamir Singh the younger of the two Singh children was feeling rather tired. His father lifted him up onto his shoulder. At that height and with his mind wandering, Aamir found himself on the same level as the British Legion stand. Its lights were on and flashing and the Father Christmas doll seemed to be smiling at him. He stretched out his arm and touched it just as Graham West ended the service.

'And now may the grace of our Lord Jesus Christ, the love of God and the fellowship of the Holy Spirit be with us all, evermore. Amen.'

Jingle Bells, Jingle Bells, Jingle all the way.....................

For Goodness Sake

Chapter Thirteen

Money, Money, Money

Coming up with new ways of raising money was on the mind of Graham West as he walked across the green towards the Church hall one evening in March. An east wind was blowing, keeping spring at bay, forcing him to pull up the collar of his overcoat and lengthen his stride.

Why was raising money so often in the minds of the members of the Parochial Church Council (PCC) of St. Wulfstans Parish Church, he thought. It was on tonight's agenda.

As he passed the notice board, he mused that there was always some event or another designed to raise money. He supposed it was a constant problem in every church which was asked to pay its contribution to the Common Fund by the diocese each year. It always went up, never down. Thats life.

The PCC spent more time on *Finance* than anything else judging by the agenda items. He was the chairman, so why didn't he change it. Good question he thought as he unlocked the door to the hall.

The chairs for the quarterly meeting had been set out around the two long tables. It occurred to him as he took the pile of agendas from his briefcase that he didn't know how many would be there. MMM....he counted the chairs.....12....very biblical he thought. Should be enough, after all, this was the governing body of the parish that he chaired. It was important, but it was part elected and part appointed. Priests; Readers and those who could lead services, were *ex officio*. He smiled to himself, that really meant don't need to be there, and don't need to give apologies. The Synod representatives three co-options; and the rest elected at the Annual General Meeting tended to take it more seriously. Twelve would probably do it.'

He read through the agenda. It was their last meeting before the AGM in April and he would need to be sure that the right people produced the right reports to inform the members who assembled once a year.

He laid the copies of the financial report next to the agendas in front of the 12 chairs. He glanced at it. The financial situation was not dire... income...could be better...interest on capital, that saves us, he thought.

Momentarily he focused on those people who had left money in their wills so that the regular income could be underpinned by interest on the capital.

He conjured the scene in his mind was determined that the church would not be complacent to rising costs, but that the proposed budget for the following year should include some fundraising for charity. This was always controversial and he knew it would be difficult to gain agreement. Why did people always believe charity begins at home. Not in the church it didn't.

Graham tried to visualise the outcome he wanted. He remembered the diocesan personal development course in which it was suggested that if you visualise the goal you wish to achieve, you would be more likely to achieve them. The trouble was no matter what he tried to visualise for the PCC meeting he couldn't get out of his mind the picture of a boxing match.

In the red corner was the treasurer, Peter James. 'Old School' summed up Peter. Now in his early seventies, he had been, and actually still was, a family Solicitor. James and James had been in Ely for at least three generations. Curiously it was Peter's father and grandfather who were the original James and James, and it was rather convenient that over the generations the name had not needed to be changed. Indeed Peter's son Malcolm had also followed in his father's footsteps and actually did most of the work. A smile crossed Grahams face as he realised his image of a boxer was one least likely to fit Peter. 'Narrar,' fen folk would have called him. Over six foot in height, and long limbed, he weighed no more than eight or nine stone. Always formally dressed, he had once been described as man being eaten by his suit, as they seemed to dominate his increasingly fragile appearance. His white hair long nose and slightly stooping stance, hands perpetually clasped behind his back gave him the appearance of a crane. Indeed he once had gone to Cyprus for a month in January and the idea of him flying south for the winter seemed very appropriate. For Peter, things had to be done precisely. He zealously guarded the church accounts as his territory. In manner, he erred on the side of pessimism, no risk, and as little change to life as was possible.

In the blue corner was Jane Winter. In appearance Jane modelled herself on Miss Marple, the Margaret Rutherford version. She realised she was slightly overweight, and liked her grey hair to smell of lavender; it reminded her of her parents garden in north London. In summer, she liked clothes that seemed to float around her, so she wore dresses somewhat too big for her almost reaching to the ground. In winter she reverted to twin sets and a large black cloak that she could hide inside. Jane had won a substantial amount of money on the lottery, some of which she had given to the church, so she had a personal interest in its finance.

The battleground between them covered different aspects of church finance. The Income came from fees (weddings, funerals, etc), service collections, planned giving, fund raising and capital interest; expenditure for the common fund; administration; building maintenance and charitable giving.

The debate was essentially about how the money was raised. Peter felt that the traditional method of fetes and teas and sewing groups were part of the fabric of the church and should continue. He was all in favour of efficient planned giving but not to the exclusion of the social activities that raised money. He wanted the 'fun' in fundraising to continue.

Jane wanted to get rid of fetes and stalls which took such a lot of effort to organise and put more effort into increasing direct giving. Too many people, she thought, put minimal amounts into the collection plate, but would spend quite large amounts on things at the fetes. It ought to be the other way round.

Peter accepted it was human nature, Jane emphasised the discipline and responsibility that came from faith.

As people started to arrive, Graham determined to tread a middle way, at all costs not be seen to be taking sides, and in his mind he rehearsed his position. The church had clear social responsibilities and provided it was practical he felt it should support needs within their community and beyond. He also recognised that the church had a responsibility for stewardship, to use its resources wisely and ensure that it did not put itself at risk. They needed to ensure that their buildings were in good repair, but not to the exclusion of other responsibilities. There were always more demands than they could meet.

He thought they had established a sensible practice. The money that came through the collection plate funded the central work of the church and charity would get two collections per year; Harvest festival and Christmas day for charities chosen by the members of the church. As well as this, he had proposed that the church run an activity once a year, the proceeds of which would be exclusively for a single charity. Last year had been the first activity, as a good cricketer he had chosen a cricket match, and it had been fairly successful. Held at Random's cricket club ground, players were asked to gain sponsorship for the number of runs they scored. Teas were sold to players and spectators alike; the sun had shone and a good time was had by all, raising just over a thousand pounds. However it had been really difficult to find a date when the ground was available, and one lady had fallen over damaging her knee ligaments. Nothing had been said but he had felt the church might be vulnerable to an insurance claim. Perhaps something gentler was required.

'Thank you, Peter, for such a lucid presentation of the accounts and clear documentation which I'm sure will be appreciated by the AGM. Now has anyone any questions?'

Jane Winter drummed her fingers on the table.

'Yes Jane?'

'Thank you. Peter, I note that under expenditure for last year, we gave just under £2000 to the two nominated charities, which is not a lot of money, yet there is nothing in the budget for this year. Should we not have included in the budget a target for our charitable giving?'

'Thank you Jane. Peter?'

'It's not something we normally do, because we do not know in advance what the sums are? They are from two cash collections, and the cricket match. If I remember correctly the sponsorship depended on the number of runs scored and wickets lost, or something like that.'

Jane coloured and fiddled. 'Why then do we have a budgeted amount of £500 in the hardship fund. We don't know in advance how much hardship there is going to be, do we?'

Peter sighed. 'It's a notional figure, Jane. We increase it from time to time at the request of the Vicar and the church wardens, who are responsible for it, but since it has never been fully spent we can assume it will be sufficient. If Graham needs more he can ask for it and we can top it up.

'So why can't we do the same with a charity donation?'

'Mainly because the same amount that comes in for charity goes out; we are simply acting as a post box, so the effect on the accounts is neutral. You can decide you want to raise more than last year if you wish, by having more activities, and you can say what you hope to raise; but the sum raised will be the sum raised, if you get my drift. It will make no difference either to the accounts or the budget.'

. 'But we do know what is required in some areas. The food bank, medical equipment, overseas aid projects for example. We know what we raised last year, why don't we try to increase that by 20%,' Jane persisted.

'Why don't we leave that decision to the AGM?' Peter suggested, collecting his papers together into a neat pile on his lap. 'Thank you Peter. Now if there are no other points let us move on to the activity, has anyone any ideas for the charity activity that we can propose to the AGM?'

John Panther raised a finger in the air. 'Why can't we have the cricket again?' Graham responded. 'Well I did make enquiries at the club but the groundsman is very reluctant as they are running more teams this year. I didn't press it, and in any case because Ruth Ginns twisted her knee last year, I thought perhaps something a little safer and less strenuous might be a good idea.

John pressed the point. 'She's had that bad knee for years, slipped in the shower one Christmas she claimed. The fact that she demolished half a bottle of dry sherry the night before was an unfortunate coincidence I suppose. She couldn't hit the ball, that's what really happened! If we leave it to her we'll only have tiddlywinks left, and then she'd probably sprain her wrist or something.'

'Thank you, John, let's move on. I wondered about Rounders, it's a little less dangerous? I understand that the Junior school has the equipment and might be willing to loan it to us for the day; and they would be prepared to let us use their games field.'

Jane intervened, waving her pencil in the air.

 'How much money would it raise though? We can make something on drinks and teas but I can't see much scope for sponsorship. I know we all want to have a good time but do let's remember the reason for doing it.'

'I imagined we might ask people to be sponsored for how many rounders they scored either as individuals or as a team.'

John cut the discussion short. 'OK Vicar, let's do it. I propose we put it to the AGM.'

'Just a moment.' Peter delved into his briefcase and drew out two folded pieces of paper. 'Before we close the discussion, I have a couple of ideas I want to put forward for consideration if you don't mind. 'The cricket and rounder's game is great if it's a sunny day, but if it rains we are in a mess and considering the summers we've had that's a big risk. We got away with it last year but I think we'd be pushing our luck. Secondly, it's alright for you sporting types, but not all of us are good at sport. I want to suggest something that will have a wider appeal that is not dependant on the weather.'

'Ok Peter what are you thinking of?' Graham asked conscious that time was getting on and this was potentially a big item.

'This!' He a piece of paper to reveal what looked like a marketing hand-out. "Use your talents to double your money."

'I hope it's not what I think it is, said Elisabeth, 'If it's that calendar thing, I'm not taking my kit off for any amount of money.' There was a titter around the room.

'I think you are going to have to explain that to us, Peter?' Graham encouraged him.

'As I understand it, a church in Nottingham did it and raised a lot of money. The idea is that the church gives you an amount of money, say £5 or £10 pounds, this one was £10 for period of time, three months I think.. During that period you do something or run something or sell something which doubles your money. At the end of that time you give back to the church double the amount you were given, just like the people in the parable.'

Graham noticed the silence around the room and the look on peoples' faces.

'That sounds interesting-what kind of things did people do?' he said.

'They made and sold things, like cakes and chutney and ran coffee mornings for their friends; board game evenings, films; that sort of thing. They raised an awful lot of money.' Peter concluded with a victorious smile

Everyone listened and nodded to each other.

Then Jane raised her hand again. Was this the battle that he thought might happen? Jane began. 'Before we all get carried away with this, can we face reality? I seem to remember that in the parable one of them buried the money and did nothing with it, and what happens if someone loses money on a venture, or puts in on the horses. And if we did launch a 'talents' programme when would we do it? People only have so much surplus cash; we don't want to harm the other main fundraising charities. I have an alternative. The talents programme looks to me like a great deal of work, I think we should look in a different direction.'

She took out her purse, and brought out her debit card. 'As most of you know, I went to San Francisco in February to see my daughter Beth. Well, on the Sunday we went to church. It was a huge place and the congregation was well over a thousand people. Worship was conducted from a stage with all the ingredients you'd expect, hymns, bible readings, a very long sermon etc. At various times people would come onto the stage and deliver testimony about how God had helped them. Some of them were very moving. But behind all this was a huge cinema type screen which projected credit cards numbers and different ways of giving, including mobile phones, and ways of paying by credit card. This set me thinking.'

'Jane. You are not suggesting we put a screen like that up in the church somewhere are you?' interrupted Elisabeth.

'No, of course not, but it's got me thinking about how people give. We are one of the few organisations that don't offer people ways of giving that certainly most charities do now. We are still largely cash based. I have to go to the bank especially to put cash in my envelopes. You still see people fiddling with their purses and wallets for cash when the plate comes round, especially visitors. Then I saw this. It's an advert for a contactless payment system.'

'What's that?' asked John.

Jane waved her debit card again. 'It's a way of paying relatively small amounts of money for something. It has a limit of thirty pounds. Most of you will have it on your bank card. You don't have to use a pin number. It's quick, cheap and efficient. It's used in the cathedral tea shop for example. Why couldn't it be used in church?'

'Oh,' said Graham, slightly nonplussed, 'I can think of a few practical difficulties.'

John reacted quickly. 'What as part of the collection?' Can you imagine carrying a cash point reader round with you in one hand, and the plate in the other one? How would you give them a receipt?'

'There is no receipt, I understand', said Jane. She continued.

'Yes I grant that we would have to think about how we could use it. Could we have a collection for people on the way in or on the way out instead, for example.'

'Not on the way in. That would seem like paying an entrance fee.' said Graham.

'Entrance to heaven,' muttered Elisabeth.

'There is something quite persuasive about having a plate thrust under your nose', and it would take longer if a lot of people used it,' commented John.

'What would it cost?' asked Graham

'I haven't gone into all the details, but it was designed for small organisations so I can't imagine it would be expensive.'

Graham intervened. 'Look it's a huge issue, can I suggest we save it until the next meeting as we are short of time now.

I think we could put these ideas to the AGM in Peter's report as things to be thought about and so encourage a wider debate. Peter, Jane can I borrow the leaflets, I'll get some copies made?'

'How did it go?' Judy greeted her husband without looking up from the papers strewn around her as he sank into the armchair just after ten o'clock.

'OK, I think. We've got the potential for a good discussion on fund raising at the AGM; but I do wish I could get Jane and Peter on the same side. They just rub each other up the wrong way with me as the referee. In their own way they both have a lot to offer and I need them both. I need a coffee? Do you want one?'

'Mmm..yes please. I'm trying to finish my notes for tomorrow. What was the disagreement about this time?'

'Jane wants a charity giving target and Peter doesn't see the need.'

Graham raised his voice as he rattled the mugs, waiting for the kettle to boil. He leant through the service hatch.

'But you haven't heard the best bit,' laughed Graham. Jane wants to introduce credit cards for the collection. I'm not sure what Peter thought of it. He came up with one idea which is a talents activity. Jane was quite critical.'

'So Jane came up with the idea of credit cards, did she? That's interesting. Do you mean credit cards?'

'Well to be fair, I think she said a contactless payment scheme,' said Graham returning with coffee.

'Good for her, at least someone's got some imagination on that group. What did you say?'

'Well I wasn't sure of the practical implications, it would need a lot of thinking about.'

'Honestly Graham, you are a stick-in-the-mud sometimes. You should grab ideas like that and bring the church into the twenty-first century.

We didn't have time to explore either option properly, that or the talents; one is pretty traditional, the other very left field.'

As Graham sipped his coffee, Judy continued.

'So was there a row?'

'No, not really, they were both polite. Just different emphases I'd say.'

'So what's your problem? In fact they both sound very positive. It sounds to me as though their disagreement might be territorial. Perhaps Peter thinks she's treading on his toes; invading his realm.'

'Really?'

'It has been known. Finance can be a bit like that. It's specialised but it affects everybody.'

'Well you're the management guru, what would you advise?'

'Well my standard response would be to first ask yourself whether it's something they are aware of and are concerned about. Secondly ask yourself why you are worried about it. Is it having a negative impact? Doesn't sound like it. Some element of disagreement can be very healthy.'

'They must be aware of it.'

'Why must they? They may not be, or they may not be worried about it in the same way you are. Why don't you ask them? It could be that you just don't like disagreement. Now leave me alone for a few minutes to finish my work.'

Graham went upstairs to read the bedtime story. He was nearing the end of a fairy story. In a crackling voice he chanted,

> '"Merrily the feast I'll make.
> Today I'll brew, tomorrow bake;
> Merrily I'll dance and sing,
> For next day will a stranger bring.
> little does my lady dream
> Rumpelstiltskin is my name!"'

'Daddy that's rather scary,' complained Sarah.

'Don't be such a wimp. It's only a fairy story,' commented Stuart.

'Now children, it's time to go to sleep.'

Sarah was still curious, 'Daddy can you really turn straw into gold?'

'No darling, I'm afraid not.'

'King Midas could, he could turn anything into gold,' said Stuart recalling a lesson at school.'

'Who was King Midas? Did he live in Random?' Sarah continued.

'He was a Greek King wasn't he daddy?' said Stuart in an elder brother kind of way

'Yes but I don't think he was real either,' said Graham.

'Anyway settle down now, lights out. Goodnight.'

'Goodnight daddy.'

'Are you ready for supper darling?' called Judy.

There was no answer. Graham West was thinking.

'Supper, darling?'

'Out of the mouths of babes and sucklings.....

'What?'

'It's from Psalm 8.'

'Graham for the third time, do you or do you not want your supper or shall I give it to babes and sucklings?'

'What darling? Oh yes please.

'Yes please what.' Graham will you please come out of your dream and pay attention.'

'You see darling, Sarah has just reminded me of something. Rumplestiltskin!
We have to be very careful not to spend lots of time trying to turn straw into gold.
I've been so focused on raising money. I'd forgotten what we were really about.'

The receptionist picked up the telephone.

Good morning, James and James, how can I help you?'

'Oh good morning, is Peter in this morning by any chance?'

'I'll try for you. Who can I say is calling?'

'Graham....Graham West.'

'Putting you through.'

'Hallo Graham. What can I do for you this morning?'

'Hi Peter, I wondered if you could spare me five minutes sometime today. I have an idea I want to talk to you about.'

'Sounds intriguing- can you give me a clue?'

'I'd rather meet you. It's very much at the rough stage at the moment and I need help to develop it.'

'I tell you what. I'm free at lunchtime.. Let's have lunch at "The Lamb"- my treat. Can you get to Ely for twelve thirty?'

'Yes...yes I can.'

'Will an hour be long enough?'

'Oh goodness. Yes. That's very nice of you.

'See you then.'

'Oh, see you there. Goodbye.'

As Graham walked into 'The Lamb,' Peter was already at the bar.

'Hello Graham, what will you have to drink?'

'Oh just an orange juice would be fine thanks. I'm driving.'

'Ah, I walked from the office, so I might just indulge in a glass of red.'

They moved to the restaurant and sat at a corner table. Peter, as if by habit, straightened the knives and forks in front of him and aligned the napkin at a right angle to the plate.

'So what's this idea that you have, and why do you want to talk to me about it.'

Graham cleared his throat.

'I want to talk to you about it because I know you will thoroughly analyse the implications and come up with issues that I might not have considered. I don't want to be wrong, so I want to think about it carefully, and before the AGM; and it relates to finance.'

The pause was long enough for Peter to turn the napkin around ninety degrees and back again.

'Ah, is this a nice way of telling me you want me to resign as treasurer?'

In mid-sip, Graham spluttered in his orange juice.

'Good God. No. That's the last thing I want. No it's nothing like that. I have been thinking about our fundraising. Perhaps it's just me, but raising money in general seems to have become much more professional, especially in the charitable sector, and the church is getting left behind. Our discussion the other evening was not strategic. We have to recognise, as you have often reminded me, that our people have a limited cash surplus, and there are increasingly more good causes vying for their contributions. I think we need a more strategic view. I think it's too big for the PCC agenda so we need a new approach. That's part one.'

At that point scallops au gratin arrived. Graham was thinking about whether he had put the case. Peter was thinking about how hungry he was.

'These look good. I enjoy almost anything in a cheese sauce,' and so saying took a mouthful before beginning a kind of preamble. In reality he wasn't sure where Graham was heading.

'Interesting, there isn't very much to disagree with from a business point of view. Should we be strategic? Yes we should. After all, it only really means should we have a plan?'

'Yes exactly.'

Peter was a little hesitant. 'Let's pause there. Did you say that was part one? What, I wonder, have you in mind for part two?' He sipped his *Chinon* wine

'I want to set up a finance working group to write the plan, and I want you to chair it.'

'No'

'Oh. No to the working group or no to the chair?'

'The chair. Now listen, I am happy to be part of your group, indeed I have to be I think. But it is your plan and you need to chair it. My argument would rest around the

171

notion that this really should be a stewardship plan which includes fund raising, and stewardship is much more to do with faith than business. It's your territory Graham.'

'Rumplestiltskin,' said Graham without really thinking. You've just reminded me of a thought I had when I was reading to the children. You know the story it's about turning straw into gold. I knew there was a better way of doing it but i just couldn't make the link.. We should focus on stewardship.'

'Yes I think I do believe anything else is too narrow. We want people to feel that they can give time and prayer as well as money.'

'You are right. Thank you for that. Ok let's call it the...um...the Stewardship Working Action group? What do you think?'

'Do you want the acronym "SWAG?"', smiled Peter. 'rather appropriate don't you think?

The conversation had taken them through the main course and into the dessert. Graham had his pen and notebook alongside the crème brule and had begun a list which began G.West and P.James. 'How many should we have on it?'

'I was always taught five or seven, depending on the particular circumstances. Never have an even number, because it avoids stalemate!'

'Five then, us two, then three more; one of the churchwardens, say John Panther. How about Jane?'

'I think she does represent a particular point of view which should be included. She will be strong on fundraising judging by her performance at the PCC last night. 'Ok. Good. Good Let's leave one place for an AGM nomination. That's it. Brilliant. Thanks Peter. I think it's a real step forward. Mmm! Good coffee.'

'Now what was that item Jane came up with at the end of the PCC meeting, something about contact lenses?' said Peter in a mischievous tone

'Peter don't be naughty. Contactless payments. It's an interesting idea. Perhaps you might do some research to see if it flies. I'm going to talk to the Archdeacon, to see if he knows of anyone else doing it. Let's not dismiss it out of hand.'

Doris and John Panther had finished their supper and were settling down to an evening's television.

'Who was that on the phone?' asked Doris.

'The Vicar.'

'What did he want?'

'Oh nothing much really, something about stewardship; he wants me to be on another committee. I told him as long as it did something and wasn't just another talking shop.'

It's a funny word isn't it, said Doris, 'Stewardship. I always think it must be about showing people to their seats? I'm a "welcome" steward. I'm on the rota. It's not easy because I have to get robed up for the choir. I asked the Vicar what I should do and he said robe up first and join the choir in the chancel afterwards. I said it would look a bit strange but he didn't seem worried about it. It sounds like he could have set up a committee to sort it out? Bit over the top isn't it?'

'Doris you know perfectly well what it means. People give more than just money they also give time. Can I listen to the news now?'

One evening in March, the Stewardship Working Action Group had its first meeting. The five had gathered in the vicarage study and after coffee biscuits and an opening prayer, Graham outlined what he believed the purpose of the meeting to be.

'Welcome everybody. I haven't printed an agenda because I wanted us all to discuss what our priorities should be. I've nailed my colours to the mast by calling this group a stewardship working action group.

'That's swag!' said John laughing.

Graham raised his eyebrows. 'Yes I know john, not inappropriate.'

Others joined in.

'Are we planning to rob somewhere then and flee with our ill-gotten gains?'

'Should we all wear striped jumpers and a black mask' said Jane.

Even Elisabeth laughed, 'and carry a bag over our shoulders marked...well... SWAG'

Graham tried to regain the initiative, 'does it really matter?'

'We could leave out action. We ought to take that for granted, said John helpfully.

Is this because we couldn't decide at the P.C.C. whether to play cricket or rounders or neither?' asked Jane.

. 'I wanted to rebalance our discussions. Graham spoke quietly. The discussions on fund raising were getting out of hand; partly because the PCC agenda is too full. I thought we had forgotten what we were here for. It happens to churches. We become so obsessed with making sure we have enough money to pay our way, we forget why we are here. It was Rumplestiltskin that did it for me.'

There were puzzled faces around the room.

I was reading Sarah a fairy story a month ago in which turning straw into gold was the main object of a character in the story I thought we had become so focused on raising money that we had forgotten why we were here. Our mission is saving souls not saving money! Rumplestiltskin, you remember the story. I'm sorry to say if it upsets anyone, but I think it did have to be said.'

'Thank goodness you did', Elisabeth continued, 'I for one was getting fed up with the endless discussions about raising money. Aren't we supposed to believe that prayer and worship should be at the centre of what we do?'

Then John Panther had his say. 'That comes first of course, and as long as we can meet our obligations, we should not constantly be thinking only of ourselves within the church. We should concentrate on outreach.'

There was a moment when no one spoke

Then Peter James responded. 'I think what we are all trying to say is that we agree with you, Graham. I think we started off with a few misunderstandings. Why don't we get SWAG, us...to start again and look at the accounts and the budget and see what the minimum is to keep the church afloat. Then look at our offering income and see whether it covers the bare necessities. I suspect it does. Perhaps we can ensure we do the basic collections more efficiently; increase direct debits, expand the envelope scheme. We can do a survey of members to find out whether the contactless debit card is a goer. Make the paperwork easily available to people and ensure we speak to newcomers. Other activities which incidentally raise money but also include an element of fun can be given to charities of our choice; and be flexible so we can react to need as it arises. If at the same time we have activity which spreads itself across the year because the fellowship improves our faith, then so be it.'

'Can I make a suggestion, Graham?'

Graham grimaced. It did seem as if the meeting was beginning to form a consensus. He had hoped to avoid confrontation. Everyone else had spoken. Jane had been the grit in the oyster at the PCC. Reluctantly he concurred.

'Please do Jane.'

'I like the idea of the survey.'

Everyone relaxed and smiled and Jane continued.

'I wonder if we could ask Peter whether he could write down what he has just said with perhaps some figures to back it up and send it round to all of us. We don't seem to have much disagreement now do we?'

Graham couldn't quite believe his ears and his response was instant, 'Could you Peter?'

'If you wish, I'll try, but the rest of you need to offer comments on the first draft so it truly represents us all.'

'I think we can all agree to that,' said Graham looking around the room.'

He closed the meeting with a short heartfelt prayer that confrontation had been avoided. 'Would anyone like another coffee before they go?' I think we can afford it.'

'Yes please Graham,' said John, 'I can't go home yet, Doris would never believe we've finished a finance meeting this early. We could draw up a list of volunteers while were waiting, to pose for a calendar.

'John Panther you are incorrigible, said Elisabeth.

For Goodness Sake

Chapter Fourteen

The Parish Newsletter

The Reverend Graham .West sat with his family at the breakfast table feeling good about life. He was relaxed, up to date with his work, services for the weekend had been planned, and he was looking forward to the day. Of course there was the chaos of a school morning, but that was normal. Judy was late in leaving for her commute to Cambridge and that was normal too. He stretched and yawned then laid back in his chair and sipped his coffee.

He was not even concerned when daughter Sally raced down the stairs and flung her arms round his neck. 'Daddy, daddy give me your arm, give me your arm.'

'Good morning young lady, and why do you want my arm?'

'Give me your arm and I'll show you.'

He stretched out his arm.

' A pinch and a punch on the first of the month and no return,' she said with appropriately timed punches and pinches. Stuart taught me that.'

'Oh did he? Thank you, Stuart.'

It's alright daddy, you taught me it.' They all laughed

Oh did I? Ok Sally come and eat your cereal or you'll be late as well.'

Graham sat up and thumped his fist on the table. They all looked at him. He had his head in his hands and then raised his eyes to the ceiling, or perhaps in his case to heaven. The children were silent.

'Its the first of the month isn't it?' He looked down at his watch for confirmation.

'Oh it would be. Damn and double damn.'

Judy his wife, remained calm. She knew. She continued to check the contents of her briefcase. 'You always forget, Graham, why on earth don't you put it in your diary.'

'I forget.'

'You mean you don't want to remember it, that's nearer the truth. Please try not to swear in front of the children

'I know, sorry.'

'What is it daddy?' asked Sarah.

'Oh nothing really Sarah, just that blasted parish newsletter.'

'Graham. Not in front of the children please.'

 Sarah looked quizzical. 'What does blasted mean, mummy?'

'Ask your father.'

'Never mind Sarah, it's not important.'

'Daddy is cross because it's the first of the month and it's the deadline for the parish newsletter,' Judy explained

'What's a deadline mummy?' asked Sally.

'Ask your father. I've got to go. Kiss kiss.' She blew to them all and left by the kitchen door.

'Come on you two, coats and bags please, let's get the show on the road.'

The 'show on the road' ended at *Kingsmere Primary School*, with Sarah sitting cross-legged on the classroom floor for 'newstime,' the morning ritual of conversation where the children were encouraged to talk about what was happening in their lives. Melanie Francis, the year 3 teacher, enjoyed it. It helped her get to know her charges by giving small insights into their lives, and it developed their vocabulary and confidence.

For the most part *newstime* was uneventful- a birthday, a trip, a television programme and this particular morning was no different. That is until Sarah West, aged 6 3/4 put her hand up.

'Please miss', said Sarah, her arm stretched as high as she could get it, 'Please Mrs Francis.'

'Yes Sarah.'

'What does "blasted" mean?'

'It means to explode, make a big bang. Why do you want to know that?' Sarah.

'My dad was cross this morning because it was the first of the month.'

Mrs Francis, not seeing the connexion, but not wishing to open a can of worms, thought she should be calming and tried to move on.

'Oh dear,' she said to Sarah, 'never mind, don't worry, perhaps you misunderstood. I'm sure it means nothing.'

'Now to a six year old the teacher is like God, all seeing all knowing, but to Sarah this did not make sense.

.'Please miss, what's a blasted newsletter? Daddy said it was a blasted newsletter.'

'OK, I think I understand. Sometimes our mummy and daddy say things when they are cross, tired or busy, that they don't mean. It's nothing to worry about.'

Ok, form three, let's all go back to our tables and I'll take the register.

At 3.30 in the afternoon of the same day, Graham West stood in the playground outside the year three classroom with the other mothers, fathers and grandparents. As he arrived, Mrs Francis stepped out into the playground and watched, partly to check that each child was met by someone they knew. As Graham walked up to the door, she mouthed , 'have you got a minute'....as she caught his eye between the milling parents, and pointed to the inside of the classroom. Graham followed her inside.

'Have you got a minute?'

'Certainly, is there a problem?'

'Nothing serious, I'm sure. It's just that Sarah asked a question in newstime this morning. She asked what 'blasted' meant, something to do with a newsletter. It's very Sarah, she likes to know things but she was more worried because she thought it was making you cross.'

'Ah,' said Graham, 'the first of the month. She reminded me of the date and was upset because it made me cross. Blasted newsletter ...mmm..... yes I think I may have said that. Sorry.'

Mrs Francis smiled, 'You don't have to apologise to me, I just thought you'd want to know.'

'Well yes....thank you...I'll talk to her.'

Joan Watson, the sister of Fred Watson, the church organist, was the editor of the Random Parish Newsletter. She had been doing the job for over 10 years and she was very proud of that achievement. She had never married. Rumour had it that she had once been engaged to be married but he had died in a car accident before the wedding, and she had never recovered from the loss. She had worked in the local Estate Agents and consequently had a very good local knowledge and a wide number of contacts which proved very useful. She had a regular group of contributors to the newsletter which covered a number of interests and it was quite a task to bring them all together at the same time to produce the monthly title.

The church charged 50p per copy which covered the costs. She had collected over the years a number of readers who lived overseas and paid for the postage. The newsletter made a small profit.

She had noticed that technology had changed things. She no longer had to use the typewriter. She had learned to use *Word* on her computer. But she still typed the whole thing out and produced a proof copy which could be photocopied.

And she was not unaware that a lot people like her, of her age group, were starting to use email. In deed many of her contributors were now sending their columns to her by email. There was only one or two who couldn't.

The only thing that made her job harder was not receiving information and articles on time, the first of the month. It could have been anytime really. She chose the 1st because it was memorable. It gave her a little leeway; she could start with pieces that came in early, since she always used the same format. She ensured that the newsletter was distributed on the 1st of the following month, so it was important for everyone to understand the timescale.

The only person who did not seem to understand her needs was the Vicar. She did her best. He very rarely sent his letter on time; she always had to remind him. He always wanted to change things at the last minute which made the information in the newsletter incorrect, sometimes. The sub heading-'*all dates correct at the time of going to print*- did nothing to mollify those who got the wrong information.

It was true she did occasionally get things wrong, but most people didn't mind, They thought it was funny rather than serious, except the Vicar. Last month she'd included in the intercessions, *'Please pray for those who are sick of the community and the church.'* People knew what she meant.

In his last pastoral letter he had mentioned that the church was going to develop a website. They were hoping to get a student to work on it. People might have email, but using a website....she didn't think so.

The door bell rang and Joan got up, switched off the television and went to answer it. The front door was opening as she got to the hall and with a 'Yoo hoo, it's only me.' Melanie Francis. Form 3 teacher at Kingsmere Primary School put her head round the door, 'Hallo Auntie, are you busy?' I've brought the paper for your printer.'
Oh hello Melanie, and how's my favourite niece? I was just about to put the kettle on, could you do with a cuppa?'
'Yes please Auntie Joan, I'm parched.'

They walked through to the kitchen and as Joan brewed the tea, Melanie sat at the small kitchen table.

'Have you had a good day Mel, you must be tired? I don't know how you manage it. I know I couldn't; especially the little ones.'

Melanie added sugar to her tea. 'There are worse ways of earning a living, I suppose. By the way I only brought you one pack of paper was that alright?'

Joan picked up the packet and turned it in her hand. 'Yes that should be enough. I only have to produce one copy. The rest are photocopied on the machine at church.'

'It's quite a job isn't it, and every month. How long have you been doing it for?'

'Funny you should ask that, i was thinking this morning, It's ten years this month.'

'Don't you get fed up with it?' wondered Melanie.

'Sometimes, but not often; when I can't get hold of the material on time perhaps.' Joan paused for a moment. 'But most people are pretty good. I have to nag the Vicar, but I know he's busy and he does his best.'

'The blasted newsletter?' said Melanie to herself, recalling the mornings newstime.

'I'm sorry? said Joan, wondering if she'd heard correctly. 'It's not quite that bad. 'What made you think that?'

'Oh nothing, just something I heard someone say,' said Melanie, 'I was wondering whether you feel taken for granted sometimes. It often happens when someone has been doing a job for a long time.'

'It's inevitable isn't it, but it also means you can be relied upon. I think that's important too. There is no one else longing to do it, as far as I know. I don't particularly want to do it for ever. Of course the Vicar wants to change things, he said so in the newsletter. He wants a website. One of these days he'll get round to telling me about it. It's important we keep up to date, after all communication is what the church is all about. People rely on the newsletter for their information.'

At the Vicarage, Judy was home and the children Stuart and Sarah were having their supper of fish fingers, mashed potato and peas. Sitting at the table, Judy shouted 'Graham, do you want some tea?'

Graham shouted back from the study 'Yes please, two minutes.'

As he joined the family, Stuart looked up from his watch and said, One minute, forty three seconds.'

'What Stuart?' replied his Father.

'You said two minutes and you were one minute forty three seconds.'

Stuart, sometimes when we are speaking we use words or phrases which are not meant literally or exactly. So when I say two minutes, I mean a short period of time.'

Stuart replied, 'I do know that Daddy, It was a joke. You mustn't take me literally.'

'Ok clever clogs'.

'Like the "blasted newsletter," said Sarah.

'Oh Sarah,' said Graham, 'why did you tell Mrs Francis about the blasted... I mean the newsletter.'

He turned to Judy to explain. 'Mrs Francis spoke to me after school, apparently Sarah was upset in newstime because she thought I was cross with her for mentioning the first of the month, which i wasn't. She asked what 'blasted newsletter' meant.'

'Oh dear,' said Judy, 'of all people it had to be Melanie Francis.'

Graham frowned. 'Why is that a problem?'

'You do know I suppose that Melanie Francis is Joan Watson's niece.'

'She's not?'

'She is....so that will teach you not to swear in front of the children.'

'Blast it' said Graham, 'Oh sorry. Now what am I going to do?''

Gulam Singh, the proprietor of the *SPAR* grocery and newsagent shop was not a regular visitor to the vicarage. But he had been a friend to the church on a number of occasions and he played for the same cricket team as Graham.

Graham opened the door and smiled broadly.

'Gulam, good to see you, come on in. How are you? Can I get you a tea or coffee?'

'Could I have a milky tea, Graham?'

'You most certainly can. Let's go to the kitchen, we can chat while the kettle boils.'

'So how are you, Gulam? What brings you across the road this evening, a social visit or something else?'

'I have an idea that might prove to be profitable for us both.'

'Pull up a chair then. Ok that sounds interesting. Tell me more.'

'I have a nephew in his first year at Cambridge University.'

'A clever lad then.' said Graham.

'Indeed, he doesn't get it from my side of the family, I assure you. I have a favour to ask. His family is going to India for six months to visit relatives in the Punjab. So I have said he can stay with us. He is going to live here during the university holidays and some weekends. Now he can help in the shop, but I'm looking for something perhaps more interesting that he could do. 'I wondered whether you might know of anything or hear of anything in the IT line. He's a real whizz-kid at computers.'

'What is he reading...er...studying.?' asked Graham.

'Maths I believe'.

'Wow. What his name?' said Graham getting out his pen to make a note.

'Bal. It's Balwinder actually, but everyone calls him Bal.'

'And he's Singh, I take it...

'He is.'

'Now Gulam, don't take offence but I'm not sure how to put this but....Um.... does he need to be paid?'

'I'm sure he would like that. Depends on what he's being asked to do I guess.'

'Hmmm.' Graham sat for a moment or two looking into space, sipping his coffee. 'There is something that might be available. I just need to get my head round it and see if it's possible.'

Graham continued. 'There are one or two things that I've been thinking about. The church needs a website. Would that be within his ability?'

'Gulam smiled. 'Oh yes, most certainly. I confess I had that in mind.'

'You did?' said Graham a little surprised.

' I do read your newsletter, you know. You mentioned it in last month's edition.'

'So I did, so I did.' Graham laughed. 'And we have a budget for that. It's all the other things that go with it. It needs to be maintained and kept up to date, and that, as they say, is a different kettle of fish. We will need to train people to do it.'

'Let me come clean, Graham. My idea for him was to advertise his services in the shop; to help people in the community to set up and run their e-mail etc; to use *Word* and *Excel*. Not too expensive, simple stuff, you know? But I needed a project to get him started, which is when I saw the newsletter.'

Graham rubbed his hands together, 'I think we might have something, my friend, I think we might have something.' Then he stopped and frowned. 'The problem is Joan.'

'Joan?', repeated Gulam.

'Joan Watson, she edits the newsletter.'"

'Of course, Fred's sister. Oh how I like her. She is very funny. Let me think. Oh Yes. *"the prayer meeting was hell in the Church Hall"* and what was the other one. I know. *"If you enjoy sinning, join the choir."* Very funny, very funny. I look forward to each edition.' Gulam had a fit of the giggles.

'Gulam, it's not supposed to be funny.'

 At the end of that week, Joan Watson popped into the *SPAR* shop for some milk. Gulam's wife Manjit was serving, resplendent in her red sari.

'Good morning Joan', said Manjit

'Good morning Manjit, you do look splendid in your sari, what a gorgeous colour?'

'Thank you Joan how kind you are. Now you must come round for a meal sometime. When Balwindwer arrives next month would be best I think, so you two get to know each other.'

'Balwinder,?' said Joan.' Do I know a Balwinder?'

'You know, Gulam's nephew, he's agreed to help you with the website. We're very excited to have him stay with us and do something useful. He's a very clever lad, well you have to be to get into Cambridge.

'Really, I get into Cambridge every Saturday,' said Joan, totally misunderstanding, 'if you know where to park it's not complicated. What website?' She began to get irritated? 'I don't know anything about a website? Are you sure you've got the right person?'

'Oh I'm very sorry. I didn't mean to upset you. I must have got it wrong. '

Joan paid for her milk and left the shop.

Later that morning, Gulam returned from the *Cash and Carry*. She realised Joan had been upset but didn't know why? She consulted her husband.

'She was definitely upset. All I did was suggest she came for a meal to meet Bal. Oh I told her he was at Cambridge as well.'

'Maybe she was just having a bad morning?' wondered Gulam. 'People do.'

Graham West finished his pastoral piece for the newsletter and pressed the send button with a sigh of relief. He knew it was three days late but there was nothing he could do about it. He had been so busy. Pentecost and then Trinity, special services when Junior Church stayed for the whole service. There had been a piece of drama for Pentecost which had to be written and rehearsed and his Trinity sermon for the following Sunday always took a long time to prepare. He recalled the words of his Tutor at theological College when asked what he would do about Trinity Sunday said, 'Invite the bishop.' He had done his best and written a note to Joan

Dear Joan

Attached is my monthly letter for the newsletter. I'm sorry it's late. I have been extremely busy and I do hope you will forgive me for not meeting your deadline.

I would like to talk to you about the 'communications strategy' that I am putting to the PCC on Friday next week. So perhaps you could give me a couple of possible dates after next Friday when we could meet.

Yours in Christ

Graham

At about the same time that Graham had pressed the 'send' button, Joan Watson was finishing her editor's letter for the next edition and pressing the 'save' button.

My dear friends,

This edition of the newsletter is my 10th anniversary of becoming editor. It has become part of my way of life and I have enjoyed it, well most of it, immensely. It seems a very good time to stop, but rather than it come as a complete surprise to everybody, I am giving notice that I shall resign in September. This will give the church time to find a replacement if they wish. I hope that this will enable the church to pursue a new path without hindrance. Thank you for your support over the years.

Joan Watson

Editor

Now she had everything she needed to put the edition to bed, to have the proof copy ready for the end of the week. She walked over to her sideboard, found the bottle of dry sherry, poured herself a full glass. She raised it to the computer in the corner and said, 'Here's to the blasted newsletter.'

Truth be told she felt relieved, happy even, and why not? What was the point of being angry? It was clear to anyone with any sense that the world of information was changing. She had been following the demise of newsletters in paper form for a long time. The diocese newsletter recorded it ironically. What made her cross was the assumption that she was stupid. That she would be obstructive. \The fact that no one had bothered to talk to her about what the future looked like made her sad rather than angry. She smiled. They thought she would be a problem...well let them think it. Who should she tell? No she couldn't tell anyone, not even Melanie. Let them find out in print. It would be a scoop. Neither would she respond to Grahams email requesting dates. It wouldn't be necessary now anyway.

Graham and Judy with the children were invited to supper at the Singhs, to meet Balwinder who had come for the weekend. His parents had gone on holiday to India and now that he had finished his examinations, he could prepare to move into the spare room. They had discussed the requirements of the 'communications strategy', planned the initial steps and agreed the terms of remuneration. They decided that meeting Joan was important to the second stage of Bal's work and Graham agreed to prepare the ground.

On the next Saturday morning, Melanie Francis happened to meet Judy as she walked into the bank and they exchanged pleasantries.

'We are so pleased with Sarah's progress, you know. She is so much more confident than she was. She found it difficult to cope with Stuart. He sails through things, and she didn't feel she could compete. She's much more her own person now.'

'She's such a delight to teach. Like a sponge, she soaks up everything , and has such a desire to learn. There was one other thing, can I ask you something, between ourselves.'

'Of course, about Sarah?'

'No actually, about Auntie Joan. You know that silly business of the "blasted newsletter". Well I didn't tell her directly about it. I just asked her about her work with the newsletter. She's been doing it such a long time, this edition is her tenth anniversary, and I wondered how she felt about it. Did she find it stressful? How did she feel about criticism and so on. Well it was nothing specific, but I did sense she was not entirely happy, and there was a tension building up. I think she was expecting there to be a row and that she would have to fight for its existence.'

'Can I tell Graham about this?'

Melanie looked around. 'I'd rather you didn't say it came from me. And I wouldn't like to offer any advice as to what to do about it. Do what you think best.'

'Ok, thank you for telling me.'

When Graham had got home mid afternoon after a wedding, Judy was anxious to talk to him.

'When was the last time you had a conversation with Joan Watson about the future of the newsletter?'

I can't remember off hand, what I get mostly are nagging emails about how late I am with my pastoral.'

'I saw Melanie coming out of the bank, and she felt someone should talk to Joan. Joan had heard about 'the blasted newsletter,' and wasn't happy. She'd been doing the job for ten years, this was her anniversary edition; did you know? Are you going to do the newsletter if she walks away? Maybe it's time someone told her how much she's appreciated.'

'No I'm not, how am I expected to know these things if nobody tells me.?'

'Well you know now, what are you going to do about it?'

'We could recognize it in some way. We have a couple of weeks before it's published. What about a bring and share lunch after service on the Sunday it's published? No even better, I'll ask Jeremy if he could do a bangers and mash lunch for a fiver. We can buy a cake with ten candles. We just have to make sure she's there. Better mention it to Melanie and Fred.'

Judy felt there was a piece of the jigsaw missing.

So she said, 'why don't you go and see her, anyway. Now the PCC has agreed the strategy surely you can discuss it with her. Aren't you expecting Bal to work with her? Doesn't she get a say in that?'

'Ok, Ok .I'll go first thing on Monday morning. How would that be?'

'Don't ask me, it's not my responsibility. Just don't go expecting a fight, because that's exactly what will happen if you do.'

It was eleven o'clock on Monday morning when Graham appeared on Joan's front doorstep. Her apron, hairnet and pink rubber gloves suggested she was not expecting visitors and by her armful of clothes, it was clearly washday.'

'Good gracious, she exclaimed,' what are you doing here at this time in the morning? Well you'd better come in, now you're here. You'll have to excuse the mess, I'm in the middle of doing the washing.'

Graham followed her down the hallway to the sitting room.

'Have a seat, she said, I won't be a minute. Coffee with milk and no sugar? Thought so.'

She returned with a tray of two cups and saucers, a coffee jug, milk jug, and a plate of chocolate digestives. 'I bet you didn't have breakfast,' she said.

She sat down on the chair opposite him, the tray in front of her, and as she poured the coffee, she said,' Ok, have a biscuit, then over to you, I'm all ears. It must be important for you to come on your day off.'

Graham noted the fact that she knew it was his day off, and then began to explain how it was that the Council were insisting that they are the body who are required to take decisions, and they felt he was by-passing them. So that by the time things were brought before them, decisions had already been made. It meant that he had to put the 'Communications Strategy' to them before he could talk to anyone else about it.

'On reflection,' he said, 'I ought to have found a way of preparing the document for council with the help of one or two others, yourself included. I was worried it might look like a fait d'accompli. They have now agreed to it, on Friday as it happens, and having heard on the grapevine you were worried about it., I decided I should see you asap. So here I am. Here is a copy of the strategy for you. I would be grateful if you could read it and come back to me with your comments.'

He passed the document across the coffee table.

Joan took it, flicked the pages and took it over to her desk in the corner.

'I won't read it now, but I will read it today. How would you like me to respond, by email?'

'What would you prefer?'

'I think emails fine in the first instance. Although sometimes. it's difficult to deal with misunderstandings on email. Have another biscuit.'

Can you answer me one question.' Graham nodded. 'Who is Bal?' What has he got to do with the strategy?'

'Bal is Gulam Singh's nephew. He has nothing to do with the strategy itself. He is what I would call an opportunity. We need a website, he can design a website, and he is available now.'

Joan explained. 'Is that the reason Manjit Singh invited me to supper? I hadn't a clue what she was talking about. I take it you assumed that since I might have some role in the content of the strategy and perhaps the website, we should meet. Would I be right?'

Graham frowned. 'I'm sorry you learned about it that way. I had to find out if Bal was available and in the end too many people got to know about it. Time was of the essence.'

'I must apologise to her. I was just very confused.'

'I'm sure she understands,' said Graham.

'Do I get the impression that a lot more people are talking about me than I would like? I do feel rather uncomfortable about it.'

'People are concerned about you. That's not a bad thing. It shows how much people value your contribution. In the end that's what counts. I mean people laugh at the mistakes and your deadlines, but that is not serious. I don't see many people rushing forward to do it, do you?'

'Oh, people don't know what they can do until they try it. They won't get the opportunity if I carry on, will they?'

'Change is coming and we have to embrace it, but I need someone who understands what the implications are. I cannot do this without your experience.'

'Ok, let's leave it at that for now. I'll give you my thoughts by Thursday. Do you want another biscuit before you go?'

'No thanks, if I have any more it will look like bribery.'

'Oh you can take the proof copy of the newsletter with you if you like, it'll save me another journey.'

From her front window, Joan watched Graham drive away. 'You didn't tell him Joan, she thought to herself. 'What's he going to think when he reads the proof copy and sees your resignation? Yes, you ought to have consulted me, Graham West, I'm not going to let you off that easily.'

'Well, she didn't resign,' Graham shouted to Judy from the front door, 'and Jeremy has agreed to cook. Thank the Lord for the catering corps, that man is a genius. I need to send out a load of emails now to tell everyone about the meal after church.' He went straight into his study, put the proof copy of the newsletter on his to do pile and began e-mailing.

Judy pocked her head round the door. 'So what did she say?'

'Not a great deal. I gave her a copy of the strategy and asked her to comment, she's going to look at it and get back to me by the end of the week. I think I got away with it.'

'Don't be so smug. Remember pride comes before a fall. Do you want a coffee?'

Meanwhile, at about the same hour Joan Watson was coming down her garden path having hung out her washing and looking forward to her coffee.# and chocolate digestive, when she heard the front door bell. 'Oh goodness, has the world gone mad, who is it now. No peace for the wicked. She opened the door and there stood a tall and distinctly handsome young man wearing a turban.

Good morning, I'm not sure I've got the right house but are you Joan by any chance?

'Joan Watson, yes, what can I do for you?'

' My name is Balwinder Singh. Does the name mean anything to you?'

There was a moment's hesitation, and then it clicked, 'You're Bal.'

'At your service.' he said and bowed.

'Well, I have heard about you, but I wasn't expecting to meet you quite yet. Anyway you're here now. You'd better come in.'

Later that day, Melanie her niece, popped in on her way home from school.

'Had a good day, Auntie? I've come to see if you're going to stay for the bangers and mash lunch a week on Sunday. My treat.

'Oh I expect so, said Joan, without looking up from what appeared to be a loose leaf file of some sort.'

'What's that you are reading?'

'It's called a project outline- brief for Joan Watson. See, she said holding up the cover.'

'Oh very professional,' said Melanie smiling. Just for you?'

'It's just my copy, there's one for each of the actors. That means the people involved, not a play or anything.'

'Oh I see, very impressive. So where did this come from.'

'Bal....that's Balwinder . It means "gift of God," you know. He's the project coordinator. He came round just before lunch. He's a student at Cambridge and very bright but modest too. He said he's always found maths easy so he didn't think of himself as clever. He needs my help. He can do the technical stuff, but he can't design the content without my help. So we spent a couple of hours talking about what might be needed. We looked at two or three sites in the diocese where they have already done it. As Bal says, no need to invent something if we don't need to. Pinch the best ideas. We are going to spend a day a week over the next month. We design it and then he puts it together.'

Melanie thought her auntie wasn't going to stop.

'So he stayed for lunch.'

'Um, yes, only leftovers. He's a vegetarian.'

'Well bully for him.'

'So what happened to the resignation?'

'Oh I got it back. I told Graham I'd spotted some mistakes. He hadn't read it of course, so I replaced the letter with something seasonal.' She laughed.

'Well well,' said Melanie, I didn't see that coming. Good for you Auntie. Now put the kettle on I'm parched.'

'Graham had agreed with Bal that they would meet once a month. Each month had a plan with specific objectives attached.
Graham had re-read the project plan in preparation for the morning's meeting and was determined to keep tabs on progress. He knew IT projects were apt to get out of hand.
The front door bell rang.
Graham stood speechless for a moment. He was expecting to see Bal, but not Joan Watson. 'Well good morning to you, do come in.

Later that evening, when the supper things had been cleared away and washed up; Judy was preparing a report and Graham was checking his sermon. Judy asked about his day. She asked it seemed, more from duty that any real interest but Graham was clearly not happy with the outcome whatever it was.
'I have been shafted, if you will pardon the expression. That's the only word I can think of which describes how I feel.... shafted.'
Judy was used to Graham's sudden outbursts, although to be fair, they didn't last long.
'Why? What happened?'
'Joan turned up with Bal this morning for the report back. She led us to believe how upset she was; that she was going to resign. I even organised a lunch to celebrate her ten years of being the editor. I gave her a cake, for goodness sake. Meanwhile she's teamed up with Bal. They are designing the website. She did the presentation to me, all set against the project objectives. Whenever I asked a question, she answered. Bal just sat there nodding. I know what will happen, she will become the mistress of everything she surveys. Mrs Website. I don't know whether to be pleased or angry. She'd even bought herself a brand new laptop, top of the range.'
'Never mind darling move on, the secret of good management is delegation, even if you didn't intend it.'
'Blasted newsletter,' said Graham.

Printed in Great Britain
by Amazon

19410013R10112